RETURN TO ROBINSWOOD

JEAN GRAINGER

CHAPTER 1

Brighton, England, 1946

DERMOT MURPHY SAT OPPOSITE his son-in-law and said nothing.

'Well? What do you think?' Sam Kenefick asked, trying to figure out what was going on behind Dermot's inscrutable face. Kate's father had hardly changed a bit in the war years. He was tall and as strong as an ox, and his dark copper hair was thick had very little grey. Kate and Aisling looked nothing like him – they were Mediterranean-looking, all dark and curvy like their mother – but Eve, Kate's other sister, was his spitting image.

The murmur of conversation, the occasional burst of laughter, the general hum of a busy Brighton pub all around them seemed a million miles away. The euphoria of the war being over at long last was wearing off, and life was still hard for people. But the old-world pub with its brass fittings and dark wood interior seemed to help melt people's cares away, and there was a general air of bonhomie.

'What do I think?' He repeated the question.

Sam swallowed. Dermot Murphy was a man he admired

immensely, and he had done so all his life, but his father-in-law didn't suffer fools gladly. Sam needed to convince him to return to Robinswood.

'Look, Dermot, it's a good offer – well, it's the best offer I can make you at any rate. Kate wants to go home, and for her, home has always been and will always be Robinswood.'

'With all due respect, Sam, the fact that Robinswood was my family's home didn't seem to bother you too much in 1940 when we were thrown out by your mother. I know it was she who did the evicting, but you'd inherited it by then, and you did nothing.'

Sam knew Dermot's lifelong mistrust of the English had not melted away when his daughter became the new Lady Kenefick. British titles did not impress him. He decided honesty was best. 'You're right. And I'm deeply ashamed of that. I should have taken more of a role, but I just wanted to fly, and I was caught up in the excitement of the war. I should not have left the management of Robinswood to my mother, nor should I have allowed her to leave you all homeless. Your family and mine have worked together for a very long time, and it was shabbily done. My father would have been appalled.'

Dermot took a sip of his pint and grimaced. Warm British beer was no match for a creamy pint of Guinness in the pub in Kilthomand. 'My family worked *for* yours, Sam, not *with*. I worked for your father, God rest him, and Isabella and the girls worked for your mother. So let's not sugarcoat this. Also – and I don't mean any offence – but what in the name of God do you know about farming? You're not an outdoor man, and you look like a gust of wind would knock you over.' He winked to show he wasn't being unkind.

Sam always felt like a schoolboy around Dermot, and the man was right – he was slight and boyish looking. But he desperately wanted to go home, to put everything right. He really believed things were different now; the class structures of the past were just as demolished as the buildings of London, and it was a new era.

He grinned. 'I am actually tougher than I look. And you're right, I don't know much about farming, but I'll learn. And who better to teach me than the best groundskeeper Robinswood ever had? And now that we have Jack to consider, it's for him as well. I've inherited the title and not much else, as you know, but I really think if we went back together, we could make a go of it. There's nothing you don't know about running the estate. Goodness knows, you did it all single-handedly when my father was distracted by whiskey and horses. The point is, none of us thought we'd make it through the war, but here we are, in one piece, and it feels like another chance, an opportunity to put things right. Not just for our generation, but for little Jack as well. I know he's only tiny, but one day he'll be Lord Kenefick, and I want that to mean something.' Sam knew he sounded like an overenthusiastic schoolboy, but he and Kate really wanted to go back to Robinswood, and the only way it would work would be if Dermot and Isabella came as well.

Dermot smiled at the mention of his first grandson, though the idea that Kate's son was going to be a peer of the British realm, the country Dermot and so many others had fought tooth and nail to remove from Irish soil, was odd to say the least.

'Well, it is certainly something to think about. I'll talk to Isabella, see what she thinks. As you've no doubt come to realise, the women are the decision-makers in this family.' He smiled and took another sip of his pint.

Isabella had insisted on coming over to Brighton for the birth of Kate's baby. The whole thing had gone smoothly, and little Jack Kenefick was a lovely little lad who was thriving under his mother and grandmother's devotion. They were due to go back to Dublin tomorrow.

'The ladies' rule is something I am well aware of.' Sam smiled. 'But Kate and I are in complete agreement on this. The only way we can do it and not end up in the poorhouse is if you and Isabella are in on it with us.'

'Right, so explain to me again – and in detail this time – what you have in mind.' Dermot sat back.

Sam, encouraged, went on.. 'So, our plan is to return to Robinswood and not open all of the house yet. It was in terrible

3

condition when we left, and that was six years ago, so I can only imagine the state of it now. But Kate thinks we could open the small back wing – remember where Father had his study and sitting room? We could manage in that section for a while until we got the house back into some kind of habitable condition.'

Dermot said nothing, but he thought they were being overly optimistic at best and, at worst, positively delusional.

'Meanwhile, we take the land back from Charlie Warren – he's on a rolling year-to-year lease – get it into full production and start producing food for export. I gave him twelve months' notice six months ago.'

Dermot was impressed. At least the lad had been thinking it through; it wasn't some mad notion.

'The whole of the United Kingdom is crying out for food, and we can make a killing supplying it to them. I haven't a clue of how we'd do it, I'll be honest. But you do, and I am willing to work day and night if need be.'

'Go on.'

'Well, we are living, as you know, off my RAF salary and the rent of the land, but since Mother has remarried, she is no longer my responsibility, financially speaking. Perry Goodall has quite enough money for both of them. She sends her love, by the way, and is very sorry she wasn't here when Jack was born, but Perry needed her to play hostess for some business contacts of his in Nice. They are all British, but he's entertaining them on his new yacht, I believe. Now that the war is over, people can't get enough of travel and the good things in life, I suppose.' Sam shrugged.

'Is he good to her, that Perry Goodall?' Dermot asked.

Sam smiled, and Dermot knew why. The idea that he would come to care about Sam's snobby upper-crust mother was an odd one. But life was strange, and over time, resentment had turned to grudging respect and now, after all these years, was bordering on affection.

'Lord Goodall, as she refers to him when he's not there – Perry darling when he is – is actually besotted with her. They make an odd couple, no doubt about it. He's about a foot shorter than her for starters, but he is loaded, and he knows everyone, and he's thrilled to bits to have my mother on his arm, so it's all working out fine. Kate gets a great kick out of him, and he really enjoys her – he thinks she's hilarious.'

'I'm glad. Give her our regards when you speak to her. By the way, have you mentioned your harebrained scheme to her?' He grinned to take the sting out of his words.

'Actually, I have. In fact, when we spoke about it, she was the one who said the only way it could be done is if you and Isabella were in on it with us. She's even given over all her entitlements to my father's estate to me to help out financially, her only proviso being she never has to go back there.' Sam chuckled.

'She was never happy there anyway, that's for sure.'

'No indeed.' Sam nodded. 'She has no love of Ireland, and she remembers Robinswood as draughty, cold and damp. She was endlessly trying to make ends meet while maintaining a façade of wealth and attempting to manage my father as part of the bargain.'

Dermot chuckled at the memory of the previous Lord Kenefick. 'Old Austin was a great man for the horses and the bottle, and he was known all over Munster for his generosity, but he didn't want to face the facts. He left your mother in a right old mess. I did try to warn him, but he wouldn't listen, so I can't say I blame her for never wanting to darken the door of that place again.'

Sam paused, then asked the question he had debated about as he prepared for today's pitch. 'And you? Can you go back in there, after everything?'

His father-in-law shrugged. 'I could, I suppose. It's just a house. And to be honest with you, I saw so much during the Troubles with the British in the twenties to haunt a man, that what happened in Robinswood was nothing by comparison. So no, if I refuse this, it's not because I'm too scared or upset to go into that house again.'

'All right. So here's my offer in a nutshell. You and Isabella move back into your old farmhouse, which I will sign over legally to you. That is your home, you should never have been forced to leave it, and now you never will be. Charlie Warren's lease of the land will be up in the time it will take us to get organised. I have three months left on my commission before I'm discharged. We work the estate together, and we split the profits fifty-fifty.'

Dermot held his hand up. 'That's generous, Sam, but I don't need your charity. We're fine and settled at the Hamilton-Brooks place. Eve is with us, and we've a home there for as long as we want, so we don't need handouts.'

Sam cursed inwardly. He'd overdone it. Dermot Murphy was a proud man, and it had hurt him deeply to leave Robinswood six years ago.

'It's not charity, it's a plea. I want this so badly, and so does Kate. Whatever terms you dictate will be fine with us.'

Dermot gazed at him, saying nothing. Sam held his nerve. Eventually, the older man spoke. 'If I do it – and it's a big if – I'll have to talk to Isabella, and she may not want to. She likes it in Dublin, and she loves Georgie and Arthur. If she agrees, I'll take the house, but it's a seventy-thirty split to you. It's your land, for God's sake.'

'Fine, fine, whatever you say. This could be fantastic. The harder we work, the more we make. Then as we make money, and I'm sure we will, you can either keep your share or you have the option to buy some land from me at half of the market value. The only other thing I'll ask in return is that you help me get Robinswood habitable again. Kate has an idea that we open it up as a kind of country house hotel, Isabella doing the cooking – just a restaurant to begin with, but converting the rooms into guest bedrooms eventually.'

'Your mother would have a canary at the idea of riff-raff wandering the corridors of Robinswood.' Dermot chuckled.

'She doesn't care. She has Perry's very plush mansion to swan about in. And anyway, it's not hers, it's mine, and I just want to find a way we can live there. That house is too big for Kate and me, and everything has changed now. All that nonsense about class and position is a thing of the past.'

Dermot raised one eyebrow sceptically. 'It has and it hasn't changed, then, young Sam. It has and it hasn't.'

CHAPTER 2

*K*ate crept down the stairs in their lovely terraced home on the Brighton seafront. Her feet sank into the plush carpet, and the mirror in the hallway reflected the sparkling chandelier. She had joked with Sam the previous night about how the mirror was admonishing her every day for her still flabby belly after having Jack. She felt frumpy and out of shape. Sam was so gorgeous, with his grey eyes, curly hair and tall, slender body. She adored him. Mammy assured her she'd be back to herself in no time, but she longed to fit into her cinch-waisted dresses.

She knew she was just like their mother, dark hair that would hang in corkscrew curls if she didn't tie it up, red lips, green flashing eyes. Mammy always said she was descended from the Spanish traders who brought wine to Galway, and Sam always said that Kate looked every inch a beautiful senorita.

Mammy and Jack were having a snooze upstairs. She could still hardly believe she and Sam were married, with a baby and a home of their own. Jack was delicious, and she could look at him for hours. Her eyes fell on the new phone. While she was in hospital, Sam got a telephone installed as a surprise, and she was able to make calls to Eve and Aisling, which eased the pain of being away from her sisters. She felt very posh having a phone of her own in the house.

Who should she ring? Eve was in Dublin, working at the same house as their parents, where she'd been since her husband of just over a year died in an accident at work. They thought for a long time that Eve would never get over losing Jack. But slowly, she was coming back to herself, though it had taken six years. She was coming to visit Kate and the baby once their parents went back to relieve her, and Kate couldn't wait. She worried for her sister, stuck all day with another widow and her two children. Elena and Georgie and Arthur were nice, but it was such an isolating life. Eve would never meet anyone else if she stayed cooped up there. And she was gorgeous. She could have had any man she wanted, but she was living like a nun. Anytime Kate brought it up about her getting back out there, Eve shut her down instantly.

Aisling was in a village in Devon with her husband, Mark. Something wasn't right there, though it was hard to pinpoint what exactly was wrong. Sam and Mark had been great friends when she and Aisling started seeing them, but Sam went up through the ranks quickly – all due to his title and nothing to do with his ability according to him – and Mark had a good war, she thought. But Aisling and Mark never called to see them in Brighton, nor did they invite Sam and Kate to Devon. Once the weather got warmer, maybe she could suggest it, and she and Jack could take the train down to visit.

She could call Framington Hall, Perry's incredibly beautiful house, except Perry and Violet were in France. Anyway, she'd only have to thank him for the hideous silver mug he'd sent for Jack, and she was a terrible liar. She had promptly put it with all the other horrible old stuff in the attic. She wanted all new, shiny, clean furniture, none of those big old heavy wooden things she'd had to dust in Robinswood as a child.

She and Sam had been to visit Framington Hall often, and it made Robinswood look like a broken-down old doll's house. Perry was a good sort, though, and he always made Kate feel so welcome. He wasn't all 'Lord of the Manor' at all; he was quite ordinary in fact. It was one of the reasons she liked him.

She was still taken aback when people called her Lady Kenefick. She wondered what on earth the people of Kilthomand would make of little Kate Murphy, the groundsman's daughter, coming back as the mistress of Robinswood with the title and all. They'd hate her for it probably.

She decided on Eve. She dialled the number for the Hamilton-Brooks home in Dublin, really hoping Elena didn't answer. Elena probably didn't mind Eve using the phone, and Kate always called Eve, not the other way around, and always waited until the children were in bed, but she would still rather if Eve didn't have to feel beholden. The rest of the Murphys didn't care too much about working for the gentry over the years, always tipping the cap and bending the knee to them – though she suspected Daddy hated it more than he let on – but it always rankled with Kate. Still here she was, Lady Kenefick herself now… Incredible. Still, she couldn't be any worse than the last Lady Kenefick, she supposed. She'd have given a hundred pounds to see their faces back in Kilthomand when word got out.

Admittedly, Elena was nothing like Violet. She was in her late thirties and really beautiful in that very peaches-and-cream English way. Eve and she were very close, Kate knew.

She spoke to the operator. 'Dublin three-one-five, please.'

The usual few clicks and then the ring. It never ceased to give her a thrill. Imagine – she could just talk to her sister, all the way over in Dublin, whenever she wanted.

'Hello? Hamilton-Brooks residence, Eve speaking.'

'Eve, it's me!' she said, trying to keep her voice down so as not to wake Jack but still be loud enough for her sister to hear her.

'Kate, hi! How's everything? How's Jack?'

Kate felt the familiar tug on her heart as her sister mentioned her son's name. She had asked Eve when she was pregnant if she would like the baby, if he were a boy, to be named after her Jack, and Eve was so touched. Little Jack Kenefick was named for his

Uncle Jack O'Neill who died when he was only twenty-five years old.

'Oh, he's great, though how I'm going to manage him next week without Mammy around, I've no idea. My boobs are killing me, and I won't even mention what things are like downstairs, if you know what I mean...'

'Kate!' Eve admonished with a scream of laughter. It was good to hear her laugh. 'You'll be the talk of the parish!'

Kate could picture her sister laughing, her gorgeous red hair tumbling over her shoulders as she threw her head back. Eve had the most infectious laugh, and there was a time when they feared they would never hear it again.

Her sister died a bit when she lost Jack, her gorgeous curvy figure becoming thin and her green eyes unable to hide the deep pain she felt. These days, however, she was better, and Kate loved to see it. If only she didn't lock herself away.

'Ah, it's all right, Eve. This isn't like Kilthomand, with the operator listening in to every conversation. We're not interesting enough for them in London or Dublin. Two old sisters wittering on about their aches and pains.'

'Ha, ha! Remember that, when people would make a call at home? People used to say goodnight to Mossy as well as to whomever they were talking to.' Eve giggled at the memory of the old postmaster who ran the telephone exchange in Kilthomand. He was nice but notoriously slow.

'I do. Speaking of Kilthomand, tonight's the night. Sam is meeting Daddy to ask him about going back.'

'So you two are really doing this?' Eve replied, fascinated.

'Oh, I'd love it. We've a nice life here, and a lovely house and everything, but England is just so dreary now, and I miss home. I really do. I've had enough of the big lights to last a lifetime. I think we could make a go of it too, but only if Daddy can be convinced.'

'I'd have thought he'd jump at the idea. He loved it there.'

'Well, fingers crossed. You know Daddy can be prickly, and he's not getting any younger, either.' Kate was trying to be rational.

'He's as fit as a trout, and he's only in his fifties. And Mammy too. I presume you told her first?'

'Of course I did, but Sam thinks I didn't, and Daddy will think the first she hears of it will be from him, you know.' Kate laughed, and Eve joined in. She knew exactly.

'If anyone can swing this, it will be you.' Eve said. ' Especially if Mammy wants it, then you'll be heading back to Robinswood for sure.' Eve was convinced. 'Hey, imagine the old biddies calling you Lady Kenefick. 'Twill stick in their throats.' She giggled.

'I was just thinking that exact thought. It would be worth going back to see the look on old Ma Lacey's face. I wonder if she's still buttering her little Seanie's toast for him?' Kate grinned.

'He was a right eejit, all right. When I think of the way he treated our Aisling...' Eve was still cross at how the local draper's son had humiliated their younger sister. 'Still, she has Mark now.'

'Hmm.' Kate was non-committal.

'Have you heard from her? I wrote, and I got a really short reply, not like Ais at all.'

'Yes, I thought the same. I figured I might have been imagining it. She seems kind of distant or something.'

Both women were worried about Aisling. She was the gentlest of the three. She had Mammy's Spanish looks, just like Kate, though her hair was poker straight and she was much more low-key.

'Well, if you two wind up back in Robinswood, at least she could go over to visit. It would be good for any troubled soul to wander round the grounds at least.'

'And how about you, Eve? Do you want to come back? We've always room for an extra pair of hands – there'll be so much to be done.' Kate deliberately kept her voice light, but she knew the seriousness behind the words.

There was a brief pause.

'I don't think so. Thanks for asking, though, and I have thought about it. But Elena and I have plans for here, and we both need to be here. And I know Georgie and Arthur will be going away to school, but still… And especially if Mammy and Daddy do go back, Elena needs me. Is that all right?'

Kate had known what her sister's answer would be, but she still had to ask. 'Of course it is. I understand completely. But know this – Robinswood will always be a home for you should you ever want or need it.'

Eve smiled at the intensity of her younger sister's promise. Kate was passionate and fiery, and woe betide you if you got on the wrong side of her, but she was loyal and kind and wanted to do the best for everyone.

'Thanks, Kate. Or should I say, thank you, ma'am.' She chuckled.

'Oh, dear God, don't you start that. 'Tis going to be bad enough going back without you lot all teasing me as well. Sam thinks I'm paranoid that everyone in the village will be talking about me and saying what a gold-digger I am, bagging the lord of the manor. And if only they knew we haven't a brass bob.' Kate sighed.

'It's going to be weird, though, isn't it?' Eve mused. 'I mean, leaving like we did, thinking we'd never go back, you and Ais joining up, me heartbroken over Jack, and now here we all are. Life is odd some-times, isn't it?'

'It certainly is. I have to pinch myself all the time. I just pray Daddy agrees. In my head, we're going back already, and I have so many plans for the place…'

'Not wanting to be a wet blanket, Kate, but how are you going to pay to get the house up and running again? I mean, I know Charlie Warren has been working the land, and he's a good farmer, whatever else he is, so Daddy could take the estate over again fairly easily. But wasn't it lack of money to fix it up that made Lady Violet leave in the first place?' Eve didn't want her sister to get herself into something that was going to prove to be impossible. Kate always was a great one for big ideas.

'We've talked about that. I was thinking we could just open the east wing. It's the bit you could section off most easily – it even has its own door. Remember, Austin got that put in so Violet wouldn't know what time he got back from the races. We could turn that small drawing room into a living room, and Daddy could make a little kitchen out of Austin's old office. There's that storage room behind and then the bathroom and the small bedroom. Those few rooms would be enough for Sam and Jack and me, and we could do the rest of the house bit by bit.'

As her sister digested this plan, Kate mistook her silence for disapproval. 'You think I'm mad, don't you?'

Eve heard the disappointment in her voice. 'No, I don't. I'd probably do the same in your position, actually. Sam is Lord Kenefick and you are now Lady Kenefick, and you should be there, raising your family at Robinswood. It's Jack's family home too, and it's such a lovely place to grow up – we should know. So no, I think you are doing the right thing, but it's going to be a lot of hard work.'

They chatted about life in general, Kate moaning about how there was hardly any nice food to buy even though the celebrations of VE Day were almost a year ago.

'I'll send another parcel tomorrow,' Eve promised.

'Please do send a parcel, but make sure you keep it under the five pounds weight, or they'll take it off our ration. A woman down the street got done last week for using the ration books of two people that were dead. Honestly, it's worse now than when the flipping war was on. They've cut soap and bacon and loads of things. If Sam didn't bring things home from the mess, I swear we'd starve.'

'You'll miss that when he's discharged.'

'We will, but I'll be glad to have him out of uniform. Another three months, he reckons, and he'll be out.'

'And then the real work begins, and you'll be Lady Kenefick the Third!' Eve laughed. 'And speaking of Lady Keneficks, how's Lillian? Last time we spoke, she was dreading Beau going back to America.'

'I haven't seen her. Beau was sent back almost six months ago, and she's not been seen since. I'd say she'll probably have to find some chinless wonder with a load of cash, and she'll provide an heir, and everyone will be happy. She had a phone conversation with Sam the other day, presumably about him paying her rent. Some things never change.'

'Ah, don't be mean,' Eve admonished. 'She's improved so much. Remember what a snobby cow she was when she was young? She'll talk to you now at least. Do you really think it was just a fling with Beau?'

Kate sighed. 'It's hard to know. She did seem mad about him and him her, but wartime is different – anything goes. I know, she *is* miles better...still a snob, though. And I do feel sorry for her. At first, I was sure she was only knocking about with Beau to scandalise her mother, but she really loved him, and him her too, inexplicably. Beau is a sweetheart, such a nice man and so gentle and mannerly, though he does talk about God a lot. They have a different kind of way of going on about religion, I think. Anyway, he asked the Americans if he would be allowed to stay, but they were having none of it. I thought they might even get married here – mixed marriage isn't illegal – but the U.S. Army wouldn't allow it.'

'So what's going to happen?' Eve asked. She found the idea of Lady Lillian Kenefick having a black man as a husband fascinating.

'Nothing, I'd imagine. She'd marry him in a heartbeat, I'd say, but Beau told us that it was actually illegal for him to marry her in America. I can't see him coming back to England, so I suppose she'll have to forget about him and move on to marry anyone who'll have her. I do hope it's soon, though. We can't support her, and she seems to expect it. Though having had relations with Beau isn't going to do much for her already dodgy-looking prospects.' Kate chuckled. She and her sister-in-law had reached an entente cordiale but were by no means friends.

'Still, it is sad for them. He was good for her, softened her or something,' Eve mused.

'Don't I know it! She'll no doubt be back to the entitled madam she was before now that Beau isn't here to put a bit of manners on her. Oh, that's Jack wailing. Mammy stayed up with him last night so I could rest, so I better go. Mammy and Daddy will be back in Dublin with you next week, and I'll have to be a mammy all on my own!'

'Give my darling nephew a cuddle from his auntie Eve and tell him I'll see him soon.' Eve hung up.

CHAPTER 3

*A*isling ate her dinner in silence; Mark didn't even touch his. His blonde head was bent over his plate. He was big and brawny, a typical West Country farmer's son, with ruddy cheeks and blue eyes. He'd always looked like nothing could beat him, but now he was more like a shell. He seemed the same on the outside, but it was like he was hollowed out. The clock ticked on the dresser. She wanted to ask him about Kate and Jack coming for a visit; Kate had asked outright on the phone the other day – she knew something was up. Aisling longed to see her sister and meet her little nephew, but she dared not bring it up.

She tried making his favourite – ham, egg and chips – to see if it would cheer him up, but nothing worked. He lay beside her at night, turned away, his back like an impenetrable wall between them. During the day, he either stayed in bed or sat in the little sitting room, not reading or listening to the wireless. He simply stared into space.

He'd been back seven months, and they had barely spoken. It was as if he were miles away. He drank most nights down in the Spreading Chestnut, not coming home until very late. He often slept in the small spare room, muttering that he didn't want to wake her. They had not had any physical contact since he returned, and when she tried to hug or kiss him, he stiffened and seemed to endure the moment until it was over, then he would retreat back into himself.

The outbursts of rage were terrifying. She noticed his knuckles were cut and hoped he had not been fighting. She raised it with Delilah, who was just as mystified as she was as to her brother's behaviour. Delilah assured her that he wasn't fighting. In a small place like Portwye, such stuff was grist to the gossip mill and they would have heard about it. Two nights after that conversation with her sister-in-law, she looked out the bedroom window. It was a moonlit night, and there she saw him, hitting the wall of the shed with his fists as hard as he could. She tried to bring it up, but he just stormed out, and she never mentioned it again.

Mammy knew as well that everything wasn't right, and she wrote frequently, asking Aisling to come home for a visit, or tentatively offering to come to Devon, but Aisling couldn't do it. She would be embarrassed in front of her parents if Mark behaved like he had been, and she could imagine her father's reaction if he saw one of Mark's outbursts. Mark would never hurt her; she was certain of that. But Mammy and Daddy would insist she come back with them – she just knew they would – so it was best to keep her distance until he got better.

Mrs Belitho, Mark's mother, was nice enough, but she suffered with her nerves. She chain-smoked and seemed a bit disconnected from the family. She didn't even really help Delilah out with the boys – apparently, they were too much for her. Aisling, on the other hand, was glad to pitch in. It filled the days, and Harry, Davy and Terence really liked her. It felt nice that someone did these days.

'Delilah had to take Harry to Doctor Crossley today. She allowed them to go fishing, and as Davy was casting off, he caught Harry's face with the hook. I met her at the butcher when I was getting the ham. She said he needed two stitches but he's all right. Poor Davy felt terrible.'

Mark didn't respond, and she waited. Eventually, he looked up, realising he was going to have to say something. 'I'm glad it's not more serious.'

Those were the first words he'd said all day.

Aisling smiled and hoped she could continue the conversation. 'There's always something with those lads. Poor Delilah is at her wits' end.'

Silence again.

She leaned over the table and took his hand in hers. She swallowed and blurted out, 'Mark, can Kate and the baby come to visit? I'd love to see them, and Sam's gone over to Germany again, so she's really lonely since Mam and Daddy went back home.'

She saw the flash of panic in his eyes.

'No... I... I don't want people...' He pushed the chair back, slid his hand out from under hers and got up from the table.

'Please, Mark...just for a few days...'

'I said no!' he shouted, and slammed his plate into the sink, causing it to shatter. He turned to leave.

She ran and stood in front of the door, blocking his exit. 'Why not?' she demanded, sick of tiptoeing around him. 'It's my home too! Surely I can have my sister to visit?'

He stopped and closed his eyes, wincing like he was in pain. Eventually he said, 'Please don't make me, Ais...please... I can't.' All the anger seemed to have dissipated, and he was deflated and so sad.

Her heart went out to him. 'All right. I won't invite her. But, Mark, we have to talk. Please, darling, I love you and I want to help, but you have to talk to me. I... I don't know what to do any more, I've tried everything...' A tear sild down her face.

Mark stood there. He didn't hug her or reach out in any way – he just stood and stared at her. 'Go home, Aisling.'

She looked at him, confused. 'What? I am home...' Sometimes he was incoherent, but that was usually when he drank. He had not been drinking today. Yet.

'No. To Ireland. Please. Go home. Leave me. I'll do whatever I need to. We can get a divorce, and you can start again. This is not fair to you.'

Aisling felt her stomach lurch. Was he telling her their marriage was over? Surely he couldn't be. Blood pounded in her ears. She tried to keep her tone even. 'Mark, I am your wife, and you're my husband, and we love each other. I am not going back to Ireland or anywhere else – I'm staying here where I belong, with you. So please don't ask me to leave you, because I never will.'

'My father says I should never have married you, and he's right. I'm no good for you, Ais. I'm…' His voice caught in his throat.

'Don't you love me any more?' she said, her voice barely audible.

The sound from her tall, strong husband sounded more like an animal than a man. It was sheer pain. 'Of course I do. You're the best thing that's ever happened to me, but I'm no good to you any more, I'm…' He stopped. He had no more words.

She led him by the hand into the sitting room and to the sofa. She sat beside him. 'Tell me. For once and for all, tell me and we will deal with it. What happened, Mark?'

He looked at her, hunted and afraid. He was barely recognisable as the funny, charming and adorable man she'd married. Then he turned away from her, facing forward, his elbows resting on his knees, his eyes gazing unseeingly at the empty fireplace. He seemed so far away.

After a long silence, he began to speak. The sheer effort of talking could be heard in every word. His lovely soft West Country accent even sounded hard. 'When I was stationed at Ahlhorn in Germany last May – it was all but over by then, more or less – we were ordered to scramble. There were three ships on the Baltic coast they said, full of escaping SS trying to get away. We were ordered to bomb them, and then to strafe the waters for survivors, and we did it. Seven thousand people, maybe more…'

He didn't sound like himself at all, and his voice had a hard, bitter edge.

'But, Mark, you were doing your job. Hitler and the Nazis had to be stopped. What kind of world would we live in if –'

'They were Jews, Aisling.' He choked out the words.

'What? I don't understand…'

'Jews. The Germans were hiding them. They didn't want the evidence of what they'd done, so they shoved them on these ships out of the way. We killed thousands of innocent people. They walked from those camps. They could have made it, Ais. They would have been reunited with their loved ones, but' – his breathing was ragged – 'we killed them.'

'But how?' She still didn't understand.

'I don't know. We thought they were SS. There certainly were SS on board, but they were guarding those poor unfortunates. They marched them north and put them on ships, and then we killed them all.'

His shoulders were heaving, and he was crying with hacking dry sobs. She couldn't bear to see him in such distress.

'But, Mark, darling, it was a mistake, and not your mistake. The top brass obviously had misinformation or something. It was a horrible thing to do – I'm not saying it wasn't a tragedy – but it wasn't your fault.' She put her hand on his back, wishing she could get through to him.

'Ais, I strafed the water as those people tried to swim to shore. Me... I did it. Orders or no orders, I was the one to do it. I close my eyes at night, and I see them, screaming, the fire, the bodies. I can't live with this...with what I did.'

He allowed her to pull him into her arms, and he cried like a baby. After what felt like a long time, he sat up.

'But, Mark, can't you see? You're not responsible. The Germans did that. They were never going to let those people just go free – they were just getting them out of the way. I'm not saying what happened wasn't horrific or tragic, but it wasn't your fault.' Her dark eyes burned with the injustice of it all.

'My father is ashamed of me, and before, he was so proud. I'm an RAF pilot, but he told me a few weeks ago that I was a disgrace to the family. He told me to get a job and stop lying about, that I was good for nothing and pathetic...'

'Don't mind him. I don't give a hoot what he thinks, for goodness' sake...'

'No. He's right. I am a disgrace. I should be able to put this behind me, but I can't.'

'But you were just following orders,' Aisling said, trying to be reasonable.

Mark spoke slowly. 'That's what the Nazis are saying now. That's their standard defence – I was just following orders. It won't stand up, nor should it. And it's the same with us. I don't want to live with this forever, and I don't want you to waste your life with someone like me.'

'I am *not* wasting my life!' Her temper was riled now. 'Tell me this, Mark. If I were like you are now, hurt and upset and damaged, what would you do? Give up on me? Tell me to pull myself together? Leave me?'

'Of course not, but it's not the same...'

'It *is* the same!' She was almost shouting now. 'For better, for worse, in sickness and in health – remember those words, Mark Belitho?'

'Till death us do part.' He gazed at her, and he didn't need to say any more.

She put her hands on both sides of his head, drawing her face close to his. 'We will find a way to get you better, Mark. I will, if it's the last thing I do. But if you take your own life, I swear to you now, I will never forgive you. Do you hear me? Never.' Her breathing was laboured from the sheer emotion of it all.

'Stay with me, please, my love, stay with me. I couldn't bear to lose you. There has been so much loss, so much pain and grief and tears. Look at poor Delilah trying to manage without Terry. So many men from this village alone will never come home. All around the world, the same thing – mothers, fathers, wives, children, all sitting round their dinner tables with an empty place that won't ever be filled. Do you think they would want their sacrifice to be for nothing? We won. We stopped Hitler and drove him and his evil regime back to hell where they belong. And you survived, you are still here. And I know it's hard. I can't imagine what it feels like to have done and seen what you did. But can't you see, Mark? You lived. They all died but you didn't, so honour them by living your life. Come back to me, be my husband again.' Aisling was crying now; they both were.

He put his arms around her and together they sat, clinging to each other.

CHAPTER 4

*L*illian held the letter, her heart thumping wildly.

My dearest Lillian,

I'm writing to you from the hospital. It has come to the attention of some of the folks round here that I had a relationship with a white woman while I was stationed overseas, and they don't like that. You know who I mean. I don't think his sinful pride will let him get over you refusing to dance with him. I guess the fact that I refused to accept the blue ticket when I was being decommissioned didn't help my cause. They want to send all us black soldiers out on the blue ticket so we don't qualify for the GI Bill and get to go to college. I said I wasn't willing to accept it, so it had to go to a committee. I did get an honourable discharge in the end, but some folks sure were not happy about it.

Even now, to be in a coloured hospital, kept separate from whites when we were good enough to die with them and for them for all those years, seems very hard to take. My two brothers died for this country, my mother gone too – she couldn't take losing them – and we fought for people to be free, and yet I come back to this. Not one single thing has changed, and it all seems so much worse now. I suppose I shouldn't be writing you this sort of thing, and I apologize, but we did say we would always be honest. And this is me being honest. The way we were treated before the war, it was hard and wrong, but since coming back, I don't know, Lillian, it's harder.

I think about those times every day, when we were together, and I miss you. I pray to the Lord Jesus that he'll protect you and your family, and I told our pastor and my cousin Ruth all about you. Lillian, this is the hardest thing I've ever had to write, but I think you should forget about me and move on with your life. During the war, things were different. Nobody knew what was going to happen, so there was a sense that all the rules were no longer in force, but they are back now with a vengeance. Lying here, broken bones and bleeding, I got a reality check. Your society won't ever accept me, and mine won't ever accept you. All they see is the colour of my skin. They don't under-stand what we had – sometimes I don't even understand it myself.

My cousin Ruth is going to post this for me in Chicago. I've told her all about you. She's kind of like a sister to me. She lives there now and is going back soon. It's safer.

The day they put me on that troop ship and took me away from you was the hardest day of my life. I wish you happiness and joy. Nothing will erase the memory of you, my beautiful Lillian, brave as a lion.

Always yours,

Beau

She angrily wiped the tear from her eye. How could this be happening? She had seen how Beau and his fellow black soldiers were treated by their commanding officers and was appalled. British people were generally very grateful to the Americans, all of them, regardless of the colour of their skin, but this was so difficult. She had wanted Beau to stay, but of course, the military had other plans. They flatly refused to let them marry, or to let him stay; he had to go back and finish his service in America. The plan had been for him to come back and for them to marry, but in hindsight, she wished they'd have just married without his commanding officer's permission. What could he have done about it?

It was all so unfair. White GIs were allowed to marry and bring their brides back to America if they so wished, but no such privilege was allowed for men like Beau. The day he left, she made him swear he would come back, or that she would go to America after him. Beau had explained that there was no way Lillian could go over there. If he were seen with a white woman… It just wasn't acceptable. It would put her in danger and might even mean he could be killed. The whole situation seemed impossible.

She found herself wishing her mother was in town, something she could never before have imagined in her wildest dreams. She and Perry had been swanning about in the South of France for the last four months, and apart from an occasional phone call and the odd postcard, she'd heard nothing.

She and Violet had never really gotten along. Lillian was her father's pet, not her mother's, but in a funny way, it was Beau who had drawn the two women closer.

Lillian would never forget the first time her snobbish mother laid eyes on Beau. She was horrified. But over time, Beau endeared himself to the point where Lady Violet Kenefick almost flirted with her daughter's lover. Lillian was used to it; most women who met Beau had precisely the same reaction. He was incredibly good-looking, standing six feet four, with broad shoulders, a gorgeous rumbling voice, and eyes of liquid chocolate. His face was etched in her memory – it looked like it had been carved from ebony. He turned heads wherever they went, and she was so proud to be on his arm. He made her heart thump every time she saw him, and when he fell in love with her, she was in heaven. Many of her friends were appalled when they heard that she was involved with a black man, but she didn't care. Secretly, though they'd never admit it of course, they were jealous.

She looked around the sparse and dank flat. Between her allowance from her mother – siphoned off her own allowance from Perry – and the miserable sum she got from Sam, she just about managed to keep a roof over her head. She scurried to the shops when she needed food, but other than that, she didn't venture out. It was easier than seeing the inevitable glances, and she didn't want to run into anyone she knew. But that strategy wasn't going to work for too much longer. She needed advice and help, and there was no one she could turn to. Her society friends were just that, society people. Nothing embarrassed them more than poverty, and her current problem would cause them to run a mile. Most of them dropped her when she got together with Beau anyway. Her mother had liked Beau, but as far as she was concerned, it was over and done with – sad but that was how it was. Sam didn't have a clue, and anyway, he was so caught up with Kate and the baby and being fussed over by the Murphys every five minutes, he was a dead loss.

She sat down and pulled a writing pad towards her.

My darling Beau,

What have they done to you? Are you all right? I can't bear to think of you in a hospital. Please write back soon and tell me the extent of your injuries. I miss you so much, days seem like weeks. I simply have to see you. I know you said I could not come to America, that we would not be accepted, but surely that cannot be true everywhere?

Or you could come back here, to England. You know people are more accepting here. You would be respected, and you could get a job and we could live happily.

She paused.

How far should she go? Maybe the last letter was an excuse. Maybe he just didn't want to come back? Immediately, she dismissed it. He loved her. She knew he did. She wouldn't plead and beg; she had too much pride. If he came back, it would have to be because he was hers, one hundred percent.

Please, Beau. Give me some hope. I don't want to live without you.

Ever yours,

Lillian xxx

She sealed the envelope quickly in case she decided to change the letter. She knew it sounded so needy – desperate even – but that's what she was.

CHAPTER 5

*D*ermot and Isabella found a seat by the window aboard the *Irish Mist* and watched as the stevedores undid the ropes that bound the ship to the Welsh port. The journey across England and into Wales had been tiring, and Isabella was sad to leave Kate and the baby, but Dermot was glad to be getting home. England was fine, and it was home to two of his three daughters now so he had resigned himself to visiting there occasionally, but in his heart, he would never fully trust English men. He had seen too much of what they were capable of during the Troubles, and while he liked some of them individually, as a group, he wasn't happy in their company.

He settled Isabella with a cup of tea and a bun and sat opposite her. She had aged a little over the years. Her jet-black hair now had streaks of grey, and her curvaceous figure had softened, but he loved her every bit as much as he did the day he married her. He still caught his breath every night when she took her long curly hair out of a bun and let it fall over her shoulders. She had stood by him through everything – his time in the IRA when the girls were small, all the years working for the Kenefics that had ended with them being homeless and almost destitute. She never once blamed him. When Eve, Aisling and Kate were young, she was the perfect mother, and nothing had changed. She adored each of their girls with all her heart, and now that she was a grandmother, she relished the role.

He was going to wait until they were back in Dublin to raise the matter of returning to Robinswood, but he thought that now might be better. There were only a few passengers. Even though the war was over and travel restrictions were loosened, most people had neither the money nor the inclination to cross the Irish Sea from either direction.

Once they were back at the Hamilton-Brooks home, it would be the usual chaos of children and matters to attend to. Here on the boat, he had her undivided attention.

The more he thought about it, the more he wanted to take Sam up on his offer, but he wasn't sure Isabella would want to go back. She liked Dublin. She got on very well with Elena and had been a great support to her in the years after her husband's disappearance. She loved Arthur and Georgie as if they were her own. The Hamilton-Brooks children would be going off to boarding school in England – a barbaric practice in Dermot's opinion – and Elena had plans to open up the house as a kind of training centre for orphans who were finished in the care system. He would teach the boys skills that would make them employable, and Isabella and Eve would do the same for the girls in the house. Isabella was looking forward to the challenge.

Elena was a powerhouse when it came to causes, and it would be hard to abandon her and her plans. They had been a great support to her when her husband was taken to Germany in 1940. He was most likely dead now, as the Germans would have been happy to get their hands on a high-ranking British spy. Dermot did feel guilt; Thomas was taken to Germany because of his actions, and the fact that Dermot did what he did to save his own daughters was cold comfort.

'Thanks, love, I'm parched.' Isabella sipped her tea and settled into the seat.

'Are you all right now? Not too lonely for them?' Dermot asked. He hated to see the sadness in his wife's eyes each time she said goodbye to one of their daughters.

'Ah, I'll be grand.' She gave a weak smile. 'There's no fear for Kate.

She's taking to motherhood like a duck to water, and Sam tries to be around as much as he can. To be honest, it's Aisling I'm more worried about.'

He nodded. 'I know, but what can we do, Bella? We need to give her space. She's not a newlywed, I know, but it's the first time she's had Mark at home for any length of time. I remember when we first married, I wouldn't have wanted your mother landing up.' He gave her a playful wink.

'If it was just that, I'd be fine, but I get the feeling there's something else wrong.'

Dermot placed his hand over his wife's. 'I'm sure she's grand, but even if she's not, we have to let her come to us. Mark is her husband, her closest relative now – we'd be doing wrong to stick our noses in. Aisling has a good head on her shoulders, you know she has, so she'll be all right.'

Isabella wasn't convinced. 'I just wish she'd talk to me. Every letter is all cheery bright, but I just know by her, something isn't right. Just last week when I phoned her from Kate's and offered to visit, she was all evasive. And what about his family? We've never even met them. I know the wedding was rushed because of the war and everything, but in all the years since? I brought it up with Aisling in a letter – I know you probably think I shouldn't have, but I wanted to know why – and all she said is the Belithos don't leave their village. I mean, did you ever hear such codswallop? Don't leave the village indeed.'

Dermot smiled at the indignant look on his wife's face. Mark had mentioned a few years ago that his family were all ex-military, so his guess was that some of them probably served in Ireland at some point and, as a result, would have no love lost on the Irish. He didn't voice that opinion to Bella, though, for fear he'd make the situation even worse.

'It's an odd one, all right.' He sipped his own tea and bit into the dry bun. He grimaced. 'I can't wait to get back to proper food. This is like eating sawdust.' He put the offending confection back on the plate.

'They have to skimp on the butter, as they only have margarine, and even then, it's not enough. And that powdered egg… Well, it was never near a hen is all I can say.' She examined her own bun. 'I'll make a nice brown cake when we get back and a batch of scones. Arthur will be delighted – he loves a scone with butter and jam.' Isabella smiled at the thought of the Hamilton-Brooks children. They were ten and twelve now, and she'd looked after them since they were five and seven. She loved them, and the feeling was entirely mutual.

'He does. I doubt he'll get that kind of feeding when he goes over to school in England in September,' Dermot said ruefully.

'Don't.' She raised her hand to stop him. 'I can't bear the thought of it. He's only ten. And Georgie is twelve, I know, but she's only a little girl really. I tried convincing Elena to leave them in Dublin as day pupils, but Thomas always said he wanted Arthur to go to his old school, and Georgie is to go to someplace that every woman in her family has attended since God was a child, so she's not for moving.' Isabella shook her head. 'I don't know, Der. They are like us, but in some way then, so different. We would never in a million years have let ours go to boarding school.'

'We couldn't have afforded it even if we wanted to.' He smiled.

'That's true.' She smiled back. 'But even if we could have, we never would have considered it. Children need their parents.'

Dermot nodded, and an easy silence fell between them. Now was his chance. 'Bella,' he began, 'Sam wants us to go back to Robinswood with him and Kate.' He outlined the whole plan, hoping he sounded as neutral as possible; he didn't want to influence his wife's decision.

She sat and listened until he was finished. 'Do you want to go back?' She faced him and fixed him with a questioning look.

He paused. 'If you do, then I do.'

'I suppose when Arthur and Georgie go away to school, there won't be much for us to do, but what about Eve? And Elena's plans for the orphans?'

'Well, Eve is all right now. I don't think she'll ever get over losing Jack completely, but she's managing. Imagine he's six years dead now? Hard to believe. And it will do her good to make her own life, I think. Elena too is managing. They don't need us as much any more. I think it might be the best thing for them. For as long as we're there, they won't ever stand on their own two feet.'

'I suppose you're right.' Isabella lowered her eyes as she sipped her tea.

He knew that gesture. She could not look into his face and lie to him. 'You knew, didn't you? About Sam's suggestion.'

She looked out the window, a smile playing on her lips.

'Isabella Murphy, I've known you too long for playing games.' He looked at her with mock sternness.

'All right. Kate told me that Sam was going to speak to you. She wanted to get me on her side, but I told her what I always tell them, what we've told them from the start – that we always agree on everything.'

Dermot laughed. 'I remember some right fiery conversations between you and me over the years for a pair that always agree.'

'Ah, but they don't know that.' She winked. 'Any good general would tell you to always pose a united front, no matter what's going on behind the scenes.'

'So, General Murphy, what do you think?' he asked.

'I'd miss Elena and Eve, and I would feel bad to bail out on them with everything they've planned. But then I think it would be lovely to have our own home again, and I think the idea that we could buy some land would give us a bit of stability for when we're old. And I like the idea that we could offer a home to Eve and Aisling too if they ever needed it. Of course, it's going to be all hell of a job to get Robinswood up and running again. I don't think either Kate or Sam has the faintest clue what they're dealing with. They were only children when they left, and they've this lovely romantic idea, but I remember it well and so do you. Dry rot, wet rot, leaking pipes, no heating, cracked chimneys... 'Twould be easier to say what's right than list all that's wrong with that house, and you're not getting any younger and neither am I.'

'Still, it would be nice to wipe the smile off Charlie Warren's face, wouldn't it? To get the land back, to farm it again? And what do you mean, I'm not getting any younger? I'm in my prime, I'll have you know. There's nothing I can't do.' He winked and gave her leg a playful squeeze.

'Go on away out of that, you auld chancer, I'm well aware of your abilities.' Her giggle took any sting out of the words.

'Of course, there are plenty of people, not just Charlie Warren, who won't be happy to see us up in the big house,' Dermot said.

'True. In lots of ways, you can't blame them, I suppose. We fought so hard to rule ourselves, to own our own land, be masters of our own destiny, but independence hasn't meant what people thought it would. Seeing us, the former servants, up in the big house, living like gentry, will certainly rankle with a few of the locals, but we can't let that stop us. Warren will hate you to the day he dies because he thinks you abandoned the cause once the Treaty was signed. Nothing will change that, so we shouldn't even bother to try.'

'So we'll do it?' he asked, allowing the excitement to creep into his voice.

'If Eve is all right with it, then yes, I'd love to go home.'

CHAPTER 6

*E*ve took the apple tart out of the oven as Elena entered the big sunny kitchen. It overlooked the beautifully tended lawns through a wall of glass panels, the middle of which were folding French doors that opened onto the old stone patio for fine days. The house was a large one in the wealthy Dublin suburb – twelve bedrooms and a self-contained series of connecting rooms on the top floor where Eve and her parents lived.

The kitchen was at the rear of the red-bricked and ivy-covered house, and despite there being several other rooms on the ground floor – drawing room, sunroom, office, downstairs cloakroom, formal dining room, everything a house of this size should have – Elena and her children and Eve and her parents mainly congregated in the huge, bright kitchen. It had a lived-in feel, with children's sports equipment and shoes stacked against one wall. One end of the huge table had drawings they did, books and several pieces of correspondence that Elena was in the process of dealing with. There was a large dining table, pitch pine, that could seat sixteen easily, and a marble-topped island. Eve and Isabella did all the cooking, and now that it was going to be a classroom of sorts, at least they had no worries about space.

'Oh, Eve, that smells divine!' Elena inhaled appreciatively. 'What time do you expect them?'

Eve smiled. Elena's perfectly coiffed blonde hair was in a chignon, and she wore an immaculate coffee-coloured skirt and ivory blouse. She didn't look like a woman who ate apple tart, but Eve knew she had a very healthy appetite. The difference was Elena never put on any weight. Eve only had to look at a cake and she felt her waistband tighten.

'The boat is docking at three, so they'll probably be back by four or half past, I'd say. I've sewn the name tapes on the children's uniforms – do you want to write their names on yourself?'

She placed the hot apple tart on the countertop and smiled. Elena was a wonderful employer, never speaking down to the Murphys and so appreciative of everything they did for her and the children. So different from when they worked for Lady Kenefick.

'Oh, heaven's no, they'd want you to do it. You have such better writing than I have. I'm glad Isabella and Dermot will be back before they go, though it will be like the valley of tears, I know. They think I'm hard-hearted, sending them off like this, and it is horrid, but it's what Thomas would have wanted.'

Eve saw the familiar shadow cross Elena's face at the mention of her husband. He was dead, she knew that, though there was no body or official confirmation, but she missed him, and a glimmer of hope remained. She never encouraged any of the men who had shown an interest in her. She was an attractive woman, and Eve knew how she felt.

Jack had been dead just a little longer than Thomas was missing, but in her heart, in lots of ways, it felt like yesterday.

'They'll be fine,' Eve said noncommittally. She agreed with her parents. Despite Arthur and Georgie's parents being British aristocrats, the children were Irish, and they loved the local school. They had lots of friends and were always being invited to birthday parties, and Arthur played rugby and Georgie was in the Girls' Brigade. They came home every day to Isabella, Dermot and Eve, whom they loved, and their mother, when she was there, whom they adored.

'Of course they will. It didn't do me any harm, probably.' She gave Eve a conspiratorial wink and popped a bit of pastry from the tart into her mouth. 'Mmm… Eve, you have your mother's touch in baking, that's for sure. Poor old Arthur and Georgie will hate the food in school, everyone does, but they really are going from riches to rags in gastronomic terms.'

'They'll be home in the holidays, though, won't they?' Eve asked as she sifted icing sugar on top of the tart.

'Of course. I'm not a complete dragon.' Elena laughed. 'Besides, we'll be so busy with everything once the children are in school. You and your parents are part of our family now. Neither I nor Georgie nor Arthur could ever bear to lose you.'

Eve thought about the conversation she'd had with Kate. It was up to her parents to make any decision for themselves, and she could almost say with a hundred percent certainty that they would go back to Robinswood, but she wanted to stay on.

'These children who grow up in the institution need so much to enable them to get employment. You and Isabella will be so busy teaching housekeeping, cooking and so on, you won't have time to miss Georgie and Arthur. And that new shed Dermot built in the grounds, it's going to be perfect. There's plenty of room for the work-shop, so we should be able to take seven or eight boys at a time. Dermot is designing the curriculum, teaching the boys about…well… I'm not sure exactly, but manly things. These young people are going to get a real shot, and who better to teach them than the Murphys?' She giggled.

Eve smiled. Elena was a little scattered, but her heart was in the right place. 'Well, Elena, I know they'll want to speak to you, but I wouldn't bank on my parents if I were you. They've had an offer to go back to Robinswood with Kate and Sam, so I wouldn't be surprised if they took it.'

'Oh…' She looked crestfallen.

'I'm not definite or anything, but I think they will be going back. I just thought you should know.' Eve hated bursting her bubble. 'And

I'm happy to stay, so if we got someone to replace Daddy, then we could just go ahead?'

'Well, I can understand why they'd want to, I suppose. Your father loves the countryside. I always felt he was rather a fish out of water in the city...' Elena sat down despondently.

'But even if they did go, we could still do it, couldn't we?' Eve sat beside her. 'We get a man in, and that big shed could have one end turned into a little flat, so it could be a live-in position. It's not the end of the world.'

'I know but... Look, you're right. And I mustn't make them feel guilty. Dermot and Isabella have done so much for me. Thank you for putting me on notice. Now I can react with excitement at their new plans.' Elena seemed genuinely thrilled and relieved. 'And you're right, we can do it together. Now, I've to meet with the board of governors, but I'll be back this evening and we can all discuss it then.'

Eve watched her drive erratically down the avenue, wincing as she rolled clean over a hydrangea her father had planted before he left for England. Elena had only learned to drive in recent years despite having a car since before the war, and she never really got the hang of it. Dermot had given up after about ten lessons, fearing for his life.

She wondered if her parents would decide to stay in Dublin. She doubted it. Her father was an estate manager first and foremost, and while doing odd jobs and gardening for Elena provided a roof over their heads and a good wage, it wasn't what he wanted. He never said, but she guessed that he hated living in someone else's house as well. When they were at Robinswood, they got a house as part of the package, and though it wasn't their own, it always felt like it was. Until the day they had to leave.

As the afternoon passed, Eve reminisced about those days. She made up her parents' bed with freshly laundered sheets. They had been heartbroken at leaving their home. Kate and Aisling had taken off for England in the middle of the night to join the British air force, much to their parent's horror, but all Eve felt was jubilation. In those days before they left Robinswood, she was engaged to Jack O'Neill.

She married him the week they left and went to live with him and his mother in Cork.

She felt a stab of guilt about her mother-in-law. She'd only seen her twice since Jack died. She should visit more often, but it was all the way down in Cork, and besides, Eve always felt Jack's mother blamed her. If Jack hadn't been working so hard to save up a deposit for a house for them, he might have been paying more attention and the accident might not have happened. Her mother-in-law never said that – well, not since those horrible days after the funeral – but Eve knew in her heart that's what Mrs O'Neill felt. It was sort of by mutual consent that they gave each other a wide berth.

Jack would be thirty years old today. She tried to picture him as older, but she couldn't. In her mind, he was always young and handsome and making her laugh. She wished she could remember his voice. It upset her more than she admitted that she could no longer hear it in her head. She could picture him as clear as anything, and sometimes she would get a smell as a man passed her on the tram or in the street and it would be his scent, but his voice was lost to the mists of time, and she hated it.

She heard a car door slam outside, so she went to the window. Her parents were getting out of a taxi. She ran out to meet them and found herself enveloped in her father's arms.

'Hello, Evie, how's things? I see Elena drove over my flowers?' Dermot rolled his eyes in exasperation, walked to the bush and tried to repair the damage.

Eve giggled. 'I take it you didn't notice that half of the pillar is missing below at the gate then?'

'What? I only just repaired it after the last time she demolished it. That woman shouldn't be given a tricycle, not to mind a car.'

'Come in and don't worry about it. You can take a look at it tomorrow.' Isabella hugged her daughter. 'You all right?' she asked quietly. She'd remembered it was Jack's birthday.

Eve nodded, not trusting herself to speak.

'Now, let's get in and get the kettle on. I need to get out of these shoes.'

35

Over tea and apple tart, Eve told her parents about the conversation she'd had with Elena. She saw them catch each other's eye.

'I know about Kate's plans,' she said to reassure them. They'd been so good to her since Jack died, holding her together in so many ways. 'And I think you should go. She asked me too, but I want to stay here and help Elena set up the training centre. But for you, Robinswood is always going to be home.'

'But what about you, pet? We can't leave you here alone,' Dermot said, holding her hand across the table.

'Daddy, I'm twenty-nine years old, not five. I was in a bad way after Jack died, I know that, and I'm so glad I had you and Mammy. I don't know what I would have done. But I'm all right now. Honestly, I am. I still miss him, every day, but I can breathe again. Remember, the night Jack died, you told me that all I had to do was breathe in and out, nothing more. I'm fine, and you need to get on with your lives. I'd actually like it, I think, helping young girls to get some skills so they'd be able to support themselves. I was so lost, and such a burden, so I thought it would be nice to help other people.'

Isabella put her arms around her daughter. 'You were never a burden, Eve. You are our child, and no matter what age you are, you'll always be that. You were dealt a very hard blow, losing Jack like that, and we were only happy we could be there. But you're right. You're on the mend now, and I think we will go back to Robinswood.'

CHAPTER 7

*K*ate tiptoed out of the bedroom, hoping that Jack wouldn't wake. He loved to fall asleep as she nursed him, and if Mammy hadn't shown her the trick of tickling his toes to wake him up, she would spend every hour of the day and night sitting under him. She adored her son. He was the most beautiful baby, and when his blue eyes locked with hers, she could melt. But she was exhausted.

Sam was in Germany most of the time; the operations there were ongoing even though the war was over. He promised her he would be decommissioned soon, but when exactly 'soon' was, was not clear. He was working so hard and trying to gather enough money to at least get them started up in Robinswood. She didn't want to nag, but it was lonely without him.

He had offered to get a nanny, and she had hooted with laughter. 'The class divide thankfully doesn't enter our lives much, Sam.' She grinned. 'But the irony of who your nanny was when you were small seems to have escaped you.'

Sam coloured with embarrassment. 'Of course, your mother was wonderful, we loved her, we still do…but…'

She gave him a squeeze to show she was only joking. Apart from the fact that they couldn't afford one, no child of hers was being pawned off on somebody else to rear.

Having Mammy and Daddy over was wonderful, as they were so capable, but she knew they were happy to get back, Daddy especially. She hadn't heard from them since they left, but she was fairly confident it would be a yes to the proposal of returning to Robinswood. Kate couldn't wait.

London looked worse if anything since the war ended. The camaraderie of the last six years was fast dissipating, and people were fed up with everything. Nothing worked properly, the city was in a shambles, and rationing meant there was nothing nice to eat. Some of the men were back in civvies, but they were either physically or psychologically scarred so badly it was hard to imagine how life would ever be the same. Mr Churchill had gotten the boot, which she thought was unfair considering how much he did to rally everyone during the war, but that was politics, she supposed. She longed for the tranquillity and beauty of Robinswood. At night, she dreamed about Irish food, and more than anything else, she wanted Jack to grow up there, to love it as much as his parents and his grandparents – except Violet of course – did.

It was hard to imagine Sam as Lord Kenefick and impossible to visualise herself as Lady Kenefick, but it was the reality. She had decided she would not like people to call her Lady anything – not that they would anyway – as she had always been just Kate Murphy and that was who she was happy to stay. They could be lording away with Sam if they wanted to, but she was just going to be Kate.

She reached the bottom step and stopped, listening, holding her breath. A heavy shower that had been threatening all day was now hammering the roof of the glass conservatory off the kitchen, but so far, it hadn't woken Jack.

She was going to write to Aisling. This time, she was going to say what was on her mind. She was so worried about her all the way down there in Devon, and she still had the feeling that things weren't right. Something in Aisling's voice when they spoke on the phone – she sounded tired or something. Kate wondered if her sister was pregnant; she knew she had been exhausted in the first months with Jack. But if she was, that would be great news, so why would she not say?

She put the kettle on the gas and sat at the kitchen table with her pad and pen. The house was spotless after Mammy's visit; Kate had just been too exhausted to clean before her parents arrived. The room was much brighter now as well since Daddy cut all the trees that were blocking the light into the back of the house. He'd even made a little crib for Jack to be used downstairs so she didn't need to lug the heavy Moses basket up and down during the day.

Just as she lifted the pen, there was a knock on the door. Her heart sank. *Please don't let it wake Jack.* She ran to stop the caller banging again and opened the door to a sodden Lillian. Kate was gobsmacked, not just to see her sister-in-law who had only called to see them once in the past year – and that was with Beau before he had to go back – but to see the version of Lillian that stood before her.

'Lillian! Come in... You're soaked.' Kate ushered her into the kitchen where a gas heater was on so the room wasn't cold.

'I got caught in that bloody shower all the way up at the station, and there were no cabs, so I had to walk.' Lillian's chocolate-coloured cloche was soaked, and her fur-lined cape was dripping on the kitchen tiles. Kate arranged two chairs in front of the fire as a clothes horse and turned as Lillian peeled off her wet things, down to her chemise.

'Here, give me your cape and hat, and we'll lay them here to dry. I can lend you something to wear if you'd like...' Kate turned, and the words fell away. Lillian was not the svelte woman she had been only a few months earlier.

'Oh... I... I... Sorry, I was just...' Kate tried not to stare at Lillian, who was quite obviously pregnant.

'Let me get you something to wear.' Kate pulled a dress and cardigan from a basket of washed clothes she had yet to replace in the wardrobe.

Lillian pulled them on.

'I need your help.' Lillian's clipped accent was still sharp, but there was a tremor in her voice that Kate had never heard before.

'Sit down. Let me make you a cup of tea.' Kate fussed about, playing for time. Lillian was pregnant? Was the child Beau's? The timing would be right, she reckoned, doing a quick calculation.

Lillian said nothing but accepted the cup of tea and sipped it. Her hand shook as she replaced the Royal Doulton china cup back on the saucer.

'How far along...' Kate began eventually.

'Six months.'

'And Beau?'

'Is gone back to America and doesn't show any signs of returning here.' Lillian sighed, and it sounded like it came from her toes.

'But surely he would want to come back, marry you, now that you're...' Kate couldn't believe someone as decent as Beau would just abandon his pregnant girlfriend.

'I haven't told him.'

Kate instinctively took Lillian's hands across the table. They were like ice. 'But you must tell him. I know there might be some raised eyebrows, and there's bound to be a bit of talk, but if Beau is by your side, if you got married...' She didn't need to say how a girl who found herself in trouble out of wedlock would be treated, not to mention if the child were black as part of the bargain.

'He's in hospital. He was beaten up by police for nothing. One of his white superior officers knew about us, even though we kept a very low profile, never flaunting our relationship. But this man knew about Beau and me, and he couldn't stand that a black man had succeeded where he failed. This man had tried it on with me one night in a club. I rejected him, and then he saw me and Beau together. He didn't do anything while here, but once he got back to America, he made sure his friends got to hear about it, and Beau has been a target.' Lillian's voice was strong and clear, but Kate knew she was torn apart inside.

'That's awful. Why doesn't he just leave? He's been decommissioned, hasn't he?'

Lillian nodded, her eyes bright. 'He seems to think we have no future, that society won't accept us.'

'So you can't go over there to him?' Kate struggled to understand. She, like many others in England, was shocked by the way the black soldiers were treated by their fellow countrymen.

'Definitely not, it seems. You saw how they treated them with your own eyes, and that was over here. I can't imagine what it must be like over there, when the law is on their side.' Lillian was resigned.

'But you have to tell him. I mean... Violet will have a fit, for one thing. I take it you haven't told her?' Kate asked, already knowing the answer. If Violet had even a hint of it, she would have chewed Sam's ears off on the subject.

'No, of course not.' Lillian was dismissive. 'I haven't told anyone. I've been in my flat apart from rushing out to get a few groceries every few days. I wear this when I go out.' Lillian pointed to a gold band on her ring finger.

'Well, that'll work on people you don't know, and until this baby decides to join us, but then...' Kate tried to be diplomatic, but both she and Lillian knew the harsh reality.

The two women had never been close, but Sam's older sister had softened somewhat from the insufferable brat she was growing up, or at least she had around Beau. But now that he was gone, the old Lillian could well return.

She shook her head. 'I know. It's hopeless. I should have had it seen to. I know you're probably shocked, but it can be done if one knows the right people. But I couldn't bear it – it might be all I have of him. And now, well, now it's too late even if I wanted to.' A single tear escaped from the corner of her eye.

Kate tried not to think about how women got rid of their babies. She understood why sometimes people felt that they had no choice, but then all she could think about was her lovely baby boy upstairs.

'Look, Lillian, it's not right you're dealing with this alone. Beau would want to know, and you need him. I know it seems hopeless, and London is not ideal, and Sam and I and Jack are going back to

Robinswood...' The words were out before she realised it. What had she done?

Lillian looked as if she were drowning and someone had thrown her a rope. 'Oh, are you really? Well, that's simply perfect.' Her face was transformed. 'Oh, Kate, this is marvellous. How wonderful, wonderful, to be able to go back to our home. I loved it there as a child. Our children can grow up together there, ponies and tennis parties. Oh, why didn't you say before? It would have saved me all this worry.'

Kate tried not to backtrack, though every fibre of her being wanted to give her sister-in-law a few home truths. Firstly, Lillian had done nothing but complain about Robinswood all the years she lived there; she went on and on about how much she hated it. Secondly, there would be no ponies or tennis parties; it was going to be scrimping and saving and working hard. Finally – and this was the thing that could never be said but was true – however difficult it would be to be a mixed-race child in England, the idea of a little black boy or girl running around Kilthomand was just inconceivable.

'Well, we don't really have... You see, my parents are coming as well...' Kate tried.

'Better again – this is perfect. Nobody there would dare judge us. My father was an earl, and I am Lady Lillian Kenefick of Robinswood. My brother is now Lord Kenefick, and Jack will inherit his title, but my child will be part of that household.'

Kate started to panic – this was getting out of hand rapidly. San would go mad. 'Well, I don't know if that would work. I mean, the house is falling to bits, and it might not be a suitable place for a newborn...'

'But you're taking Jack, are you not?' Lillian fixed Kate with a stare, all vulnerability gone. She had been thrown a lifeline, and she was never letting go.

'Yes, but that's different. My parents will be working on the estate –'

Lillian interrupted her. 'Oh, Kate, I don't mind your parents going back there. Dermot and Isabella are wonderful servants, always were.

They can take care of two as easily as one. Jack and this little one will be company for each other.' She patted her rounded abdomen, relieved and satisfied. 'When is the move?'

'I don't know, and anyway, I'd have to talk to Sam. He might not...' Kate was desperate now. For that split second, she was little Kate Murphy, the servant's child, and Lillian was the earl's daughter. She could not stand up to her. Sam would have a fit when she told him. She changed the subject back to Beau. 'But I still really think you should tell Beau.' She was firm on that at least.

'I want to, believe me. Nothing would give me greater relief. But I don't want to be one of those women, wheedling and needy, begging him to come back. If I tell him – and I almost did when I wrote – I would never know for sure whether he came back for me or for the child.'

'Listen to yourself. You're pregnant with a black man's child and no wedding ring on your finger. He needs to know, and you need him to come back and marry you.' She paused. 'You *do* want him back, don't you?'

'Of course I do. I... I just can't beg. What if I was just a wartime fling? So many girls had a romance with an American just to be left high and dry. And I love him, I truly do, but now that it's all over...' Lillian's voice was barely audible.

'But he's written, hasn't he?'

Lillian nodded. Kate wondered if there weren't more to this. Had Lillian suddenly realised the opposition she was going to face in society with a black husband?

She sighed heavily, wondering how on earth she was going to get out of this one.

CHAPTER 8

*V*iolet looked across the ballroom of the Royal Excelsior Hotel at Perry laughing uproariously at something a beautifully dressed lady in her sixties was saying. Violet didn't recognise her or the other man in the trio, but they certainly looked a jolly lot. She nodded graciously as an impeccably dressed waiter offered her a glass of champagne. From the large stone balcony, one could see the glittering lights of yachts anchored at the port of Nice, waiting patiently as their owners sipped cocktails all along the French Riviera. In many ways, when one was here in such beautiful surroundings, it was hard to believe the war had ever happened.

She'd said as much to Perry the previous night as they were falling asleep in the master cabin of their 160-foot yacht, *La Violette*. It was Perry's latest toy, named after his wife, and he loved it. Of course, he knew precisely nothing about sailing, but that didn't matter. Captain Royston and his crew managed all of that expertly, so all she and Perry had to do was relax and enjoy it.

'Mmm...' he'd mumbled, kissing her neck. She had hoped a conversation might dissuade him from such amorous advances, but unlike most people, he didn't want to talk endlessly about the war. 'It's over and done with, old girl, let's move on. It was quite dreadful enough while it lasted – why prolong the misery by dwelling?' was one of his favourite lines.

Lord Perry Goodall was not a physically attractive man in the conventional sense, or in any sense, she admitted, and she did rather have to lie back and think of England once or twice a week, but it was a very small price to pay for the life she now enjoyed. She didn't marry for money as such – she had learned during the war to fend for herself – but she liked him. He was clever and funny, and he absolutely adored her; he had from the moment they met when she held a little drinks party in 1943 to ask those of her class to consider building houses on their land to shelter all those families who had lost everything in the Blitz. She convinced the charity she volunteered with to rent a room in the Ritz, and they trusted her that the investment would pay off. It did, and several hundred acres of potential building land were committed by the end of the evening. She had made a speech, appealing to their sense of duty, to the fact that they were the British nobility and they had a responsibility to their people. And finally, her ace in the hole – once the war was over, they would have a grateful and available workforce for their estates. They would get rent from the houses and rejuvenate their crumbling old piles in the process. The way she explained it, they were, in fact, giving up nothing and gaining a tremendous amount. She was quite proud of herself. The added boon that she met Perry was unforeseen but most welcome.

She had managed better than she anticipated once she accepted her new position in life after leaving Robinswood, that of an impoverished gentlewoman, and funnily enough, she had enjoyed the experience of being one of the ordinary people. She'd had quite a good war, living in her little rented house in Hampstead with Samuel and Kate and Lillian and Beau around, but it was rather lovely to be back in her rightful place.

Perry was an earl, as Austin was – in fact, Perry's older brother Reginald had been at school with Austin – but her second husband was a very different type of man. Perry enjoyed the good things in life and was generous and kind, but he was no fool. He didn't wager on horses, and while he enjoyed a glass of Bollinger or a nice single malt, he was not a drinker in the way her former husband was. There were no leaking windows or threadbare carpets at Framington Hall, and because Perry was such a generous and well-liked employer, he had managed to retain a reasonably extensive staff, so life was really very pleasant.

How he'd never married, being as eligible as he was, remained a mystery, but it was her good fortune to have caught his eye that night, and it had been plain sailing ever since.

'Violet, that dress is truly spectacular. I've been eyeing you jealously since you arrived.' Lady Esther Cavendish sidled up beside her. Violet remembered Esther as one of the women who had shunned her when she first arrived in London because she no longer had money or position; but still, one had to be polite.

'Oh, I've had this forever, though I will be relieved when the clothes rationing ends, won't you? It really is tiresome.' Violet sighed, but she knew the other woman was right. Now that she had the money to attend Knightsbridge's finest hair salons and beauty rooms, she looked very good. She'd maintained her figure thanks to rationing, and Perry loved her blonde hair, which she wore dressed back from her face in soft waves. He didn't need to know the blonde was helped along by a tint. Make-up was still almost impossible to get in the shops, but Perry had some sent from the United States when he heard her bemoan her lack of lipstick. Couture too was slowly becoming available to those who could source or afford it, which she thankfully could, though she didn't go overboard at home – it didn't do to look too glamorous when everyone else was still so drab. But down here on the Riviera, people felt free to splash out, and she loved it.

'I agree. And to think that the war is over yet they continue to reduce the coupons. Well, frankly, I don't understand it. They no longer need to make uniforms, so what on earth can the delay be about?' Esther looked thoroughly put out as she glanced once more at Violet's outfit.

The new Lady Goodall noted with satisfaction that her amber

dress, worn to a summer ball at Robinswood in 1935, was still quite acceptable, whereas Esther's rather lumpy frame filled out a silly-looking baby-pink dress unflatteringly.

'Though the law does not seem to apply universally,' Esther muttered so only Violet could hear.

Violet followed her gaze to Wallis Simpson, who was telling some story to an enraptured audience. As usual, Duke Edward stood to her side, gazing adoringly.

Wallis's rail-thin figure was clad in a rather masculine jacket and pencil skirt that reached almost to her ankles. Despite the austere cut, she looked very attractive, Violet thought.

Violet's expression was non-committal following Esther's catty remark. *Of course the former king and his wife don't have to get their clothes with coupons, for goodness' sake, and Esther would do well to keep her opinions on them to herself. They may be persona non grata in Buckingham Palace, but they are still a force to be reckoned with in society.*

She caught Perry's eye across the room and gave him an almost imperceptible wink. It was their secret signal that they needed to be rescued. When one socialised as much as they did, one needed an invaluable manner of extrication from tedious or awkward situations.

Perry beckoned her over immediately.

'Oh, I think Perry needs me, Esther. It was lovely meeting you again. Regards to Clive.' She gave a sweet smile and made a beeline for her husband.

She knew Esther and others had made some very unkind remarks about Beau and Lillian, and because their circle was large but fuelled by tittle-tattle and scandal, she had heard about it just a few weeks ago. She got upset and told Perry, who was outraged on her behalf but also because he was fond of Lillian and had met and liked Beau enormously.

Violet had hidden a little smile. Perry did a lot of business with the oily Clive Cavendish, and she had a feeling that could change quite soon.

She greeted people as she crossed the elegant room, a hum of

47

conversation and clinking glasses not quite drowning out the string quartet in the corner entertaining the guests.

'Darling, let me introduce you to some American friends of mine, Gerald J. Grosvenor and Daisy Williams-Smyth.' Violet shook both of their hands and tried to remember where she'd heard the woman's name before. Once she spoke and Violet registered the American accent, she recalled instantly. She was the sole inheritor of the famous Von Hacker fortune. Her husband, now dead, was reputed to be one of the Astors as well, so she really was American royalty.

The tall man shook her hand and smiled. 'My pleasure, Lady Goodall.' He had a slow drawling accent.

Then she shook hands with the lady.

'How nice to meet you, Lady Goodall. Your husband has been telling us all about your war work.' Daisy smiled warmly.

'Oh, it was nothing in the great scheme of things, really. It was the generosity of the owners of the stately homes of England who stepped up and did the patriotic thing. I merely asked the question,' Violet replied.

'Well, I think it's marvellous. This terrible war has had such a devastating effect on the entire world, but amid the rubble and the grief, there is hope to be had when humanity and kindness shine through, don't you think?'

'Well, absolutely. Perry was most generous.' Violet smiled.

Daisy gave a chuckle. 'Oh, Perry can certainly be kind. I presume he never told you how he had a brush with the law stateside?' Merriment and mischief twinkled in her eye.

'No, he did not.' Violet looked at her husband, an eyebrow raised.

'Well, picture the scene…a speakeasy serving illegal liquor, during prohibition, you know?'

Violet was intrigued, and Perry and Gerald grinned guiltily like a pair of schoolboys.

'Well, a certain young man from the state of Mississippi was studying on the East Coast. Now this young man, whose parents had high hopes for him, was where he shouldn't have been, drinking something he should not have been drinking and dangling a young lady on his knee who would have sent his poor mama into a dead faint.'

Gerald had the grace to blush slightly. 'Daisy, I'm sure Lady Goodall...'

'Oh, Governor Grosvenor, I'm sure she would like to hear what sort of a man she married, aren't you?'

'Daisy, you are a stirrer!' Perry said good-naturedly. 'Violet, my darling, Gerald here was about to be arrested, in fact he was, so he told them he was Lord Goodall of Framington Hall, England, and I said I was his friend, Lord Loxley, and we got away with it. Though his Mississippi drawl nearly gave us away!' Perry grinned. 'Now that he's an upstanding member of the community, though, state governor no less, he's mended his ways.'

Violet laughed. 'And nothing ever came back to you on it?'

Daisy interjected again. 'No, Perry and Gerald know the right people, my dear.' She tapped the side of her nose with her index finger and chuckled again. 'But know that your earl was seconds away from being a convicted felon.'

'Well, to be fair, it was I who was caught in...well...less than ideal circumstances. I owe you, Perry. You sure saved my bacon that night.'

'I don't recall having much choice, old chap, and yes, you do owe me!' Perry clapped his old friend on the back.

Somebody else approached them, and the men began another conversation. Violet was glad to get to speak to Daisy alone.

'So you have two children from your first marriage, Perry tells me? He really is a nice man, and I'm so happy for him that he found someone to love at last.' Daisy did seem pleased, and Violet warmed to her.

'My son was in the RAF' – she tried to keep too much pride out of her voice – 'and my daughter worked at a dressing station in the West End – she even drove an ambulance, so it was all hands on deck – but our family was the norm rather than the exception.'

'Perry speaks with such pride about them and the fact that you are now a grandmother. Congratulations.' Her smile was warm and genuine.

'Thank you. Yes, I have yet to meet him. His name is John after my father, but he will be known as Jack.' Violet had decided that herself upon hearing the child's name.

'What a lovely thing to look forward to. And is your daughter married?' Daisy asked.

'No.' Violet mentally took a deep breath. 'She had a romance during the war with an American soldier actually, a coloured man, but he has been returned to the United States with his unit. She is heart-broken.' Violet had never openly admitted Lillian's relationship to anyone in their social set before, but something about this woman made her feel like she could.

'Well, Lady Goodall, I must say, I do not approve of how some of my fellow Americans regard our coloured troops, and I was just discussing this with Dwight last month when he came to dinner at my Newport house. He was full of praise for everyone who fought under our flag, regardless of skin colour.' Her eyes were compelling and showed a sharp intellect, and Violet got the impression she was kind but took no nonsense.

She led Violet by the elbow slightly away from the others. 'Not that our Southern friends see it that way,' she murmured, her eyes darting to Gerald, who was reminiscing with Perry about their times together in America.

Violet knew of the segregation and the Jim Crow laws from Beau.

'I was a little surprised at the start, to be honest, but he is a very nice man, this chap my daughter was walking out with.' Violet wanted to stick to her guns.

Daisy took a sip of her drink and said, 'I hope they can be reunited if it is what they both wish.'

'So do I,' Violet replied, and was surprised to find that she really meant it.

CHAPTER 9

*A*isling knelt down to pick up the shattered glass on the tiled floor of their cottage, trying not to cry. She was exhausted, emotionally and physically, and she longed just to crawl into bed, pull the covers over her head and sleep. Her mother and Kate had offered so often to come down to visit her and Mark in Devon, but much as she would have loved their reassuring presence, it would upset Mark too much. He became so agitated around people, and then was so contrite and upset afterwards, it wasn't worth it.

She'd bandaged his hand where he'd cut himself on the glass and given him two of the sedatives the doctor had prescribed. They knocked him out for a few hours, nothing more. She hated giving them to him – he said they gave him horrible dreams – but today she needed a break.

As she wrapped the remaining glass in newspaper, she heard a knock on the back door. Heart sinking, she went to open it.

'Oh, Mr Belitho, hello.' She tried to smile at her father-in-law, but it was hard.

'Marjorie wanted to come, but I thought I should speak to Mark alone, Asslinn,' he began, no greeting, his moustache almost bristling.

Mark's father was both a farmer and a military man. He'd served in the first war and had been, until recently, inordinately proud of his son. But Mark was not the man he once was, and former Corporal Tobias Belitho could not accept it.

'I hear he's been fighting in the Spreading Chestnut.' He glared at Aisling as if it were somehow her doing. She'd tried explaining how to say her name when they first arrived in Mark's home village of Portwye, but she had long since given up. An Irish name that sounded nothing like how it was spelled was proving to be another complication, and she didn't need any more problems, so she'd stopped correcting him.

There was no point in lying – the whole village would know what had happened by now.

'He was. Someone down at the pub said something about the Jews, made some kind of joke, and Mark got upset.' Aisling sighed. No doubt the Belithos had heard it all anyway in dramatic detail. Mark had not done any real damage this time, thankfully – an old school friend had pulled him off – but this would be the second time he found himself up in front of a magistrate. He'd been taken in for being drunk and disorderly two months ago.

She had hoped that after he told her why he was so upset, things would improve, but they hadn't; if anything, they'd gotten worse.

'This can't go on, Asslinn. It just has to stop.' Tobias Belitho's nostrils flared with fury. 'He served his country well, he came back in one piece to a lovely home and a wife – what on earth is wrong with the boy? He needs to pull himself together. He needs taking in hand.'

Aisling tried not to hear the implication that if he'd married a local girl, someone who understood about the British stiff upper lip, not some Irish girl with a name nobody could pronounce, then Mark would not be in the mess he was. The fact that Tobias's brother Leonard was shot by the IRA while on service in Ireland back in the twenties didn't do much to endear her to them either. It was why they had never met her family.

Things had been so much simpler during the war. She and Kate enlisted in the WAAF, and Sam and Mark were in the RAF. They all lived on the Biggin Hill base. They worked hard, and they risked their lives and all the rest of it, but it was fun and exciting, and she was young and in love. But now, a married woman, back in this tiny West Country village, trying to deal with a man so badly damaged by what he saw and did – it was unspeakably hard.

He'd told her to divorce him so many times she'd lost count. He told her that he'd say he had an affair – he would go to a hotel with a woman he would pay and be seen so there would be no blame to her. He begged her to leave him and go home, but she couldn't. He needed her, and besides, she loved him.

'He's sleeping now, so it's not a good time…' she began.

'Sleeping? At three o'clock in the afternoon on a Monday? You see, this is what I mean. He should be out looking for work. I could get him a job if he'd only settle to it – it's not doing him any good moping about the house all day long. He's a man, Asslinn, not a child, and he needs to start behaving like one.'

'He was having a bad day. He didn't sleep much last night, as he gets terrible nightmares and wakes up sweating and screaming. Please, Mr Belitho, let him sleep. We'll pop over to you and Mrs Belitho after our tea, and you can have a word with him then if you want to?' Aisling knew she was only putting off the inevitable, but Mark really did need to sleep, and she hadn't the strength for another outburst today.

'His mother is as soft as you.' He strode past her in the direction of the stairs. 'No, Asslinn, I need to speak to my son, man to man. Now, perhaps it might be best if you popped out to the shops or something. Don't take this the wrong way, but I think having you there to cling to isn't helping.'

The thought of leaving Mark to deal with his father alone was horrible, but she couldn't refuse to allow him access to his own son. The house they lived in was once Mark's granny's, the old Mrs Belitho, long since gone to her reward, so in fact, it was more Mark's father's house than theirs.

Maybe his father was right. She had failed spectacularly in trying to bring her Mark back. In his place was this distant, violent, emotional wreck, and she had no idea what to do about it.

She sighed and took her coat off the hook. 'Please, Mr Belitho, he's genuinely very upset. It's not just laziness or feeling a bit low – there really is something wrong with him.'

She thought she saw a flash of compassion in his eyes. He wasn't a bad man. A bit gruff and not a great lover of any foreigners, in particular the Irish, but he was all right.

'Don't worry, lass, I'll get to the bottom of this.' He patted her arm in an unprecedented gesture of affection. 'Run along now. Call on our Delilah – she'll be baking, today being a Monday. You might be lucky and get a currant bun.'

Aisling gave a weak smile and let herself out the back door.

Mark's sister, Delilah, lived at the other end of the village with her three boys. Her husband, Terry, had never come home from the war, and Aisling felt so sad about it. Delilah needed her husband, but she also needed a father for her three wild boys. She'd managed, like so many other women, for six long years and held it all together, waiting for the day he'd return, but instead, she'd had the dreaded telegram saying he had been killed in action. Aisling helped her out with the boys as much as she could, and they'd become friendly, though the boys' Uncle Mark's outbursts frightened them, so they didn't call to the house.

Aisling headed down the garden path towards Portwye's main street. Their little front garden was looking merry, as spring crocuses and daffodils were poking their heads up. She found nature so reassuring – no matter what happened, no matter that the world had been in the throes of a bloody war less than a year ago, Mother Nature still did everything in her own time. The flowers around the house had been planted by old Mrs Belitho, and Aisling had never dared pick them, but today she plucked a small bunch to bring to Delilah. As she crossed the square, she was reminded how like Kilthomand Portwye was – the same faces, the same social hierarchy, the vicar instead of old Fr Maguire ruling the roost. The Belitho family had lived in Portwye for as far back as anyone could remember. They rented their farm from the local count, someone everyone called Bunty for some reason, who had his summer residence there. Their place was a beautiful old house called Brockley Manor, and it reminded her in so many ways of Robinswood. But yet they saw her as a total outsider, with no understanding of their way of life.

She hoped Delilah wouldn't mind her calling unannounced. As she knocked on the door, she heard a crash from inside, followed by a bellow from her sister-in-law.

'Harry! Put Davy down right this minute. You've turned the dresser over on Terence's leg!'

Aisling didn't wait for the door to be opened, instead turning the key and rushing inside. She pulled one side of the heavy Welsh dresser up while Delilah heaved the other side, and four-year-old Terence wriggled out, seemingly unscathed.

'Oh, Assling,' – at least she got her name half right – 'thank goodness you're here. I'm fit to strangle these three. It's been raining all day, and I'll never dry their clothes if I let them out to play outside, but they are driving me up the wall.'

Aisling smiled at the three faces looking innocently up at her. Harry was nine, Davy six and little Terence was the baby at just four. They were tiny and wiry, hair the colour of conkers, with huge brown eyes. Aisling had expected all English people to be like the Irish, very pale with blue eyes and dark hair, but she was surprised so many of them were very tanned, especially down around Devon. Mark too went very dark in the summer, despite his fair hair. He always joked there was some pirate blood in him. It seemed like a lifetime ago that Mark had joked about anything.

'Shall I put the kettle on? Have you time for a cuppa?' Delilah asked once she was sure no lasting damage had been done to her youngest. She looked outside and the sun was peeping through. 'At last it's dried up, thank goodness. So out you go, you lot, and I don't want to see you till supper time, do you hear me? And look after your brother!' she shouted at the rapidly disappearing backs of her older sons, who were tired of being cooped up.

'Now, peace at last.' She sighed and filled the kettle. 'They will be the death of me, I swear.'

'They're so sweet, though, it's hard to stay cross with them, I'd say.' Aisling smiled.

'They can wrap me round their little fingers. I dread to think what Terry would say if he saw them half-wild. They need a firmer hand than me, I think...' She tried to keep the sorrow out of her voice but failed.

'You're doing a great job, and I bet Terry would be so proud of you.' Aisling rose and hugged her instinctively. She'd never been openly demonstrative before with any of Mark's family, but it felt right.

'I hope so,' Delilah managed, her eyes bright with unshed tears.

'He would. Mark always told me how mad about you Terry was, always going on about you and carrying your photo with him everywhere he went.'

A watery smile crossed her sister-in-law's face. 'He did. Our Harry was on the way when we got wed. A real quick job it was, but nobody said anything – we were together since we were thirteen. Even my mum and dad were all right about it. There was never anyone else for either of us. I can't believe he won't ever come back, Assling... I know his ship was sunk, and it was out in the middle of the ocean, but I still think he might. Stupid, I know.'

Aisling didn't know what to say that would provide any comfort, so she just hugged Delilah as she cried for her husband whose body would never be recovered.

The war had taken its toll on everyone. Those who survived felt guilty for doing so, and the families of those who didn't come home were just expected to get on with things. There was a real sense of 'other people have it worse, so stop moaning', but Aisling felt that was very unfair. There should be no hierarchy on grief. The mother who lost a son should not be seen as better off than the mother who lost two.

She often thought of the people she and Kate had gotten to know in their years at Biggin Hill RAF base, and all the ones who didn't make it. There was an urgency to life then, as anything could happen at any time, but now it all just felt immeasurably sad.

CHAPTER 10

*E*lena Hamilton-Brooks absentmindedly listened as her daughter, Georgie, recited the list of school items she needed.

'Mummy, you're not listening!' Georgie shouted in frustration.

'I am, darling. Two pairs of hockey socks and a gum shield...'

'You're miles away, and I refuse to be the only person at Harling without the full kit. Can you please pay attention?'

'Did Eve not see to it before she left?' Elena asked.

'We only got the list in the post on Tuesday. Eve has been gone over to visit her sister since Saturday, so no, she didn't.' Georgie was at a boiling point. At twelve, she was precocious but generally a good-spirited child; however, the departure of the Murphys from their lives was a terrible wrench.

Georgie and Arthur loved Dermot and Isabella. Elena understood why the Murphys could not give up the opportunity to return to the estate they managed for so long, particularly under the generous terms offered by the current Lord Kenefick, but the children were heartbroken.

Eve staying on was the only thing that saved them, but she was visiting Kate and her new baby in London. She'd barely taken any time off since she arrived six years ago, so Elena could hardly refuse when she asked, but the new maid, Dilly, was a total washout. Since the war, nobody wanted to be in service any more, and hiring domestic staff had become a complete nightmare. The only thing worse was trying to manage one's own household and children.

She turned to her daughter and silently vowed to give her all of her attention. Georgie would soon be gone to Harling Hall, where Elena and all her female relatives had been educated, and childhood was over once that happened. She should enjoy the last days with her daughter.

'I'll tell you what. Why don't we go into town now, take the list with us, get what we need, then treat ourselves to tea and buns in the Shelbourne? Arthur is playing rugby up at Old Belvedere, and he has been invited to his friend Aubrey's for dinner, so he won't be dining with us. We'll have a girls' day out.'

Elena stood and wrapped her arm around her daughter's slim waist, tucking a stray strand of chestnut hair behind the girl's ear. She looked so like Thomas that sometimes Elena caught her breath. Arthur looked more like her side, but Georgie had her father's eyes and a certain swagger, a confidence that he had. *Not that it did him any good in the end*, she thought ruefully. She should be angry with him for leaving her in such a mess and for risking the Murphy girls' lives the way he did, but it was a gamble that didn't pay off. The anger was long gone, as was Thomas, in a U-boat with a German agent, and she had to assume he was dead somewhere in Germany.

'Great, let me get my coat.' Georgie was pleased her mother was being proactive at last, and she dashed upstairs.

Elena turned her wedding ring. That day would have been her fifteenth wedding anniversary. 'Happy anniversary, my love,' she whispered, then inhaled and stood, smoothing down her slim pencil skirt, refusing to allow the tears to come. There had been enough of that.

Those days and weeks after he disappeared were a blur, but how kind Dermot and Isabella had been. She recalled forcing Dermot to give her the German's address so she could write to him, begging him to spare Thomas, to return him to his wife and children.

She never received a response, of course, and after months of black grief, where she hardly went out and spent virtually no time with her children, choosing instead to stay in her room, Isabella sat her down and told her that she needed to pull herself together. That Georgie and Arthur needed their mother and that Thomas would want her to live again and be a parent to them. Slowly and with little enthusiasm, she re-entered life, made it up to the children as much as she could, went back to her committees, told people Thomas had been killed by a bomb on a business trip to London... And life ground slowly, painfully on.

Georgie bounded back into the kitchen, her scarf and hat on, buttoning her wool coat. 'It's chilly, Mummy. You should wear your fur.'

Elena felt a pang of guilt. Georgie saw her as someone to be taken care of, not as her capable mother. She should really have done better, but she had never realised how much she loved Thomas or how horrible life was as a widow.

'I will, darling. Could you get it for me? I would ask Dilly, but goodness' knows where she's got to.' Elena looked around in the hope of finding the maid.

'She's down at the gate talking to Timmy,' Georgie announced.

'Timmy? Timmy who?' Elena had no idea who her daughter was talking about.

'The postman – well, he's only nineteen, so hardly a man... And he's got a spotty face, but Dilly loves him.' Georgie rolled her eyes, as if such silliness was beneath her twelve-year-old sophistication.

'Oh, for goodness' sake. That dratted girl. I'm not paying her to flirt with the postman.' Elena huffed in exasperation. As they walked out the door, she saw Timmy cycling up the gravel driveway and a guilty-looking Dilly scurrying into the kitchen. None of this nonsense would be tolerated if Isabella and Dermot were still there. Isabella would have given Dilly a piece of her mind, and Timmy would be lucky not to get a clip round the ear from Dermot.

Things really were going to pot without them, and she had the first group of girls to be trained as housemaids and boys as caretakers in two weeks' time. Eve was going to take care of the girls, and the charity had sourced a man in his sixties to train the boys. His name was Henry Griffin, and his wife was one of the committee members. Elena feared his appointment was more to do with Mrs Griffin's desire to get her newly retired husband out of the house than his skills, but it was the best they could do. She had yet to meet him, but it was doubtful he would be as knowledgeable as Dermot.

'Your post, ma'am,' Timmy announced with a flourish and a smirk in Dilly's direction. He handed her a large parcel with her name and address clearly marked on the front and foreign stamps.

'Yes, well, you *are* supposed to be a postman, so stop behaving like you've presented me with the crown jewels,' Elena snapped as she took the parcel. 'And I will thank you to in the future deliver my mail in a timely manner rather than distracting members of my staff, or I shall be making my complaint to your superiors. Am I making myself clear?' She fixed him with a haughty stare.

'Yes, ma'am.' Timmy reddened, and Georgie giggled. 'I'm sorry, ma'am.'

'Yes, well, get along with you.' Elena made a shooing gesture with her hand, and Timmy cycled away.

Elena looked down at the parcel once more and flipped it over.

Sender – Oskar Metz

No address. She paled.

'Mummy? What is it?' Georgie asked, realising something was wrong.

Elena didn't answer but tore open the package. Inside were three large bundles of letters, each one tied with string, and a single sheet of paper.

The page shook as she tried to steady her hands and read it.

Dear Mrs Hamilton-Brooks,

You do not know me, but my name is Oskar Metz. I was responsible for taking your husband, Thomas, to Germany. I was a German operative, and I kidnapped him and took him from Ireland aboard a U-boat bound for Germany in 1940.

I was a friend and old comrade of Dermot Murphy, whom I had contacted at that time to try to convince him to help the German cause. Dermot, a man I respect and admire, refused and told me that I was on the wrong side in that war. The truth of these words only fully hit me on the U-boat.

I want you to know the truth about what happened to your husband, and I wish to deliver these letters he wrote to you and your children. I am very sorry for everything, more than I can ever express, but I do want to tell you what happened.

Once we were aboard the U-boat, he was attended to by medical personnel. One of them made a remark that fixing his foot, which I shot, would only be a temporary measure, as once the Gestapo got him, they would extract whatever they needed and then he would be executed.

It was at that exact moment I realised Dermot was right. I was on the wrong side. It was too late to try to get back to Ireland, so once we were ashore in France, I thanked the crew and put on my uniform. I escorted Thomas on a train bound for Paris and then Berlin; the Gestapo were expecting us there. They trusted me to bring him in; after all, I had managed to get a high-ranking British intelligence officer out of Ireland, so my loyalty was not in question. Once we got to Germany, however, I took a train south and did not stop until I reached the Black Forest. I am familiar with the area, having visited there often as a child.

The forest is dense and impenetrable, and nobody was yet looking for us. My time with the IRA had prepared me for living outdoors and on the run, so Thomas and I set up camp in the middle of the forest, and there we stayed for the duration of the war. We lived off what we could catch or grow, and I went into a town once a month or so for things we needed and to hear how things were progressing with the war.

Thomas wrote these letters while there. He thought I posted them – I told him I did, but I didn't. It would have been too dangerous. So here they are. I kept every one. Some are for you, some for your daughter and the remainder for your son.

We heard news of the Allied landings in the summer of 1944, and

Thomas was most anxious that we leave our hiding place and move west to meet the advancing liberators. But I refused, as it was not yet safe. He spoke no German, and if we were stopped, we would have been arrested or shot.

Eventually, in February 1945, I could hold him back no more. He desperately wanted to get home to his family, so I agreed. We left the forest, travelling only on back roads. Neither of us shaved for years, and we were completely unrecognisable. We both affected injuries that people would assume had been sustained in the first war, which would explain why we were not in uniform. Three weeks after we left the forest, we were in the small city of Freiburg. Thomas hid in a church while I went to try to buy some bread. I left him there with strict instructions to speak to nobody. I was only gone about fifteen minutes when I felt the earth rumble and the bombers come. I am so sorry to tell you that the church took a direct hit, and Thomas was killed.

Elena saw a drop hit the paper, and she realised she was crying.

I tried to get him back to you. I did my best, but it was not good enough, and for that I am truly sorry. I would like to meet you, to explain, after which time I intend to surrender to the British. If you do not wish to see me, I understand. Please know that Thomas became my friend, and he told me often of his love for you and his children.

Yours truly,

Oskar Metz

'It's from Daddy?' Georgie asked tentatively, alarmed by her mother's reaction to the letter.

'No, darling… No, it's not. Daddy is dead. This is from the man who took him… He…' Elena couldn't go on.

'But he was killed in a bomb? Mummy, what's going on?'

Georgie could get no information out of her mother, so she took the keys and opened the front door with trembling hands.

She went to the telephone and asked the operator to connect her to Kilthomand thirty-five. Dermot and Isabella didn't have a phone, but the local post office did, and they had told her that in the event of an emergency, she could call them there. She was sure this constituted an emergency.

She was connected, and a man's voice answered. 'Kilthomand

thirty-five. Mossy Flanagan, Postmaster, speaking.'

'Oh, hello. I...um... I need to get a message to Mr Dermot Murphy or his wife, Isabella, please. It's urgent.'

'Well, I don't know if... Hold on there one minute... Who is looking for them?'

'Georgie... I mean, Miss Georgina Hamilton-Brooks. Please, I need to speak to one of them.' Georgie tried to sound grown up, but there was a tremor in her voice.

'Well, I saw Isabella out at the market there a minute ago – she might still be around. Just hold on there now a minute till I see...' There was a clattering as he dropped the receiver and then a knock on a window. She heard him call, 'Here, Chopper, is that Mrs Murphy over beyond?' There was a pause, and Georgie couldn't hear what the other person said. 'Tell her there's a telephone call here for her, will you.'

He lifted the receiver once more. 'She'll be into you now in a minute – just hold the line.'

Georgie waited.

'Georgie? What's happened? Are you all right?'

The sound of Isabella's voice from so far away made Georgie want to cry, but she spoke instead. 'Isabella, Mummy got a letter – well, one letter and a big bundle of letters – and she's crying, and I don't know what to do. She said it's from the man who took Daddy or something, but she won't tell me...'

Isabella didn't say anything for a moment, and then Georgie heard her reassuring voice.

'Tell your mother we'll be up tomorrow. Sam and Kate can manage for a day or two without us. Take your mother into the house and make her a cup of tea. We'll get there as soon as we can.'

Isabella knew that Dilly was useless, but she had been the only applicant. And with Eve away as well, the little family would have to manage until the Murphys got there.

'Now, darling, get your Mummy for me,' Isabella said. Georgie did as she asked and escorted Elena back inside, still clutching the letter.

Elena lifted the receiver. 'Isabella, Thomas is dead... Oskar Metz wrote...'

'I know. Georgie told me. Dermot and I will come up on the bus tomorrow. We can only stay one night, but we'll be up first thing, and we'll help you. You've had a terrible shock.'

'I don't think I can... I just...'

Isabella heard the note of hysteria in Elena's voice. 'I don't know, Elena, but don't worry. We'll be there tomorrow.'

'But what if he...'

'Elena.' Isabella had seen her like this before, in the days after Thomas's disappearance, frightened and panicked. 'The children are going to need you to explain what really happened. You can wait for us if you like, but I doubt Georgie at any rate will wait that long, so tell them. You can do this.'

Elena exhaled and finally spoke. 'I can... Thank you, Isabella. I'll see you both tomorrow.'

'You will.' Isabella hung up. It was only then that she realised all ten people in the post office were staring at her, fascinated.

'Thank you, Mossy,' she said, and walked out without a word of explanation.

CHAPTER 11

ate was emptying boxes in the kitchen of their old farmhouse when Isabella arrived. She knew instantly by her mother's face that something was wrong.

'What?' Kate asked, her heart pounding. Sam was back from Europe, demobilised and full time at Robinswood, and Jack was happily sitting on the floor banging pots with a wooden spoon, so it wasn't either of them.

'Oskar Metz wrote to Elena. Thomas Hamilton-Brooks is dead,' Isabella said.

'I'll call Daddy. You watch Jack.' Kate grabbed her coat off the nail behind the door, as she'd done thousands of times throughout her childhood, and ran up the yard. The cobbled-stone farmyard was mossy and full of weeds, some almost hip height. Charlie Warren had never used the farmhouse or the stables in the six years he rented Robinswood, so hardly anyone had set foot there in all that time. The house was musty and damp – it needed a good airing out – and there was plenty of evidence of rodents.

Kate ran up the lane to the main part of the farm and found Dermot in the barn with an oil can and a big tool bag, trying to get some piece of rusted machinery up and running again.

'Daddy, you need to come down to the house. Mammy just arrived back from the village.' Kate delivered the news quickly, and she saw the shock on her father's face.

'How did she hear that?' he asked.

'I don't know, that's all she said. I came to get you straight away.'

'Right, come on.' He and Kate hurried down the lane.

As they entered, Isabella was giving Jack a crust of bread with a light spread of jam. He was such a happy little boy, already nine months old and strong as anything. Isabella swore he'd walk before he was one.

'Kate, put the kettle on, please, would you?' Isabella asked as she sat at the table, Dermot beside her.

'Well?' Dermot asked.

'Oh, Der, I don't know what to think. I was below at the market, getting a few messages, and Mossy sent young Chopper Casey to call me. When I went into the post office, Mossy said there was a phone call and it was Georgie. The poor pet sounded distraught. She and Elena were going out when they met Timmy, and he had a letter for them.'

Dermot nodded.

'It seems it was from Oskar Metz, and he told her Thomas was dead.'

'What else did it say?'

'I don't know. The poor woman was in shock. She could barely speak.'

'Oskar made it through,' Dermot said quietly, and reached for his wife's hand.

'It seems so.' Isabella knew Oskar was Dermot's closest friend, and her husband was bound to be relieved that he survived, but she could not bring herself to rejoice. For one thing, he was a Nazi, and for another, she was worried sick about Elena and the children. 'She sounded awful, Der.'

'Sure she would. God love them, they've been through so much already.' He shook his head, not knowing what to think or feel.

The last time he saw Thomas, the man was bleeding profusely

from his foot. Thomas had kidnapped Aisling and Kate and tried to blackmail Dermot into handing Oskar over to British intelligence. They knew Oskar was in Ireland, and they knew he was hoping to recruit Dermot to the German cause. However, Dermot had told Oskar that no matter how much he disliked the British, he thought the Germans were much worse and he could never support Hitler and what he was trying to do.

Oskar shot Thomas in an effort to get him to reveal where Aisling and Kate were being held and the code word that would have to be given to their captors to secure the girls' release. Once they'd extracted the information, Dermot, Oskar and a barely coherent Thomas drove from Robinswood to the post office in Kilthomand to send the prearranged message to the kidnappers to free the girls. Dermot went in, leaving Oskar and Thomas in the car, but when he came back out, Oskar had driven away. Dermot always imagined that was the last he would see of either of them.

As the news of what was happening in Germany was filtering through, he thought often of his friend Oskar Metz. All through the Troubles in Ireland from 1919 to 1921, when they were out nightly, waging war on the British forces, they were inseparable. Oskar was with him when he met Isabella for the first time, and he was Eve's godfather. They always joked that even though his father and his surname were German, Oskar was an Irishman. He grew up there, with his Irish mother and German father, and felt every bit as Irish as Dermot did. But once the Troubles descended into internal squabbling in 1921 – the British left and the Irish turned on each other – the German had enough, so he went back to Germany to take over the family business.

Dermot could never in a million years have imagined Oskar as a Nazi, but that's what he became. And the prize of bringing a high-ranking British spy back to the fatherland was too good to pass up.

'I've told Elena we'll go up tomorrow on the bus for an overnight. Is that all right?' Isabella looked around at the chaos. They'd been moving in and unpacking boxes for weeks. So much of the contents of both the farmhouse and the main house had been stored in the outbuildings that it felt like they would never get to the bottom of it.

'Of course. This lot will be fine. Actually, I had an idea. How about we offer to bring Georgie and Arthur down here with us for a few days? They're not starting school until September, and they started their school holidays last weekend. It might do them good and give Elena a chance to figure this out?' Dermot turned to Kate, suddenly remembering it was her and Sam's place now. 'Would Sam be all right with that, Kate, do you think?'

Kate placed the teapot and three mugs on the table. 'Daddy – actually, both of you – please don't do this.'

They looked at her in confusion.

'Asking me if things are all right or not. We're doing this together, all four of us, on an equal footing, not with Sam and me being Lord and Lady Muck and you two working for him. That's how it used to be, but we can't go on like that, for God's sake. So of course, invite Georgie and Arthur, and anyone else you like. You don't need to check with me or with Sam. This is your place, your home, and Robinswood belongs to all of us now. That's what Sam wanted you to understand, Daddy – that you were coming back here as a partner, not an employee.'

Dermot smiled at his youngest daughter. 'Fine, Lady Muck.' He stood and put his arm around her, giving her a squeeze. 'I understand. Old habits die hard, I suppose.'

Kate kissed his cheek. 'You need a shave.' She grinned.

'Yes, ma'am, right away, ma'am.' He bowed mockingly, and she swiped him with the tea cloth.

* * *

SAM STARTED as Kate crept up on him and placed her hands over his eyes. He was leaning on a gate, looking over the rolling hills that swept all the way to the ocean.

'Surveying your estate, milord?' She giggled.

'I am.' He smiled as he kissed her. 'And trying to not have a heart attack at the idea of farming it all. I've no idea, literally not a clue, and I've taken on so much... Sometimes I wonder if I'm mad.'

She wrapped her arms around his waist, and he rested his chin on the top of her head and sighed heavily.

'I'm hearing a lot of "I's" in there, Sam. Last time I checked, there were four of us, not one, and the other three actually do know about farming. So if you do as you're told, it will all work out fine.'

'What would I do without you, Kate Murphy?' he asked, shielding his eyes from the bright June sunshine and looking down at her.

He looked older than the boy who'd gone off to war, but he was still the same Sam. She was so grateful for that. So many men came back different; so many relationships were in crisis. There were so many hardships to endure during the war that people expected life to be wonderful once the Germans and then the Japs surrendered. But for lots of people, the aftermath was as bad, if not worse.

His hair was longer than regulation RAF now, and she could see his curls again. He was still lean, but he had filled out a lot. And he looked every inch the handsome new Lord Kenefick.

'You won't ever need to find out.' She grinned. 'Unless, of course, you start drinking and spending all your days and all our money on the horses. Then, of course, I'll divorce you and take you for everything you've got.' She patted him on the bum.

'I won't ever do that, because while I recognise how invaluable you are as an ally, I am also acutely aware of how worthy an adversary you could be – I wouldn't stand a chance.' He chuckled as they began to walk back to the house, his arm around her shoulders.

She told him about Thomas Hamilton-Brooks and the letter, and he was silent.

'What's going on?' she asked.

'It's not my business, I suppose, but that man put you, Aisling and my mother in terrible danger, all to further his own ends. I know there was a war on, and it's a bit rich coming from an ex-RAF pilot to despise a fellow countryman for doing his job, but I can't forgive him. All three of you could have been killed. And it would have been his fault entirely.'

69

Kate heard a note of bitterness in his voice she didn't recognise. 'But we didn't die. Poor Elena and the children are the ones suffering, and after so much death and destruction, it just seems cruel.'

Sam looked at her, his expression incredulous. 'So you can forgive him?'

Kate sighed. 'I suppose so. I don't know. He's dead, so what's the point of holding on to bitterness? Elena misses him so much, and she's a good person. She was so kind to my family, and to Eve after Jack died and everything, so yes, I can forgive him.'

'You're remarkable,' he said, stepping away slightly and admiring her.

'True.' She grinned. 'Anyway, we have bigger problems. Lillian wrote to say she is getting along fine in the nursing home but is very much looking forward to having it all over and done with – her words not mine – and being able to bring the baby home to Robinswood just as soon as they are strong enough.'

Sam rolled his eyes. 'I still can't believe you sanctioned this.'

'Well, technically, I didn't. She just assumed. But you would have said the same in my position. She's devastated over Beau, and she is left not just as an unmarried mother, but as an unmarried mother with a coloured child. London society would crucify both of them. We have to give her somewhere to live, Sam. You know we do.' Kate was not any more enthusiastic about having Lillian come to Robinswood than he was, but there was no choice.

'But why won't she at least tell him? I don't understand. I'm tempted to track him down myself and fill him in. Beau is a decent chap – he wouldn't leave her high and dry deliberately.'

'I know and I agree. But she says if she wasn't enough to come back for without any child, then he didn't really want her and, in that case, she is better alone. She won't beg him – she's too proud.'

'And are they still writing to each other?' Sam avoided his sister as much as he could. She drove him up the wall, so he was happier to put Kate between them.

'She hasn't heard from him in months. His last letter sounded like a sad goodbye. She wrote a few more times, but nothing. Not even return to sender, which makes her believe he got them but is choosing not to reply. I feel sorry for her, I really do.' Kate sighed.

'So do I, there but for the grace of God and all of that.' He glanced sideways at her.

Like most young people during the war, they took their chances to make love whenever they could, even before they married. Nobody knew what the future held. Life seemed so precious and fragile then; all the old mores had dissolved in a fog of smoke and fire.

'The difference is, though, that if I'd found myself in the family way, we'd have married quickly and the baby would be white. She can go with the story that her husband died – that will be believed – but the faces of the locals here will be something to behold when they clap eyes on Austina Kenefick-Lane. She's called her after your father, apparently.'

Sam shook his head. 'Well, I hope she has more sense than he did. I can't even imagine. How is she using Lane in the name? She and Beau were never married.'

'Who knows? Your sister is a law unto herself. I think she just decided that was the name. She always called herself Lady Kenefick as well when she should be a Right Honourable or something else, apparently, but who cares? It's a load of old nonsense anyway.'

Sam smiled. There were plenty of girls in England who'd love to be Lady Such-and-such, but to Kate, it was meaningless, and he loved that about her.

'Look, Sam, she does what she likes, your sister. Anyway, Beau's surname is probably not on the birth certificate, but who in Kilthomand is going to go checking that?' Kate shrugged. 'I think she feels like she can resume her lady-of-the-manor status here and people won't dare question her – she thinks it will be easier.'

'I hope for her and that little girl's sake she's right, but I'm not confident, Kate. Nothing is like it was – can't she understand that?'

'I don't think she wants to understand it. She just assumed she could come back here and we'd all play at tea parties and hunt balls again like the "jolly good-old days".' Kate affected Lillian's clipped accent, and Sam laughed.

'Well, she's in for a rude awakening then. It's more mops and buckets than needlepoint and sundowners around here.'

'Well, your mother isn't having her, it would seem, and we can't leave her on the side of the road, so we'll have to try at least. You never know, she might surprise us.'

Sam looked sceptical. She put her arm around him and gave him a squeeze.

CHAPTER 12

*E*ve straightened her blouse and skirt in the full-length mirror. Today was the first day in her role as a teacher. Elena was so confident she would do well, but Eve was nervous. Her pupils would be coming from a Protestant orphanage in the city centre, and the idea was that she would train them for all areas of domestic duty so they could get a job and, hopefully afterwards, make good wives and mothers.

Georgie and Arthur were gone to England to school after a wonderful holiday in Robinswood. Arthur clung to Dermot and Isabella the day they brought the children back, and it broke Eve's heart to see the child so distraught. Elena wavered but stuck to her plan.

The letters from Thomas had really shaken her, and she was a much more subdued person these days. She showed one or two to Eve, and they were beautiful. Thomas loved her and the children so much, and the letters were full of apologies and vows to get back to them to make up for everything.

Their tone on the subject of Oskar Metz was surprising. Thomas constantly referred to how kind Oskar was, how capable and inge-nious when it came to survival, how Thomas would certainly be dead if not for him. Oskar did not mention it in his cover letter, but it seemed the camp became a haven of sorts for Jews hiding from the Germans. He and Thomas were not alone, and at times there were up to twenty people in the camp.

Oskar facilitated their passage through Germany. There was a line of escape run by resisters, and their camp was one rest stop on that line. He tended to the wounded and managed to generate enough food for whoever came by. He knew the dense *Schwarzwald* well and understood what could be eaten. He had traps everywhere for birds and even wild boar, and they lived reasonably comfortably.

For Elena, telling Georgie and Arthur that the story that their father had died in a bombing in London was a lie was hard, but the letters for them softened the blow. Elena bought them each a special lockable box for their precious things to take to boarding school, and the letters were lovingly stored there.

Elena originally didn't want to see Oskar; she was so angry for so long. But as she read the letters and discovered what a kind man he was, she felt inclined to meet him. He left no forwarding address – presumably his house was destroyed and he would be wanted by the British or the Americans as a Nazi despite his epiphany – so whether or not he would ever turn up was anyone's guess.

Eve knew her father was relieved to hear that his friend had survived. And when Elena told him the contents of the letters, what Oskar did and how it was Dermot's influence that made him realise he was on the wrong side, her father simply got up and left the table. Eve went to follow him – it was so rare to see him rattled – but her mother had just put her hand on Eve's and whispered, 'Let him go. He's fine, but he needs some time to deal with this.'

Eve hoped for her father's and Elena's sake that Oskar would make it home, but nobody knew what would happen.

She pulled her thoughts back to the job at hand. The kitchen had been kitted out with eight of everything: eight baking bowls, eight wooden spoons, even eight small weighing scales. That morning, she thought she might just make scones, and they could enjoy them with a cup of tea at the break. She was going to teach them a bit of knitting in the second session, and then for the final lesson of the day, she was going to show them the correct way to clean windows using white vinegar and newspaper.

Her mother felt a million miles away. She should be the one doing this as she was the housekeeper extraordinaire, but she was back in Robinswood and loving every second.

Taking a deep breath, Eve left her bedroom on the top floor and walked down to the kitchen. Elena was there before her, sipping a cup of tea and sifting through the post.

The two women had become very good friends despite the age gap, and they saw in each other the same pain reflected. Eve still missed Jack, and she doubted the void he left could ever be filled. Elena understood, and now, any secret hope that Thomas would come home was gone.

'Morning!' Elena folded the letter she was reading and smiled at Eve. 'Are we ready to do this?'

'Not even close to ready. I was awake all night, terrified I'm going to mess it up.' Eve wished for the millionth time her mother was there.

'We'll be fine. We'll start slowly. These girls have been institution-alised, and so they don't even have normal skills one would acquire growing up in a family. You Murphy girls are unique, I know. There is nothing you can't do. But then you were raised by exceptional people with skills coming out their eyes. But even I, with my silly upbringing of tennis parties and frocks, had some clue how to run a household. These girls, even if they can't get a job, at least if they meet someone, they'll be good wives and mothers once we – and when I say we, I mean you –' – she winked – 'are finished with them.'

Eve smiled. 'I think my mother would disagree. This place was chaos when she got here!'

'Now the good news. As you know, the man they found as the boy's tutor, Elvira Griffin's husband, has gone down with a bad case of gout a fortnight ago, so a replacement has had to be found at the last minute – yesterday in fact. Apparently, he's a bit unusual. They advertised the job in the paper, much to Elvira's chagrin, it would seem. She thought we should wait for Henry – she is desperate to get rid of him,

I'm convinced. And this chap applied, so we'll see. He's due this morning, which isn't ideal as he'll be thrown in the deep end, but what can we do?'

'And when you say unusual?' Eve looked suspicious.

Elena laughed. 'The Taylor sisters and General Loughton interviewed him, and while the general thought he was a perfectly fine young man, the sisters were a bit fluttery or something. Anyway, we'll see for ourselves soon enough.'

The two women often enjoyed easy banter and real conversations. On the long winter evenings, it kept both of them sane.

Elena chuckled, and Eve thought it was good to see her smile again. Starting the programme was the best thing that could have happened, as it gave her very little time to dwell on everything.

'The boys won't really impinge on what we're doing in here, but the board thought it might be a nice idea for them to eat whatever the girls make the day we do cooking? They have been kept separate all their lives, but they think a little supervised social interaction would not do them any harm now.'

'Oh, great – add to our jobs! Those lads might be like dogs off a lead seeing the girls if they've been locked up for years, and we are supposed to supervise polite social interaction. Are these people serious?' Eve rolled her eyes.

The board of the orphanages were constantly coming up with utterly ridiculous initiatives since most of them were unmarried spinsters in their seventies, and they had absolutely no idea about the reality of life for poor people in the current day and age.

'I know, it's mad, but let's just see how we get on, shall we?'

The doorbell rang, and Dilly went to answer it. A few moments later, she came into the kitchen. 'Ma'am, there's a gentleman here. He says his name is Bartley Doherty, and he wants to speak to you.' She looked quite out of breath.

Elena eyed her suspiciously. 'Timmy the postman hasn't turned up yet, has he?' She arched a perfectly plucked eyebrow.

'No, ma'am.' The girl's cheeks turned puce.

'So what has you all hot and bothered?' Elena asked, walking past her into the hall.

Eve gave Dilly a smile. The maid was a lovely girl, just a bit innocent.

They heard voices, and within moments, Elena was back, followed by a very tall man with longish dark curly hair and without a hat. His dark, almost-black eyes landed on Eve, and he gave a slight smile. His lips were a perfect Cupid's bow. He wore unusual clothes, not a shirt and tie, more like a tunic with a leather cord threaded through eyes at the throat. His trousers were working men's, and on his feet, he had a beautiful pair of brown leather boots. He looked like a handsome woodcutter from a storybook. Eve inhaled and immediately tried to compose herself.

'Eve, this is Bartley Doherty. He will be taking care of the boy's part of the training. Bartley, this is Eve Murphy. She is in charge of the girls.'

Bartley slowly put out his hand, and Eve took it. It was calloused and rough but warm.

'Very nice to meet you, Miss Murphy,' he said, his eyes never leaving hers. He had the soft accent of the North.

'And you, Mr Doherty.' She wished he would stop looking at her; something about him made her uncomfortable.

'Bartley, please,' he said.

She probably should have said that he could call her Eve, but she didn't.

'Well, then, now that the introductions are out of the way, can I get you a cup of tea, Bartley?' Elena caught Eve's eye surreptitiously and gave a smirk.

'No, thank you, ma'am. I'll get on as I've a lot to do. If someone could show me where everything is, I'd be grateful?'

'Of course. Eve would be happy to show you the ropes, wouldn't you, Eve?' Elena caught her eye, and Eve noted the mischievous gleam there.

'Of course. Follow me.' Eve smiled, then led Bartley through the

French doors to the patio, surreptitiously glancing back at Elena, who was grinning.

She led him down the path to an area behind a copse of trees in the garden and opened the shed her father had built, which was, she had to admit, very impressive. It was sixty feet long and thirty feet wide and was block built with proper doors and windows. The walls were plastered and painted, and her father had laid a timber floor. On one end was a large wood-burning stove, and running the length of the room was a workbench with long stools on either side, where all the tools the boys would need were laid out. On the walls were all kinds of shelves and drawers for nails, screws, paint brushes, bottles of turpentine and tins of paint, and everything was stacked neatly.

'So this is the workshop,' Eve began, trying to sound professional.

'It's lovely, a really nice place to work,' Bartley said quietly, picking up some tools and examining them.

'My father built it.' She couldn't keep the pride out of her voice.

'He's a talented man, surely.' He smiled and Eve was mesmerised.

'He is. He and my mother used to work here, but they've gone back to Robinswood Estate in Waterford where I grew up.'

'I know it. A lovely place on the banks of the Blackwater. I was there with my father and a horse when I was a wee lad. The Lord there loved his horses.'

Eve was surprised that someone from all the way up in Donegal would have been in the far south of the country. 'He certainly did. Lord Kenefick is dead now.'

Bartley just nodded and continued looking around.

She walked to the end of the workshop where there was a door. 'Through here are your private quarters. My father just finished this last week when it was clear Henry would not be coming.'

She opened the door and Bartley stepped inside. Again, it was lovely. Dermot had sectioned off a bit at the end with sheets of timber and built a balcony accessed by a steep staircase, where he had put a bed, desk and mirror. Isabella had placed a big multicoloured eiderdown on the bed and a new red-checked oilcloth on the table. She'd kitted out the little kitchen, and there was wood for the fire. She'd even picked a bunch of flowers from the garden to make it welcoming for whomever moved in. Eve knew they felt bad about leaving her and Elena to do the training alone, so they had done everything they could to help. On the ground level were a bathroom and a small kitchenette. They'd found another little wood-burning stove and took a fireside chair from the house. While the space wasn't big, it was very comfortable and cosy.

Eve wanted Bartley to like it; they'd gone to so much trouble. 'I hope it's all right. It's not very big, but he thought whoever was going to be here would need all the space in the workshop, so he –'

'It is the nicest place I have ever stayed,' Bartley interrupted gently. 'Thank you. I'll look after it. And please thank your father for me. He's a great craftsman, I can see.' He admired the dovetail joints on the stairs.

She smiled, relieved. 'I'm glad you like it. Bartley, we'll be working together a lot, so if you need anything, just let us know – either Elena or me – and we'll see it gets sorted out. Now I'd better get back. Best of luck.'

'Thank you, Miss Murphy.' Bartley's smile played around his lips, and his dark eyes never left hers.

* * *

BACK IN THE KITCHEN, Elena was dying to hear how she'd gotten on with him. 'Well, I don't know what I was expecting, but it certainly wasn't that. He's remarkable-looking, isn't he?'

'That's one word for it. I know he has a Northern accent, but he's like a gypsy or something. No Irish people have hair that black, and long as well. It was past his collar! There's something about him – he's very different anyway.'

'I thought he looked very handsome, like someone from a novel. I think he was out of an orphanage himself. The Misses Taylor – they are from Donegal, remember? I told you about them, frightfully sanctimonious, the two spinster sisters – anyway, they were telling me about him at the last meeting, but I tuned out because they witter on so much. I should have paid more attention.' Elena grinned.

'Yes, well, so long as he does a good job and can keep those lads under control. The last thing we need is a bunch of wild young fellas roaring around the place.' Eve stood and smoothed her skirt, then rinsed their cups in the sink. She caught a glimpse of herself in the refection of the bay window looking out to the garden.

I've become a prudish old spinster, she thought. Her auburn hair was tied back neatly in a bun, and she wore a beige twinset and a brown skirt. The skirt was one Mammy had gotten from Lady Kenefick years ago but didn't like; she said it was too drab. Eve thought it was fine, even quite respectable, but when she saw her refection, she realised her mother was right. It was drab, just like Eve was. She had always been curvy – Jack loved her curves – but in the months after he died, she lost a lot of weight. The deprivation of the war years meant there was nothing to fatten up on, and as a result, her figure was now angular and pointy. Jack wouldn't recognise her. Sometimes she didn't recognise herself.

She heard more voices and realised her charges had arrived. She put a smile on her face and went out to the hall to greet them. Elena was welcoming everyone as she arrived, and immediately, Eve's concerns melted away. Before them were a bunch of bedraggled girls, all around fifteen or sixteen years old, looking decidedly downcast and despondent. They were dressed identically in grey smocks, over which was a white apron, and on their feet, they wore regulation flat black shoes with laces. Their hair was tied back in ribbons, though some had strands hanging over their eyes. They looked terrified.

'Ah, Miss Murphy, here you are. Girls, this is your teacher, Miss Murphy. She will be taking care of you. Listen to what she tells you, and you'll pick it all up in no time.' Elena oozed confidence and kindness, and only those who knew her well could see the deep sadness in her eyes.

CHAPTER 13

*L*illian looked down at her little girl, sleeping peacefully in her crib, and tried to quell the butterflies in her stomach.

She stroked the baby's cheek. Her skin was so soft, and she was so beautiful.

'Grandmama won't be able to resist you, my darling. Don't worry.' Lillian prayed she was right.

Violet had paid for the nursing home, which was nice even if it was in the dark North. Lillian had never been to Hull before, nor had she any desire to return there, but it served its purpose and it was miles away from anyone she was likely to know. The staff were kind, and although Austina was a bit of an oddity, they didn't seem to mind. She was such a sweet-tempered baby. Lillian wore the wedding ring she had gotten to have at least a veneer of respectability, and she'd concocted a sad story of her brave American husband who died in Normandy, which people accepted without question. One midwife had asked how the black soldier was permitted to marry when the laws of his country forbade interracial marriage in many states.

Lillian had responded in her most haughty manner. 'My husband and I married in the United Kingdom, where no such bigotry and prejudice exists.' She'd stared the midwife down pointedly, daring her to contradict. Thankfully, she didn't.

Lillian had heard of many British women marrying their American sweethearts, though admittedly, not any she knew personally, and she'd never heard of a coloured man being permitted to marry. But nonetheless, she had her story and was sticking to it. The truth was, no black soldier would be granted permission to marry while on service – it was as simple as that – and they needed that permission.

Things would be better once she was home in Robinswood. Nobody there would dare question her. There would be gossip, of course, but then the Kenefics were always a source of interest in an otherwise dreary village. Her father had spent years creating scandal by drinking, gambling and general carousing, and he got away with it because of who he was. She would follow in his footsteps.

Violet had yet to meet the baby. She had travelled up from Framington Hall in Perry's Daimler, no less. It was a long journey, so she had stayed at a hotel the previous night and was coming to visit Lillian and her new granddaughter today.

Once Lillian broke the news by letter at Kate's insistence – and her mother took forever to respond – Lillian wrote often. Her mother replied to one in four of her letters, always just a few lines, hoping she was well and so on, all very impersonal. It was hard to know what she thought. The fact that she paid for the home was encouraging, the lack of any meaningful contact less so. Lillian had received a card from Perry, wishing her all the best, and she suspected he was behind her mother's benevolence, even if it was reluctant.

At least she had Sam and Kate to fall back on. It would be odd living with Kate as the new Lady Kenefick, but it was the best-case scenario. Perhaps the Irish girl was seeking to blend more easily into society and an association with her sister-in-law might help? The ways of the working class were a bit of a mystery, but Sam seemed to be besotted with her.

Lillian had never spoken to her brother on the subject of her future – in fact, she'd not seen him in over a year – but Robinswood was her home too, so he had no option but to put her and Austina up.

According to Kate, her parents were there as well, which was wonderful because Isabella was an accomplished nanny. She could take over the day-to-day care of Austina while Lillian considered her next move.

Beau. She refused to allow his name to enter her head; each time he appeared in her consciousness, she dispelled him immediately. She wrote four times after getting that sad letter saying he was in hospital and that there was no hope for them, but she never heard from him again.

A nurse tapped on the door. 'You have a visitor, Mrs Kenefick-Lane.' She smiled. Lillian had not had a single visitor in the eight months she had been there.

Lillian thanked her and then stood as her mother entered the room.

Violet was dressed more extravagantly than Lillian had seen her do since before the war. It was as if the old Lady Kenefick had returned, and the capable, all-hands-on-deck woman her mother had morphed into as an impoverished gentlewoman had retreated again.

She was rail-thin, wearing what must have been Parisian couture. An emerald-green skirt of shot silk fell just below the knee, teamed up with a black tailored jacket, cinched in tight at the waist. Around her neck was an exquisite black and green scarf, and on her head, she wore a wide-brimmed black felt hat, jauntily tipped to one side. Black gloves and emerald earrings completed the outfit.

'You look amazing, Mother.'

'Yes, well, enough was enough with that dreadful serge and plain cotton of the war years. I got this in Dior as we passed through Paris. Perry wanted to sail home, but the Bay of Biscay is horridly bumpy, so we came by train and the captain sailed *La Violette* home. Poor Perry was like a hen with an egg waiting for it to arrive in Portsmouth.'

Lillian laughed. 'How times have changed. When we all lived in Robinswood, could we ever have predicted how things would turn out?'

Violet shot her daughter a sideways glance. 'Indeed we could not.

But life is what it is, and one must move on. Now, how are you? Recovered?'

Lillian shrugged and poured the tea that the maid had quietly delivered. 'Physically, yes. Though childbirth is gruesome. Thank you for arranging this place. It's most agreeable, and the staff are very kind.'

'You're welcome. And yes, this whole business is most unpleasant. You took two-and-a-half days to be born. I thought I might die.'

'My apologies.' Lillian smiled.

'Well, do I get to see her?' Violet asked as she put her teacup down.

'Of course.' Lillian crossed the room and lifted Austina out of her crib. She soothed the baby as she stirred, returned to where Violet was sitting and placed the child in her arms.

Violet looked down at her little face, and as she did, the baby opened her eyes. They were huge and brown and held her grandmother's gaze.

Lillian waited with bated breath. The next few seconds would decide so much.

Violet didn't smile. Her face remained impassive; she just maintained eye contact. Eventually, she spoke. 'She is beautiful. Congratulations, Lillian.'

There needed to be nothing further said. The old Violet Kenefick would have run screaming from a black grandchild – it would have been enough to send her into a darkened room for days to recover from the shock – but the war had changed Violet as it had changed everyone. It had knocked the edges off her, made her more accessible, less entitled and, most of all, kinder. Lillian had tossed and turned so many nights – for many reasons, she needed her mother's approval – wondering if Violet's return to luxury and privilege would mean a return to the snobbish ways of the past, but she need not have worried.

'Thank you, Mother. It means a lot to me.' Lillian found herself wiping a tear.

'So all that needs to be decided now is what you will do next.' Violet fixed her daughter with a gaze that said 'do not interrupt'. 'I have made some enquiries, and there is a home – it is near Bristol, I believe – for babies just like this little one. She would be well cared for, and she would be with others like herself – you are not the only girl to fall for a coloured chap. I will pay all necessary fees, and we can hope that even at this late stage, you might still be able to make an adequate match. There have been rumours, I might as well tell you, about where you've gone, but I think we can get away with it, especially if you travel for a while once the baby is settled in Bristol. We can blur the dates, and Perry has contacts all over the world, so that can be arranged.'

Lillian could hardly believe her ears. There was no way she was giving Austina to an orphanage, no matter how nice it was. She was horrified her mother would even suggest it.

'Well?' Violet prompted.

Lillian's throat was dry, and when she opened her mouth to speak, no sound came out. She tried again. 'Mother, I... I don't know what you were thinking, but I shan't give her up under any circumstances. I have a plan to return home to Robinswood, and we will do well there, I'm sure.'

'You plan to return to Ireland, to live at Robinswood?' Violet did not hand the baby back.

'Yes, I think it will be for the best. The Murphys will be there, and Isabella was lovely to Samuel and me as children, so she can just do the same again with Jack and Austina. And the house is large enough that we won't be living on top of each other. I was thinking I could take the rooms on the third floor, one as a nursery, another as my room, and then I could convert the one that looks over the turning circle to a small drawing room for personal entertaining...'

Violet's laugh startled the baby, who gave a lusty howl. She immediately soothed her, and the child went back to sleep.

'Hush... Hush now, little one. I'm sorry, it's just your mama made me laugh...' Violet crooned.

'What? Why is it funny?' Lillian was confused.

Violet looked at her daughter and, not for the first time in her life, realised she needed a good strong dose of reality. 'Lillian, Beau is gone and it seems will not be returning. You are left with this bundle to manage, which by anybody's reckoning is going to be a very difficult job. I do not believe in recriminations, and I understand that during the war, certain, shall we say, standards of what was permissible in a courtship were relaxed somewhat. You found yourself – along with many more girls, I have no doubt – holding the baby in every way. So while I was shocked and dismayed – I might as well be honest – the deed is done, and this child is a reality.'

Lillian wondered where this was going, but it didn't sound good. She braced herself. 'Yes, she is. And now that she is here, I am so glad to have her.' She was quietly determined. If her mother thought she was going to give her child up, she could forget about that.

'Yes, she is a lovely child. But, Lillian, this plan you have to return… Not just to Robinswood, but from what I can see, you plan on returning to 1930. That world no longer exists. That house is dilapidated beyond reasonable repair in my opinion, but your brother seems determined to try. He has limited resources and a young child himself, but he is married to a very capable young woman with many skills. Kate Murphy will prove an invaluable asset to him in this endeavour, and even then, I fear they might fail. As for the Murphys, they plan on renovating the house and working the estate, and ultimately turning it into a hotel or some such, so they will not be at your beck and call. Besides, your brother doesn't want you there.'

She smiled at her daughter's stricken face. 'You have a lot of your father in you. You want the reward without the work. The life you have mapped out for yourself and this little one is, frankly, a fantasy.'

'But… But how can you know this? You haven't been back there for years,' Lillian protested.

'Samuel and I had lunch last week. He was in London on business.'

'So he sent you up here to break the news to me, did he? He wants his life with the servants undisturbed by my and Austina's arrival? Couldn't face me himself?' She made no effort to hide the bitterness.

'No, let's not make you the victim here. You are the one with the black child out of wedlock, and your family will support you, of course we will. But the life you are planning simply will not happen.'

'But what can I do?' Lillian spread her hands. 'I can't stay here.'

Violet nodded. 'Indeed you can't. It is very expensive, and while Perry is most generous, I do not want to wring every last pound out of him. So like I did during the war, you will need to change, my dear. I cannot force you to put this child in the home, though it is by far the wisest option. But if you refuse, then you will need to find a house and someone to take care of Austina while you go out and earn a living to support yourself and your daughter.'

Violet had to smother a giggle at the look of incredulous outrage on her daughter's face.

'You're suggesting I get a job?' Lillian said it like it was the most outlandish proposal she'd ever heard.

'Well, unless you can find a wealthy man to take you and this little bundle of joy on, then that's exactly what I'm proposing.' Violet nodded.

CHAPTER 14

*D*ermot stood up, his back aching from bending over the fencing. Charlie Warren had grown a lot of wheat and barley on the Robinswood estate for the past six years, but he and Sam had decided to revert to dairy cattle once more. It was much more labour-intensive but ultimately more lucrative, and they needed money. The demand for everything in England was seemingly insatiable, so there was an export market for whatever they could produce. In an unexpected turn of good fortune, Violet's husband knew someone at the Ministry of Food and had set them up with a very profitable contract. They just needed to produce the milk, butter and cheese as quickly and in as much quantity as they could. They would have to take people on shortly, but they had no money for wages just yet, so they had to manage on their own for a little while until the payments started coming in.

They bought a herd from a farmer who was retiring. His son had been intending to take it over, but he had an accident where he was attacked by a bull and was then unable to work. It was with a heavy heart that the old man sold up, and both Dermot and Sam felt bad, but the money they gave him meant his son could get the treatment he needed to live some kind of life again.

The herd of one hundred cows was arriving later today, and they needed the fencing in place to ensure the cattle didn't wander.

He poured himself a cup of tea from the flask Isabella had made him this morning and unwrapped his sandwiches. He could have gone down to the farmhouse for lunch, but every moment was precious today. There was so much to do before the herd arrived, so lunch on the go was a better plan.

As he chewed on a sandwich and then swallowed a mouthful of tea, he looked down at the farmhouse he had considered home for so long. All those years they lived there, it felt like someone else's house. The day he and Sam went into the solicitor's office in Dublin and Sam signed the deeds over to Dermot was one he would never forget. It was his home, in his own name, and it felt different.

Sam was generous, there was no doubt about it, but it didn't feel like charity. It felt like a partnership, and he knew Sam needed his skills. The lad was a hard worker and not afraid to get his hands dirty, but he had no idea what he was doing in any practical sense. In lots of ways, Dermot was the boss.

That morning, young Lord and Lady Kenefick were whitewashing the milking parlour and generally sprucing it up. Isabella had spent the past week scrubbing the farmhouse while keeping an eye on little Jack, and as he left that morning at six thirty, she was running up new curtains with material she got on sale in Lacey's. The new sense of it being their place meant as much to his wife as to him. Never again would they walk down that avenue, like they did in 1940, with nothing. The whole place was a hive of activity, and he loved it.

He finished his lunch, wrapping up what was left. Isabella always packed too much. He began again at the fencing. Luckily, there had been a lot of rain in the spring, so the ground was good and fertile and it wasn't too hard to drive the posts down into the loamy soil.

He hammered away until he needed to stand and stretch once more. As he did, he saw someone walking up the field towards him. The sun was in his eyes, making it difficult to determine who it was, so he waited. As the figure approached, he realised it was a male, but not Sam. Sam was tall and skinny, but this was a much shorter man.

He wore working clothes and a cap and kept his head down. It wasn't until he was within thirty yards that Dermot realised who it was.

He put down his tools and walked towards the man, and without saying a word, they embraced. It was something they would never have done in the old days, but somehow it seemed appropriate.

'Hello, Oskar,' Dermot said, releasing him. 'I never thought I'd lay eyes on you again, my friend. I'm glad to see you.'

'And I you, Dermot… And I you.'

The two men stood and observed each other for a few moments. Dermot thought Oskar looked old and tired. The last time they met in that pub in Dublin at the start of the war, Oskar was slightly stocky, with a full head of hair. He'd looked a bit older than when they were two young bucks, wreaking havoc on the British under Michael Collins, but he'd looked more or less the same. The man that stood before him now was like a shadow of that person.

He was thin, and his hair was totally silvery grey. All the blond was gone. It was brushed back off his face, the way he always wore it. But his eyes were the biggest change. No matter what the predicament, Oskar's blue eyes had twinkled with merriment. He seemed to thrive on danger and in lots of ways saw life as a big game, but now those eyes were dull. It was as if someone had switched off the light that had always burned inside him.

'Tea?' Dermot asked, offering him a cup.

'Thank you.' The two men sat in a ditch as the German sipped the tea and accepted a sandwich from the box.

'Elena got your letter and Thomas's too. It was a pity for him to die at the end like that – he survived for so long, thanks to you.'

'Yes, it was a pity. I would have written to you too, but I thought it best not to implicate you. But yes, I survived, just about. You know me, Dermot, I'm like the cat with nine lives.' The words were jokey, but there was no levity in his voice.

'So you changed horses?' Dermot gazed straight ahead. Oscar opened a packet of cigarettes, offered one to Dermot, but he refused. He lit one for himself.

'I did. You were right. I just wish I'd seen that in time. Now...now it's too late.' Oskar exhaled a line of smoke.

'It's not too late for you. You survived, and you did a good thing. Elena told me Thomas was saying all the time about how great you were, helping him and getting Jews out and all the rest, and I could just picture you doing it. You were never one of them, not really.'

Oskar stubbed his cigarette out with his boot. 'I was. In every way that mattered, I was. I'm the reason his children will grow up without a father.'

'But you saved him, and let's face it, he wasn't exactly an innocent flower, remember? I'm not saying he deserved to be handed over to the Gestapo, but he kidnapped my girls and Sam's mother and was threatening all sorts, and we had to shoot him to get the information out of him. So he's not coming out of this whiter than white, either.'

The other man shrugged. 'How is Elena?'

'All right. Not bad. I think it closed the chapter for her, and she loved getting the letters. That was kind of you.'

'Would she see me, do you think? I want to apologise to her in person...and to you. Dermot, I'm so sorry for bringing the evil of National Socialism to your door. You're my best friend, and I behaved so badly, I can't ever make it up to any of you. But I wanted to come and say I'm sorry in person.'

'I think Elena would see you – in fact, I think she wants to. And as for me, well, consider it forgotten. You were doing your job as you saw it, and once you realised, you got out. I'm just glad you had some of your lives left. You used up a good share of them here, so it's all to your credit that you're still standing.'

'For now anyway.'

'What do you mean? It's over, you made it. Are you going to stay here? By all accounts, Germany is reduced to rubble.'

'It is. It's hard to see how it could ever come back from this... But even if they could rebuild, we can't rebuild in here.' He pointed to his chest. 'So what's the point?'

'What did you do after Thomas was killed? Did you find Birgitta?'

Oskar had written in the mid-thirties to say he was getting

married, and he'd invited Dermot and Isabella to the wedding. But the girls were small and money was tight, so they didn't make it. Oskar sent a photo of himself standing beside a short smiling woman, and he looked delighted with life. That photo was on the dresser for years.

Oskar leaned his head back against the ditch and allowed the sun to warm his face. 'Birgitta is dead. I knew that before I went into the forest, otherwise I'd have brought her with me.'

'I'm sorry.' Dermot didn't know what else to say.

Oskar acknowledged his sympathy with a nod and went on. 'I dragged his body out, along with all the others. Everyone who was there was helping. He was sitting at the back. The bodies were laid out on the street, and people were there, claiming their loved ones and bringing them home to bury. It's hard to understand. There are no systems any more. It's a free-for-all. So I asked a man if he could take Thomas's body and bury it along with his father's, and he agreed. I got his address so Elena could go there if she wants to, to see where he's buried.' His voice cracked with emotion.

'Then I just made my way up to the port and got on a ship. Well, stowed away on a ship, I should say. I'd no money, but once I got to Dublin, I was all right. I had transferred the money from the family business in Germany to my Irish bank account.'

'And so you just walked up through France?'

Oskar nodded. 'We should both be dead, many times over. Life is strange, is it not?'

Dermot wanted to somehow acknowledge the huge sacrifice his friend had made. Even though he knew the other man was a German and worked for the Nazis, he had never believed Oskar was really one of them – and he'd been proven right. It was cold comfort, considering the horrors his friend had seen and experienced, but he was alive, and that was something.

'It is. But you were on the right side. Just like here in the twenties, we were on the right side. You did right by Thomas, and you helped so many people over there as well – you should remember that. Why don't you stay here? We could use an extra pair of hands, and if you've nothing to go back for anyway...'

'I'm a bad man, Dermot. I've been part of a bad thing. Worse than you can even imagine. I'm wanted by the Americans and the British, and I'll probably hang, but it doesn't matter. I might as well be dead for all the life that's left in me. My heart is pumping, my blood flows, but I'm hollow. When they kill me, it won't matter... I'm dead already anyway.' The words were entirely without emotion; he was merely stating a fact.

'I just wanted to see you, my oldest, dearest friend, to say goodbye, to say sorry for taking off like that. And I want to see Elena and tell her everything – and beg her forgiveness too, though I don't deserve it. After I see her, I'll go back, tell them who I am, and that will be that. Even if there is an afterlife, and I doubt there is, I won't be going where my Birgitta is. So it matters nothing. I also wanted to see Ireland free. We fought so hard, and it was a good fight, wasn't it?'

Dermot nodded. 'It was. They were wrong, and we were right.'

'On the right side of history, at least once in my life.' He gave a short laugh and kicked a stone with the toe of his boot.

'We are a neutral, independent country because of what we achieved. And you are an Irish citizen. Why would you go back? You and I know from bitter experience there's nothing glorious in death – it's just a stupid, pointless waste. Besides, once they figure out that you helped the Jews, they won't hang you.'

'They will. I was a member of the Abwehr, and that organisation did terrible things. I did terrible things...'

Dermot put his arm around his friend's shoulder. They were not usually demonstrative, but this was an unusual time. 'You are not a bad man. You might have done some bad things, but you did a lot of good too. I don't know the ins and outs, but I know this – you are *not* a bad man. Stay. Please.'

'And do what?' Oskar asked quietly. 'Destruction, killing, misery... That's what I've created my whole life. So many deaths, so many... It doesn't matter, you know, right or wrong...a good cause or a bad one. There are people all over England who look at a photograph of someone they once loved, a British soldier just doing his duty here in Ireland, a boy who was someone's child smiling in a uniform, a life extinguished because of me. And now, after what Germany has done, that death toll… Well, there are not even photographs. We left nothing.' He was barely audible by the time he finished.

'All right, if you feel like that, balance the books. Volunteer, work for a charity, whatever you want to do. But first, let us bring you back to life. There will be so many opportunities. Eve, my eldest, is training girls out of an orphanage in how to run a house so they'll be able to find work. She's doing something really practical. You have lots of skills, lots of talent – use them for good in the time you have left. Don't go back just to be another corpse on the huge pile. There's no point to that.'

Dermot placed his hands on his friend's shoulders and looked into his eyes. 'Please, Oskar. We've survived so much together, I'd hate to lose you now. Please stay.'

He could see the conflict in the other man's eyes. Oskar wanted to hand himself in because it was the right thing to do as he saw it, but there was something else, a despondency there he'd never seen before.

'All right. For a while anyway. Thank you.'

'You're welcome.'

CHAPTER 15

*A*isling could not believe her ears. The magistrate was giving Mark such a dressing-down, really going for him. It was as if his father were on the bench. All that 'pull yourself together, you're a disgrace' stuff. She wanted to stand up and scream at them all. *Do you have any idea what he did? What he saw? What he had to live with every single day of his life?* Delilah must have sensed her outrage because she placed her hand on Aisling's knee as if to restrain her.

The judge droned on for a few more minutes about the need for civil society and how Mark's violent outburst was unacceptable. How he'd had a warning before, and this was the final straw. 'Therefore, I am left with no option. Mark George Belitho, I am sentencing you to six months penal servitude to be served at Dartmoor Prison. Take him down.'

'No!' Aisling heard the scream but did not realise it came from her until everyone turned to stare.

Mark's eyes pleaded silently with hers as he was pulled roughly from the dock to a staircase that presumably led to the cells below. Delilah and Mrs Belitho were on either side of her, both in tears. Mark's father had refused to come.

They took the bus back to Portwye. The clerk said that there would be a visiting order sent in the post in the coming days and she could go to see Mark then.

She sat in their kitchen alone. Delilah had to pick the boys up from Terry's mother, who had a very short fuse, and Mark's mother had scurried sheepishly back to her husband. Aisling struggled to be fair – at least she came. It could not have been easy to defy the dogmatic and bombastic Tobias Belitho.

Mark was in prison.

The words tumbled over her head like rocks. Her lovely, kind, funny Mark, the man who couldn't hurt a fly, was on the way to Dartmoor Prison to serve a sentence for 'grievous bodily harm'. Apparently, someone down at the pub made some crack about Jews or something – it was hard to tell exactly – but Mark saw red and lashed out. The man had a broken jaw and a fractured skull and was lucky to be alive. Another man tried to intervene and got a black eye and two cracked ribs for his trouble.

Her eye caught their wedding photograph on the wall. She and Mark were laughing and so in love, both in uniform because they had nothing else to wear. And he looked so handsome. How could it be that amid all that chaos and destruction, bombs falling and Sam and Mark being scrambled at a moment's notice, never knowing if this was going to be the last smile, the last kiss, how on earth could those times seem calm and peaceful compared with the present?

She would have to tell her family something. Not the truth, but something. She'd kept them at a distance for months, writing back long newsy letters about the weather, the rationing, Delilah and her boys, the life in the village, but never anything personal or honest. Mammy asked her in every letter how Mark was, but she skirted around the issue.

Suddenly, the weight of it all became too much. She needed Eve and Kate, she needed Mammy and Daddy. She could not do this on her own.

She got up wearily, went over to the dresser drawer and extracted a writing pad and a pen. She got an envelope and a stamp as well – she would post it immediately in case she changed her mind. She was going to be honest, maybe for the first time since this all began. No more treading on eggshells.

My darling Mark,

I am sitting here in our kitchen hardly believing the mess we are in. Am I really writing to you in prison?

I want you to read this carefully, Mark, and take in what I say. That magistrate is wrong. You're not a menace and a disgrace. You're a damaged and, in lots of ways, a broken man because you are a good soul who tried to do the right thing. But in a war, the lines of good and bad, right and wrong, are so blurred, it's impossible to determine which is which. I know you told me what happened, about the ship you had to bomb – that is a terrible burden to bear on top of everything else you did. You asked me a question once. 'Why are we right? How is it better that Delilah has her three boys when some mother in Germany does not have hers because a bomb you dropped killed them?' The answer is, I don't know, Mark. Maybe there's no sense to be had out of the whole thing, but I do know this.

I want my husband back. I don't know how to get you back; I truly don't. The pills just knock you out. They don't help. And nobody understands – not your father, not your community, not anyone. I don't understand it, either, but I love you, and that's the difference. I want you back, Mark, and I won't ever move on without you.

You asked me to leave, to go home, to start again. You said you wanted a divorce. I will never allow that. But this is what I'm going to do. I'm going to leave today and go home to Robinswood. Mammy and Daddy and Kate have invited us both over and over, so I'm going to go. I can't stay here in this village all on my own. When you get out, it will be March of 1947. Robinswood will be full of calves and flowers, and spring will be in the air. And I will be there. Waiting for you. Come to Robinswood, Mark. Work the land with Daddy and Sam. They will understand what you've been through in ways that others can't. I never told you this, but my father was in the IRA. He fought in the 1920s to remove the British occupiers from our country, so he knows the toll war takes on men. So does Sam. And together, we will make you better.

Please, Mark, write to me and say you'll come.

I love you always,

Your Aisling

She sealed the envelope quickly, addressed it to Mark at the prison and immediately went to the postbox at the end of the street and threw it in.

She went back and packed her bag, putting in a shirt of Mark's from the laundry hamper, one that smelled of him. She left a note for the Belithos and one for Delilah, then travelled by bus to Bristol. It was too late to catch the boat that night, so she stayed in a small hotel in Bristol and set off early the next morning for the port at Fishguard.

As the ship pulled away from the quay, the cold Welsh wind whipped around her, her thin coat no match for the October weather. Further down the railing, a man was smoking, and behind her, a mother was trying to get her children to wave to someone on the dockside below. But she didn't care who saw her. She gripped the rail and allowed the hot salt tears to come. She was going home.

The crossing was miserable, and she was overcome with nausea, so she spent most of it outside on deck. The smell of fumes and oil didn't help, but at least it wasn't the stuffy heat of bodies and odour of food inside. The lights of the port of Rosslare eventually came into view.

The words of a poem by John Locke that the nuns had drilled into them at the national school sprung to her mind. She hadn't thought about that poem since she was seven or eight years old.

Now fuller and truer the shoreline grows, was ever a scene so splendid?
I feel the breath of the Munster breeze, Thank God that my exile is ended.
She felt a wave of relief and exhaustion.

Robinswood was only seventy miles from the ferry port, but she had no idea how she was going to get there. She probably should not have been so impetuous. If she'd written to say she was coming, then Daddy would have been there to meet her, and he would have organised a way to get them home. He could even have driven to pick her up because they had a car now. But she had just needed to get away from Portwye.

She came through the terminal building and saw the bus stop. There wasn't anyone waiting, which suggested the daily bus was already gone. Deflated, she sat on a bench, wondering what to do next.

A beep from a van caused her to look up.

'I thought it was you. Do you want a spin?'

Aisling's heart sank. Of all the people in the world, Sean Lacey was the last person she wanted to see. Her immediate reaction was to refuse, but how else would she get to Kilthomand? She would have to accept the lift.

'Thank you,' she said as he put her bag in the back of the empty van.

He looked different, more confident or something, and he seemed perfectly open and friendly. He still had the same sandy hair and the same well-dressed style, but he appeared less cowed somehow. She remembered him as a soft mammy's boy, with his mother doing everything for him. He looked different to the boy who had embarrassed her by walking out with her for all to see but then kissing Eleanor Conlan at the dance. Aisling had been so humiliated that night six years ago. Eve and Kate gave him a right dressing-down in front of everyone, and while they were just sticking up for her, it was mortifying. Even thinking of it now made her toes curl.

'I just dropped a load to the boat for export. My mother's cousin has a shop in Manchester, and she can't get stock, so I supply her,' he explained. He opened the passenger door. 'Jump in.'

'How is your mother?' Aisling asked politely. Old Ma Lacey, as Kate called her, was a right old harridan, but it was a long journey, so she had better start as she meant to go on.

'She's all right. She's in the county home now, and she thinks I'm her brother Ted, who died in 1925. And she keeps asking for my father, who's gone since I was a child, but apart from that, she's happy enough. They look after her well, and she loves her grub. I pop in two or three times a week. Sometimes she knows me, other times not, but it's just a case of keeping her comfortable.'

He eased the van out onto the main road.

'I'm very sorry to hear that, Sean. Are you running the business alone now, then?'

'I am. Yerra, 'tis grand, sure what is it, only a small shop in a small village. How hard can it be? So what about you? I hear you were doing all sorts during the war.'

She waited to hear the sneer in his voice, but it wasn't there. Daddy had warned them that coming back might not be the nicest. Lots of people saw those who served with the British as traitors to their Irish heritage.

'Yes, the women's air force. I was a plotter.'

'Plotting against the king, was it?' He winked to show he was joking with her.

'No.' She smiled. 'I worked on an RAF station, Biggin Hill, taking information from radar stations and the observer corps about incoming aircraft. We would try as accurately as possible to place enemy aircraft so we could respond.'

'Go on.' Sean seemed impressed. 'That sounds interesting.'

'It was. And during the Blitz, it was hectic – long hours, constant worry. But well, it's over now.' She shrugged.

'And you're back. To be a handmaiden to the new Lady Kenefick?'

Again she wondered if he was being malicious, but he didn't seem to be.

'Well, for a while anyway. There's a lot to be done, so I'm coming to pitch in.' Even though the new Sean seemed much nicer than when she knew him, she was still wary, not giving him too much information.

'Well, there's Trojan work going on up there by all accounts, but your father was always a beast of a man for work. Old Lord Kenefick used to say having your father was like having five fellas. Charlie Warren did well out of it – the war lined his pockets well, let me tell you. When England could get food nowhere else, he was able to name his price.'

'Well, the rationing is nearly worse now than it was,' she said, anxious to get off the subject of Charlie Warren's profiteering.

'I know, sure we're the same here. I'm using the whole of my petrol ration for the last two months to get here today. And tea and cigarettes and chocolate, 'tis a right pain, but we've all slimmed down a bit, so I suppose that was no harm.' He patted his flat stomach. 'The old boys in Keoghs have taken to smoking turf, they're so desperate for something to put in the pipe. The coughing and hacking out of them, 'twould turn your stomach.'

Aisling watched as they passed green fields, small stone walls and farmhouses. After London and even Portwye, it felt so familiar, so welcoming.

'Will you have a sweet?' He opened a tin. 'Someone brought them to my mother, but sure she can't eat them, so I gave most of them to the nurses and kept a few.'

She had not had a sweet in so long, she had almost forgotten what it would taste like. Sugar was impossible to get, and all sorts of disgusting alternatives were pressed into action, but nothing really worked. The ration was set, but the trouble was the shops had no supplies with or without a stamp.

She sucked the lemon drop and couldn't help closing her eyes to savour the tangy sweetness. When she opened them, she found Sean looking at her and smiling.

'Aisling, I never apologised properly for that night at the dance. I think about it sometimes, and I feel very bad. I behaved in a terrible way, and you were a lovely girl who deserved much better. So I'm very sorry.'

She smiled. If only that were the answer to her troubles. 'Don't worry about it, Sean. It was a long time ago. We'll let bygones be bygones, all right?'

'Right.' He swerved to avoid a stray dog, and she was jolted sideways, landing almost on top of him. She grabbed his jacket sleeve to stop herself from sliding onto his lap. He looked down and saw the plain gold band there.

'You got married,' he said, and she thought she heard a hint of regret.

'I did.'

'And where is he?' he asked gently, fearing, of course, that he was yet another casualty of the Emergency, as the war was called in Ireland.

What should she say? A lie? The truth? A half-truth? She decided on the last option.

'He's still back in England, as he has some things he needs to do there. I'm hoping he'll be able to come over once he has that done, though.'

'Right.' Sean navigated a herd of cattle trotting along the road, seemingly unsupervised.

'So what else is strange in Kilthomand?' she asked, liking this new Sean so much more.

'Well, your Kate marrying Samuel Kenefick had the place buzzing for a while, but sure now that they're back and Kate is exactly the same, no airs or graces, that died down. So really nothing changed. Mossy is still in the post office, driving us all cracked. The same old faces in Keoghs. I swear to you, Aisling, it's the world's least interesting village.' He chuckled.

'Kate always used to say that.' She smiled. 'But after living through the Blitz and everything afterwards, a bit of peace and quiet sounds just lovely. She couldn't wait to get back, Mammy and Daddy too. So did you get married yourself, Sean?'

A strange look passed over his face as he turned his head to look at her, a sort of smile but something else. 'No, Ais, I never did. I had one great chance a while back, but I made a right mess of it. And well, since then, nobody has ever compared.'

She didn't know how to respond so she said nothing. He might not even have been referring to her, but she suspected he was. The thought gave her no sense of triumph or feeling like he had gotten what he deserved, exactly the sentiment her sisters would have if they heard. Instead, she just felt tired. Sean had really hurt her, more than she even let on to the girls. He had humiliated her in public by kissing another girl when he was supposed to be with her, and in front of everyone too. She was mortified, but more than that, she really liked him. The rest of her family saw him as a mammy's boy, tied to old Mrs Lacey's apron strings, and he was that. But when they were alone, he was funny and interesting, and she had hoped it would turn into something more.

The decision to leave with Kate when she went to join the war was based almost entirely on her dread of staying after the Eleanor Conlan fiasco. If she hadn't done the moonlight flit, as Kate called it, then she would never have met Mark. And if she never met him, well, things would be very different now.

'So how is wedded bliss?' he asked, again with a smile.

If only he knew.

'Good. It's hard for men who saw so much in the war to adjust to civilian life. It's as if they are just expected to pick up where they left off and forget any of it ever happened, but it's not that easy.' She heard the words come out. She had not meant to be so candid, but something about Sean was comforting.

'Did he have a bad time, your man?' he asked.

She thought for a second. 'He did. Very bad. He flew fighter planes.' A surge of pride in her husband's bravery flooded through her as she said the words, and any urge to talk about him with Sean disappeared.

'What's his name?' Sean asked gently.

'Mark. Mark Belitho.'

'I never heard that surname before. Is he English, or is it foreign?'

Aisling smiled. 'Isn't English foreign enough? It's a West Country name. His father's family are from Devon – that's where we live as well, a little village called Portwye, very like Kilthomand actually. Mark's dad could tell you all about the name. It originated in Cornwall, I think, and it's pronounced with the emphasis on the "i" in the middle.'

'So you are Aisling Belitho now, not Aisling Murphy. That will be a tricky one for the natives to remember.' He chuckled.

'Well I probably won't be back long enough for anyone to worry about it. I'm just here to visit the family.'

'Well, I'm sure they'll be delighted to see you.' He paused. 'I know I am.'

She gazed at his profile as he drove. He sounded sincere.

CHAPTER 16

*I*sabella took the shepherd's pie from the oven, savouring the aroma around her own kitchen once more. She could hardly believe she was home, and this time it was even better than before because it was theirs. Placing the pie on the worktop, she gazed around the familiar room with satisfaction. The farmhouse was more or less back to normal now, and the new curtains and the rug she'd bought really brightened the place up. The apple tart would take a few more minutes, so she shut the oven door once more.

Sam, Dermot and Oskar were out on the land, but she had warned them to be back for six at the latest. They were, all three of them, working themselves into the ground. Kate had gone to Dungarvan to get more supplies. She took the car every chance she got – that girl loved to speed along the country roads. Isabella convinced Kate to leave Jack with her, though she had wanted to take him with her.

The big house above was still a total disaster, so they were all living in the farmhouse. Kate and Sam had planned on moving into the small wing of Robinswood House, but even that proved impossible once they inspected it. There was no way anyone could live there, let alone bring a baby there. It was damp, leaking and definitely infested.

They'd had to have a rethink, and Dermot suggested that they put renovating the big house on hold until the estate was up and running properly. There was room for them all in the farmhouse, and while he knew the young couple were anxious to move into their own home, it just wasn't feasible to give it the time it would take at the moment.

'Once we start getting some money in, which will be in the next few weeks, then we can take on some labourers, and we'll have more time.' Dermot didn't want to sound like he was laying down the law, but it was the only course of action that made sense.

'Your father's right, Kate. Let's set Christmas as the goal. Does that sound reasonable?' Sam knew she was hoping to move in sooner.

'All right, we'll have a big Christmas dinner in Robinswood.' Kate smiled at her father and husband. They were working so hard, it would be churlish to be disappointed.

The cattle were settling in nicely, but the milking was still not running as smoothly as Dermot would like, and there was a lot of fencing yet to be done. They also needed to make hay for the winter when there was no growth and plant beets and swedes for the following year. The milk would bring in much-needed money, and once they had a few months of that, then they could look at the house. In the meantime, they found a double-bed frame in one of the sheds and bought a new mattress, and so Sam, Kate and Jack slept in the girls' old room.

The arrival of Oskar out of the blue was a shock, especially as he had changed so much, but he seemed happy enough working with Dermot and Sam. He was much quieter than Isabella remembered him. He was always the more congenial of the two, but now it was Dermot who did most of the talking. They never discussed the war or what happened.

The evening Dermot landed home with his old friend, Isabella nearly collapsed with the shock of it. She was very conflicted at first. Of course, he was Dermot's oldest friend, but he was also a Nazi and had been the one to take Thomas Hamilton-Brooks from his family. That said, Thomas could have had the girls killed. The whole thing was very confusing.

Oskar had waited outside while Dermot explained everything to her. He told her that Oskar had nowhere else to go, that if he went back, he'd be wanted by the Americans and the British, and the fact that he was considered an enemy of the Reich wouldn't hold much water in a court situation. As far as they were concerned, Nazis were Nazis, and that was all there was to it.

Oskar slept in the smaller bedroom that they had always used as storage, and they hardly knew he was there. Luckily, he had no German accent, having grown up in Ireland, and Oskar was not an unusual name. The few people he met – delivery men, the odd farmer at the mart – just accepted him as Oskar who worked for Dermot.

Sam had been shocked initially at the prospect of a Nazi living in his house. Again, Dermot explained everything about Oskar, their shared past in the IRA, what he'd done during the war and why there was no way he was going to allow him to face the noose that waited for him if he were ever to leave Ireland, and Sam had listened. Then Sam and Oskar had gone for a long walk. Kate was beginning to worry, as they were gone over two hours, but Dermot had sat calmly reading the paper by the range, seemingly unperturbed. The two men returned, and that was that; they had hashed out whatever they needed to, and their respective roles in the war were never raised again.

Dermot had always liked Sam as a boy, and even more as a son-in-law when he and Kate got together, but Sam's agreement to allow Oskar to stay cemented a bond between the two of them that transcended the house, Kate or anything else. In lots of ways, Sam was the son he never had.

To see the three of them walking back from the fields, smiling and talking, nobody could ever guess their respective pasts, and by then, it was meaningless. They were there in Robinswood, united in the common cause of reviving the estate.

That first night everyone had dinner together in the farmhouse, Sam brought some beer and wine and Dermot stood up and made a toast.

'This is a new beginning for every one of us. Robinswood is familiar, but the world we are going to create here will be new and different to what went before. There were times over the past few years when living to see another day seemed only a very remote possibility. We have faced death, financial ruin, near homelessness, loss of those we loved, kidnapping' – he smiled at Kate, who grinned back at him – 'awkward relatives and so much more, but we faced those things and survived. And so we go forward together, all of us, to a bright and peaceful future, and let's leave the past where it belongs. To Robinswood.'

'To Robinswood,' they chorused, and raised their glasses.

Isabella was interrupted in her reverie by the sound of a car screeching to a halt outside. She ran to the window. Kate was a fast driver, but recklessness wasn't in her, not any more at least. The passenger door opened, and Isabella couldn't believe her eyes. She ran outside and walked towards the car, arms outstretched. 'Aisling! My darling girl... What are you doing here? It's so good to see you! Your dad will be over the moon, but... Oh Lord, let me look at you...' She held her daughter at arm's length, noting the weight she'd lost, the dark circles under her eyes.

'Let her in the door, would you, Mam, before we go into the twenty questions!' Kate laughed as she carried in bags of groceries and then dropped them to cuddle her son. Jack was screaming in excitement at the new arrival, and Kate spun him around so he laughed even harder.

'Did you know she was coming?' Isabella was so delighted to see Aisling, tears ran down her cheeks.

'Indeed then, I did not. The dope never said a word, only landed up in the square. I was driving through when I saw her. I nearly crashed the car – I was sure I was seeing things.' Kate brought Jack over to where her mother and sister were locked in an embrace.

Aisling was speechless with relief and emotion, not just at seeing her family again, but at being home. It had been almost seven long years since they left the farmhouse for England. A midnight flit unknown to their parents, and so much had happened since she last set foot in the house. She never imagined she would be there again, and yet here she was. The smell of food cooking, warmth, love, protection... It was all suddenly overwhelming.

She recovered enough to take Jack in her arms. He was a big boy and the spitting image of his mother now, all dark curls and flashing eyes.

'Well, Jack Kenefick, I am very, very pleased to meet you at long last. I can't believe you are almost a year old and this is the first time I've met you, but I am so happy. What a handsome boy you are. I'm your Auntie Aisling, and I know I've not been great, but I'll make it up to you, I promise.'

Jack seemed to sense who she was and didn't cry or seek to go back to his mother. Instead, he nestled against Aisling. She held him tightly, and Kate and Isabella wrapped their arms around both of them.

Over a cup of tea, Aisling told them about her journey, about Sean giving her a spin and how she had insisted he let her out in the village. She wanted to walk back to Robinswood, but Kate had spotted her. She told them all about her life in Portwye, but she lied about Mark. She gave them the same story she told Sean – that he was busy with work.

Kate and Isabella each had an arm around her, while baby Jack sat contentedly on her lap.

'I'd have given anything to see Sean's face when he saw you. I bet he was devastated to see the ring,' Kate said. 'That eejit is pining after you still, you know?'

'He's all right. Seriously, he's changed. His mother is in the county home, and he's his own man now. We had a good chat on the way back here actually.'

'Hmm...' Kate was sceptical. 'Just don't let him go getting any ideas.' She nudged her sister to show she was joking.

'Now where are we going to put you is the next question,' Isabella said. 'Oskar is in the small room off the kitchen, Kate, Sam and the baby are in your old room...' She thought for a moment. 'Right, tomorrow we clear the attic. It's warm and dry, and we can use it as a temporary bedroom until Robinswood is some way habitable and

Kate and Sam move there. Your father put a proper floor in there years ago, and there's even a window so you won't be in darkness.'

They were sorting out the logistics of another person in the house when they heard the men's voices outside.

Kate took Jack, and Aisling ran out to the yard. 'Hello, Daddy.' She smiled.

Dermot dropped the bucket of apples he was carrying and opened his arms. 'Ais, you came home!' He was delighted.

Aisling ran to him, feeling safe and happy for the first time in a long time. He held her tight, kissing the top of her head and gently rubbing her back as he had done since she was a baby.

'Welcome home, pet. Oh, Aisling, my darling girl, it's so good to see you.' His voice was a soothing rumble, and he spoke so only she could hear. The familiar smell of him, the soft cotton of his shirt, the strength of his arms released the cold core of steel inside her – the only thing that had given her the strength to make it through the last year. She relaxed and felt like she could breathe again. Everything was going to be all right.

Sam gave her a friendly hug, and Oskar shook her hand. 'The last time I saw you, you were a baby. You've grown into a beautiful young lady, all three of you have. Luckily, you all take after your mother, not this ugly brute.' He playfully shoved Dermot.

'You're not wrong,' Dermot agreed, walking into the house with his arm around Aisling. He deliberately didn't ask about Mark, and she was grateful for it.

They ate the delicious meaty pie and followed it with Mammy's legendary apple tart with thick cream.

After dinner, Aisling sat back and patted her belly. 'Mammy, I honestly don't know the last time I felt full. Before the war, I'm sure of it. Since then, you eat, but it's never enough. And the sheer enjoyment of food – that's something that is gone. Everything is the thinnest, wateriest, least flavoursome version of what it was before. And some of the recipes that Lord Woolton comes up with... I know one thing – he doesn't sample them himself.'

They all laughed. It was so good to have her home.

She went on. 'I used to try with the meagre rations – in fact, it's worse now than during the war, which is really depressing – but I'd do my best. But when a shepherd's pie is almost all potato and very little meat or gravy and no butter or cream to mash into the spuds, well, it's always a let-down.' She ran her finger around the edge of the plate and licked it.

'Remember when we were in Biggin Hill, Ais? And we'd start talking about Mammy's stew, or bacon and cabbage, or jam roly-poly, or barmbrack toasted with melted butter? We used to nearly drive ourselves daft just thinking about it, only to be given that horrible bread that tasted like sawdust, a scrape of margarine that we wouldn't even use for baking and a tiny blob of jam made without sugar for our supper,' Kate said as she cut up pieces of juicy carrot for Jack.

'I do remember. It was the main thought of everyone, I think, apart from trying to stay alive, how hungry they were, how everything tasted nasty,' Aisling agreed.

'I went to boarding school, so I think the adjustment wasn't as bad for me. They trained us well.' Sam chuckled. 'But coming home for the holidays, I was the same, salivating at the thought of Isabella feeding me up for the summer.'

'Was it worse in Germany, Oskar?' Aisling asked, and the table went silent. Nobody ever said it, but the fact that Oskar was a German was never even alluded to.

Oskar smiled sadly. 'There was suffering in Germany – still is, I would imagine – and there has been for a long time. No food, no clean water, no fuel, fear. But we have brought it on ourselves, all of us who got sucked into the lies and the promises, so there is a price for everything. I don't think my country can ever recover. Maybe it never should.'

Silence descended on the table; nobody knew what to say.

Eventually, it was Sam who spoke up. 'Germany will recover because a strong Germany is a buffer between Russia and the rest of the world. Comrade Stalin was what we needed to defeat Hitler, but now he is strong and nobody trusts him. Germany will be rebuilt, and the people will flourish once more. German people were just as much victims of the regime as we were. Powerful men make decisions, and the rest of us pay the price.'

'Respectfully, Sam, you're wrong. In my country, we all participated. It is not enough to say that Hitler dragged the rest of us, kicking and screaming, to do his bidding. We did it willingly. That will be the scar that will never heal. Nor should it. We betrayed our neighbours, we took the precious possessions of those people the system deemed to be not in keeping with the perfect Aryan ideal – we did it. Us. The German people. The country that created Wagner and Dürer and Nietzsche also created Himmler, Goebbels and Göring. They didn't drop from the sky, something alien. No. They were of my people, the Brownshirts who smashed up Jewish property, who humiliated Jews in the streets, who shipped them off to die in conditions that do not even bear thinking about – we all did it. We drove the trains, we sold their clothes, we moved into their houses, we spent their money. And even if we didn't do those things, we kept our heads down while it all went on around us. All but a small few of us have blood on our hands, and now and for the rest of time, we must pay.'

It was the longest speech Oskar had made since he arrived.

'There is always room for forgiveness, Oskar. For those who really seek forgiveness, who are truly sorry, there is redemption.' Dermot patted his friend on the back.

They had stayed up late many nights discussing it, long after Isabella and the others were gone to bed, so he knew well the burden of guilt his friend felt daily. He didn't try to excuse or brush it away. Oskar was right; the German people were, for the most part anyway, willing collaborators, and that was something they would have to face as a nation.

CHAPTER 17

*L*illian pushed the pram along the street, praying she wouldn't run into any of the old crowd. She almost never ventured up around her old stomping ground of Hampstead, and she wouldn't dream of being seen around Belgravia, but this was her one last chance. She had checked out of the home, and it was only when she threw herself on her mother's mercy that she had been allowed to go to Framington Hall. Violet was less than enthusiastic, and Lillian suspected if it weren't for Perry, she would be homeless. Violet was adamant that if Lillian imposed on her brother, as she callously put it, she'd be furious. Inciting her mother's wrath wasn't something Lillian was in a position to do just then. It was vexing in the extreme that Robinswood wasn't an option. What harm could there be in just her and Austina, for God's sake? But it was one of the terms of the temporary accommodation at Perry's gorgeous old house that she leave Sam alone. It galled Lillian that her mother was so concerned about Sam and seemed to care nothing for her daughter and granddaughter.

Violet loved Austina and spent time with her often, but she didn't look after her when Lillian wasn't there. She had also forbidden any of Perry's staff to babysit, and initially flatly refused when Lillian suggested they employ a nanny for the duration of her stay at Fram-

112

ington. Perry had a word with Violet, Lillian was sure of it – he was so much kinder than her mother – and a nanny was hired, but Violet made sure Lillian didn't abuse the situation. Her mother didn't understand. She *wanted* to be with Austina, and besides, seeing the old crowd was never going to happen again. They were good-time Charlies, and a baby would not fit in. A brown one especially wouldn't, no matter how adorable she was.

Lillian knew perfectly well what game her mother was playing. Violet wanted her to face the music in every way imaginable. She was not going to help soften the reality of having a brown baby, no husband, no money and no prospects.

Their mother had always loved Sam more; Lillian had been her father's pet. She wished so much that Daddy were still alive, as he would never treat her like this. And now that Sam and *Saint Kate* were doing up Robinswood – apparently Sam was living with the servants – Violet was determined to keep her away. There were stories of damp and woodworm and all the rest of it, but all old houses were like that. She'd gone to weekend parties in some old mansions that were practically falling down, but that didn't matter. Framington Hall was the exception, with its central heating system and every modern convenience, but she could rough it if needs be. And anyway, she was sure Sam and her mother were exaggerating.

She dared not risk going against Violet. If she contacted Sam and he spilled the beans to their mother, she would not trust Violet not to throw her out. Every time they had the tedious conversation about what Lillian's plans were, it came back to the same thing: Violet demanding that she either work or marry someone, anyone, and Lillian explaining that she had no skills and no desire to marry anyone but Beau. Nor, to be frank, were there any men interested.

She had run the full gamut of emotions on the subject of Beau many times over. It always came back to the same thing in the end. No matter how angry she was with him for giving up on them, no matter how frustrated with the horribly unfair system in his country, no matter how many explanations she tried to invent about why he didn't contact her, she loved him and would do anything to have him back. Despite much evidence to the contrary, she knew in her heart that he wouldn't abandon her.

Purposefully, she strode up the hill. The people of Hampstead were going about their business, nannies rolling prams to walk privileged little ones on the heath, ladies frequenting one of the two boutiques that were starting to have stock trickle in after the deprivations of the war years. She stopped outside her mother's old house.

The house looked the same. She noted the brass knocker that Beau had fitted for her. The plants that Dermot had planted when they came over for Kate and Sam's wedding bloomed in the front garden. Part of her hoped there was nobody in. She walked up the little path to the front door and knocked.

A child answered, a girl about seven. 'Yes? Can I help you?' she asked.

'Yes, I... Well, I hope so. Is your mother at home?'

'No.' The girl's eyes were wary.

'Your father?' Lillian tried again.

'No. He died. In Italy.' The words were matter-of-fact, but Lillian knew that behind them there was loss and pain.

'Right. Well, I'm sorry to hear about your father. I was just wondering... I used to live in this house, you see, and I wondered if any letters had come for me since we left?'

She felt so foolish. Beau used to write to her flat, and she wasn't there any more, but he could find her if he wanted to. She'd telephoned the landlord to see if he had any post for her, but he hadn't. Beau knew Framington Hall, he knew of Robinswood; anything posted to either of those places would reach her. She was grasping at straws and she knew it.

'I don't know. We only moved in two months ago. The people who lived here before us have gone to live in Scotland. A woman and her children. Their father never came back either, and the mother was Scottish, so they went back there.'

Lillian felt a surge of hope. The family who moved in after she and her mother moved out were not Scottish, so there was a chance the forwarding information had been lost in all the coming and going.

'Well, could you check? My name is Lillian Kenefick.' She spotted the letter rack Beau had also put up for her mother and felt a pang of misery. There were lots of bits of correspondence stuffed into it, far more than it was designed to take.

Austina started to cry in the pram, and Lillian tried to soothe her, but she was hungry.

'Do you need to feed your baby?' the girl asked kindly.

'I rather think I do.' Lillian smiled apologetically. 'How did you know?'

'My little brother is just the same. Mum has just popped out to the shops in between feeds, and I'm looking after him. Would you like to feed in here?'

'Thank you, that would be very kind of you. If you're sure your mother won't mind?' Lillian could feel her breasts react to her baby's lusty cries.

'She won't. Come through. My name is Beatrice, by the way, but everyone calls me Bea.'

Lillian followed the girl into the familiar sitting room. Nothing had changed.

'It feels strange to be back here. Thank you for letting me come in.' She pulled back the blankets and lifted Austina out of the pram. Her dark curls were really growing now, and her big brown eyes were wet with tears.

'There now, my darling,' Lillian crooned as she sat down and discreetly put her to the breast. The baby sucked greedily. She had not been fed since they left Framington Hall that morning.

'She's brown,' Bea said in amazement.

'Yes, she is.'

Very few people apart from her mother and Perry had ever seen Austina, and Lillian dreaded the looks and stares. She adored her daughter; the child was the most beautiful thing she'd ever owned, and she spent hours just watching her sleep. But Lillian was under no illusions as to what the rest of the world might think.

'How come she's so brown?' Bea persisted. 'You're not brown at all.'

Lillian looked up. There was no judgement in the child's eyes, just curiosity.

'Her father is black,' she said, the word sounding strange even to her own ears.

'How did he get that way?' the girl asked. 'Was it from smoke?'

Lillian smiled at Bea's furrowed brow as the girl tried to figure this conundrum out.

'No.' Lillian smiled as she swapped Austina from one breast to the other. 'He is from America, but his family came from Africa, and everyone in Africa has very dark skin.'

'Because it's so sunny there?'

'Yes, I suppose so.' Lillian giggled.

'Bea, I thought I told you to...' A woman in a headscarf and a drab beige coat walked in the room.

'Oh... I'm sorry.' Lillian was flustered. She was not very adept at nursing yet and usually sat quietly while Austina fed. She tried to get up.

'Who are you?' the woman asked.

Lillian was taken aback by her rudeness, and then she realised the woman's eyes were fixed on the baby. She took her daughter from her breast and, with as much dignity as she could muster, buttoned herself up. Austina was not finished, so she howled, but Lillian placed her back in the pram anyway.

'My name is Lady Lillian Kenefick.' She thought using a title might improve things, but she was wrong. The woman just sneered. 'I used to live in this house, and I wondered if any post had come for me?'

The woman glared at her, then snapped, 'No. Now, if that's every-thing, I must get on. Bea, go upstairs, please.'

'But, Mummy, there are lots of letters in the box. Shall I get –' Bea wanted to help the nice lady with the beautiful brown baby, but her mother was not having it.

'Upstairs, Bea, now.' The woman's voice was like the crack of a whip. Her eyes glittered, and Bea paled. The poor child was terrified of her.

'If I could just quickly –' Lillian began.

'What you can do, Lady Whatever-your-name-is, is get out of my house and take that' – she pointed at the pram – 'with you.'

'But please, I simply want to –' Lillian tried again. She could see the letter holder; there might well be one from Beau in there.

'Get out of my house. No *lady* should ever have that' – again she pointed at Austina, who by now was silent – 'to show for getting what she wanted.'

Lillian fought back the tears. And with her head held as high as she could, she pushed her pram out into the street, the front door slamming behind her. She turned and walked away, tears almost blinding her. Was that what it was going to be like? How could someone hate a little baby?

She walked and tried to keep her head down; she wanted to put as much distance between herself and that house as she could. Eventually, she came to a bus shelter, just as it began to rain. She remembered she had left her coat on the sofa. Luckily, her handbag was in the base of the pram or she would have been totally destitute.

She wiped her eyes and tried to pull herself together. As she did, she felt a tug on her shoulder. She turned; it was Bea.

The child thrust a letter into her hand. 'Here's your letter. I have to go back,' she said. 'Your baby is beautiful.'

Bea turned and ran home, and Lillian saw her mother at the door, looking up and down the street. Poor little Bea would pay for her kindness, Lillian knew.

She looked down. One letter, postmarked America, but the writing was not Beau's. With trembling fingers, she opened the envelope.

* * *

LILLIAN WAS in shock but tried to keep her composure until she got back to Framington Hall. She asked the porter at the station to call Framington to have the car sent. Perry's chauffeur was there within minutes, and when she arrived back, it was Perry who was waiting for her. Thankfully, of her mother, there was no sign. She had not even mentioned to Violet that she was going up to London.

Perry was happy to see Austina; he was besotted with the child. He helped them out of the car. Noticing the look on Lillian's face, he handed the baby to the nanny he had employed and led Lillian to his study. He really was so much kinder than her mother. The study was just like the rest of the house: elegant, warm and beautifully decorated.

'Sit down, my dear,' he said, and offered her a sherry. 'What's the matter?' He was full of concern.

The whole story tumbled out, and his face darkened when she described how the woman had reacted to Austina. Finally, she showed him the letter from Beau's cousin, which he read aloud.

Dear Miss Kenefick,

I am writing to tell you that my cousin Beauregard has been arrested. He didn't do anything wrong, Miss Kenefick, but I know you were fond of him and you have been writing, so I thought it was only right to tell you what happened. A local man – he's very important round these parts – didn't like the idea of you and my cousin being close. He served over there in Europe too, so he knew about you two, and he decided to bring trouble to us. They pulled Beau out of his home one night, and he was just trying to defend himself, but they said he was assaulting a police officer. My cousin never assaulted anyone, Miss Kenefick, I can assure you of that.

I do not know where he is now, except he is not here in town. I only recently returned from Chicago, where I work, to visit my mother. I don't expect there is anything you can do, and I am very sorry to bring you this news, but I just wanted you to know. He always spoke about how kind and nice you were and how much you meant to him.

May the Lord bless you and your family.

Yours faithfully,

Miss Ruth Lane

Perry took off his glasses and placed the letter on his desk. His keen blue eyes rested on hers. He was bald and had a round face with the florid complexion of the country set. 'And that's all you know?' he asked.

'I didn't even know that until today. I thought he had just stopped writing...' Lillian sighed.

'And he knows nothing about Austina?'

'Nothing.'

Perry sat back and thought for a moment. Eventually he spoke. 'Now, I want to ask you something, and I want you to give me a straight answer.'

She had spoken to Perry many times but always in company; they had never been alone together before. She couldn't imagine what he wanted, but whatever it was, she was going to do her best to help him after all he had done for her. 'Of course,' she said.

'What do *you* want to do?' He held her gaze.

'Do? What do you mean?' She was confused.

'Well, I mean exactly that. I see you with your daughter. You love her and she loves you, and despite what Violet might infer, we think you are a very loving mother. But you are terribly sad, and this news, well, this is just terrible. So again, I'll ask you, what do you want to do?'

She swallowed the lump in her throat. Her mother had dismissed the idea of Beau ever coming back. As far as she was concerned, that was over and now it was a matter of deciding what to do for the best. Lillian feared her mother might have put Perry up to revisiting the orphanage idea, but she could never do that.

'I won't send my daughter away to an orphanage, if that's what you're getting at. She's not an orphan – she has me. And I know Mother wants me to, and I appreciate you putting us up, Perry, and all you do, but I can't just...' To her horror, Lillian felt tears spring from her eyes. She was mortified, as she never cried.

Perry handed her a handkerchief. 'Of course not. I don't think your mother would consider such an option either, not for a moment, you silly girl. We love her too. I have inherited a grandchild – if you'll allow me to be her grandfather, I would be delighted with that. I mean, what do you want to do about Beau?'

Lillian wiped her eyes but was still confused. 'I... I don't know what you mean?'

'Well, you have this letter from his cousin...' he prompted.

'Yes. But what can I do? Especially from over here? Nothing.' She was distraught but at a total loss as to what she could do.

'Do you know what I think?' Perry extracted something from his desk drawer and began writing. 'I think you need to go over there, to America, and see what is going on. I have some contacts, friends and so on from when I lived there, and they'll help you if I ask them to.'

Lillian looked at him like he was out of his mind. 'I can't do that. I've no money... And I have Austina. I can't take her...'

'Well, I know *you* have no money, but I do.' He smiled and pushed the cheque he was writing across the desk. It was for £500.

'I... I can't take this,' Lillian spluttered. 'Apart from anything else, my mother would kill me.'

'She will be fine. I'll speak to her,' he said calmly. 'The nanny can care for Austina, or perhaps your brother's family could help out? I understand the Murphys are experts with babies.'

He stood up and walked around to her side of the desk, placing his hand on her shoulder. 'Take it, Lillian. Go and find Beau. I only met him once or twice, but he seemed like a thoroughly decent chap and one who would not willingly desert you or his child. I have, as I mentioned, some contacts – I worked and studied over there in the twenties – and they will help you. You'll need a lawyer first and foremost.' He handed her a business card. 'His name is Walter Finkstein, and he's one of the best. He's in New York.'

She took the gold-embossed card and examined it. She was speechless.

'Walter is a New Yorker, so he doesn't suffer fools, nor does he do small talk. You can't go to him with some half-baked story – friend of mine or no, he'll shoo you out the door – so I suggest you go to Georgia, find out what you can, as you have become a very resourceful young woman, Lillian, and then contact Walter. He will be expecting your call.'

Perry smiled as if he were suggesting a quick trip to Brighton, not an odyssey across the ocean. 'But I will warn you – Georgia and those Southern states are not like here, nor are they even like Boston or New York. I knew a chap once, he was from a big slave-owning family in Mississippi, back when that was legal, and they amassed fortunes on these huge plantations, all worked by slaves. You must remember that slavery was only abolished in 1865, and I knew this chap in 1923, so less than sixty years previously, his family owned hundreds of slaves. And while he was a very amicable sort of fellow and I liked him a lot, he genuinely saw black people as inferior. It was how he had been taught to think, and it was how everyone around him thought. So you will encounter that. Be prepared. And be careful.'

Lillian looked up at Perry. He was such a nice man and had been so kind to her, but this was a huge amount of money. 'Why are you doing this?' she asked.

He smiled. 'You're astute, and you are so like your mother, much more like her than either of you'd care to admit, I'll warrant. That's why I think you can do this.'

She waited for him to answer her question.

'I'm doing it because I can, that's the main reason, actually. I have a large fortune, but I missed the boat, so to speak, family-wise. I was too busy, you see, and anyway, none of the young women who would have me really were my type. It wasn't until I met your mother that I knew what love was. We can't have children at this late stage, so I would like to be your honorary father. I believe if Austin were alive and he could fund such a trip, then he would do it. It's what fathers do for their children.' He smiled shyly. 'I hope you don't think me presumptuous?' The normally confident Perry suddenly looked vulnerable.

Lillian stood up and hugged him. 'I think you are one of the most decent people I've ever met, and if you want to take over as my father and Austina's grandpa, then I'd love that,' she whispered, and he squeezed her tight.

'Jolly good,' he said as he released her. 'Samuel seems to be doing well, but I would like to help him out as well. But all in due course. In the meantime, let's concentrate on you getting Sergeant Lane back on British soil, shall we?'

CHAPTER 18

*E*ve was so busy with the training school that by the time each day was over, she was only fit for bed. The third group of girls were due to graduate from her class on Friday. Over the months, she and Elena had tweaked the course, and now it ran like clockwork.

Each student got four weeks tuition – cookery, laundry and housekeeping, and childcare and elderly care. The orphanage sent the girls as they approached their sixteenth birthday, so in most cases, they left the institution very soon afterwards. So far, they had almost a hundred percent success rate, with each girl finding a position as a domestic. Eve was always anxious to point out to them that this was 1947 and the opportunities for women were much greater than even the generation before, so while the skills she taught were going to be useful, it did not mean that was all there was in their futures. So many girls were so bright, and given the right tuition, they could really do anything they wanted to. But circumstances meant they were never given those opportunities.

It was hard but really rewarding work, and even though some of them were unruly or difficult to manage, they almost always came round. Eve marvelled at the transformation sometimes, but Elena said it was because once they saw that Eve was on their side, that she was trying to improve their lot in life, even the most belligerent person knew not to bite the hand that feeds.

The boys, on the other hand, were not so easy. Some took to the work, but many did not. As poor Irish Protestants, they wanted to get away, to go to England mainly, where their religion would be the norm rather than the exception. They were more acutely aware than the girls how precarious their position was. In Ireland, because of its history, the Protestants were the wealthy, the landed gentry, the owners of the big estates like the Kenefics. The Catholics were the poor ones, the ones who relied on the grace and favour of their Protestant employers for their very survival. To be poor and Protestant was a misnomer and one that didn't fit in Irish society. For most of the young men, getting away from Ireland as quickly as possible seemed to be the only goal. As they drank tea and munched scones in the afternoons, she tried to explain to them that anything Bartley could teach them would be to their good and would make them more employable no matter where they went, but in the case of some at least, her advice fell on deaf ears.

Bartley rarely came into the house. He and Eve regularly bumped into each other outside, though. He grew all sorts of herbs alongside the vegetables and fruit her father had planted. Whenever they met, he was respectful but very quiet. Bartley did not do chit-chat. If there was something that needed fixing, he was prompt and efficient; likewise, if he needed supplies for the workshop, he made a list, written in beautiful copperplate, and asked Elena to get them. He spent his free time either away from the house or in his little flat. The boys seemed to like him, though, and they were in awe of his skills.

As Eve was about to go upstairs, Elena entered the kitchen.

'Ah, Eve, great, I was afraid you would have retired already. Listen, I've had an idea. How about we set up a sort of agency, where people in need of staff could contact us and we could set them up with the boys and girls we are training here? We could charge the clients, which would generate some much-needed income, and it would take the hassle out of hiring household help for busy ladies. What do you think?' Elena always ran her ideas by Eve, though she was the boss.

'I think it's a great idea, especially because we would know the temperament of the people involved and so would probably make a good guess of who would fit where. But when would we do it? We are flat out as it is with all the training.' Eve pulled her red hair out of its bun and took off her apron, examining a burn on her hand she'd received when helping a butterfingered girl remove a roast chicken from the oven.

'Hmm... Yes, that's a point. Shall we have a quick cuppa, mull it over?'

Eve was exhausted and really wanted to go to bed, but she knew Elena when she got an idea in her head. It was best to let her run with it.

'One. But then I'm going up, as I am shattered. If I were there from now until the end of time, Dorothy Lamb would never be able to make a loaf that couldn't also double as a building brick.' She laughed. Poor Dorothy had lead hands, as Isabella would say. Some people did, and the result was heavy, doughy baking.

'You'll turn her into a passable cook nonetheless, my dear, and you'll help her discover where her true talents lie. You always do. I don't know how you do it, but they come in here a bunch of woebegone and emerge as confident, well-presented young ladies. You are an inspiration. I mean it.'

Eve coloured. 'I don't know about that.'

'Well, I do. You know I've thought this for a long time. You're a born teacher.' A shadow crossed the glass doors that led to the garden. 'And he's another one.'

Elena went and rapped on the window, beckoning Bartley in. He came as far as the door but stood on the threshold.

'Yes, Mrs Hamilton-Brooks?' he asked in that soft Northern accent.

'Could you come in for a moment, please, Bartley? I need to discuss something with you and Eve.' She smiled. 'Don't worry, nothing is wrong. I'd just like your opinion on something.'

He looked hesitant. 'My boots are very dirty, ma'am. I'd make a mess on the floor.'

'Then take them off.' She waved her hand at him. 'Because you're right to be concerned. If you draw mud in here, Eve will have your guts for garters.' She laughed but Bartley didn't smile. 'Come along, there are cakes.'

As he took off his boots and entered the kitchen in his socks, Eve thought he reminded her of the foxes around Robinswood. Timid and solitary, they avoided human contact, but yet when you locked gazes with one, it exuded a quiet confidence.

'They're not afraid of you, Evie,' her father would whisper. 'But they'd rather we weren't here.'

'Hello, Bartley,' Eve said. 'The boys were so pleased with the lamps you helped them to make.'

'Good Evening, Miss Murphy.' He took the seat she offered. 'They did a great job. And some of them are going to give them away as gifts or sell them, so maybe that's why they are happy with them.' He smiled slowly.

They had tea and cinnamon buns as Elena outlined the plan.

'So, Bartley, what do you think?' she asked when she was finished.

He paused for the longest time before answering. 'I think it's a good idea, but I wonder when we would do it. It would be quite time-consuming, matching people to the lads and girls we teach here.'

Eve was surprised to hear his opinion mirror hers.

'Yes, that's exactly what Eve said, and I think you're both right, but let me be honest. You two do the lion's share of this work, and I...well, I do a lot of faffing about. Perhaps it is time I dedicated a bit more of my time to productivity. So I am going to resign from my committees and work here full time with you two.'

Eve smiled. Elena was honest, at least. Her father always said that if Elena put half the energy she had into actual work instead of flitting from one meeting to the next, she might be more use than an ornament in the world. He didn't mean it in a cruel way, but he was right; Elena was a bit flighty.

'So?' she asked. 'What do you think?'

125

Bartley caught Eve's eye for a split second, then said, 'I think it would be good.'

'Me too,' Eve agreed.

'That's settled then.' Elena seemed pleased. Eve was glad she had a project. Oskar Metz was down in Robinswood now, and while Elena was happy to hear that he was safe, she had yet to meet him. She didn't know the reason for her reticence, she confided to Eve, but she was putting it off.

As Eve cleared the dishes, Elena noticed the burn on her hand. 'Oh, Eve, that looks nasty. What happened?'

'Oh, Freda Davies was trying to take a chicken out of the oven, but it was too heavy or something, I don't know. Anyway, I was helping her, when she lurched forward and the tray burned my hand. It's quite sore actually, but we used the last of the ointment on Jodie when she dropped the pan of water on her foot last week. You should have seen me, buzzing about like a bee with the pain! I poured lukewarm water on it, but it's still quite sore, and I think it will scar.'

'I'm sure you looked much more like a graceful butterfly,' Elena joked. 'You poor thing. We must have some sent up from the chemist's first thing.'

'I don't think it's much good, to be honest, even if we had it,' Eve said, examining the red and sore skin on the back of her hand.

Bartley stood up. 'Thank you for the tea. Goodnight, Mrs Hamilton-Brooks, Miss Murphy.' He nodded once more and went outside to put his boots back on.

As soon as he was gone, Elena turned to Eve. 'He's odd, isn't he? I don't know what it is about him – he's just a bit strange.'

Eve nodded. 'He's unusual, that's for sure, but I like him. He's kind to the boys, and he teaches them the most extraordinary things, you know. He knows all about plants and flowers and their properties, and he is an exceptional carpenter. The housemaster of the boys' home told me they all made bird feeders to sell to raise funds for the home, and they were exquisite, all inspired by Bartley.'

They cleared everything companionably, and as Eve was about to gratefully go upstairs, Elena stopped her once more. 'Eve, I'm sorry, but can I ask you something?'

'Of course.'

'Well, it is rather... I don't know... Perhaps I'm being silly, but it's about Oskar Metz. I was avoiding it until now, I don't really know why, but I've written a letter inviting him to visit here. I don't know if I should send it or not.'

Eve felt a wave of sympathy for her friend. 'I understand why you want to meet him face-to-face, but you needed time to think about everything. And he's said he'd like to meet you, to explain, so I think it would do you both good.'

'It just feels so hard, so strange to be opening up this whole can of worms again. I'm afraid of what he's going to tell me, I suppose.' Elena looked shattered, and Eve could imagine the deliberation that went into writing the letter.

'Mammy and Daddy love him – he's a good man. Post it,' Eve said, giving her friend's hand a squeeze. 'Goodnight.'

'Goodnight.'

The following morning, Eve woke early. Her bedroom was directly over the kitchen now, as she'd moved out of the little flat on the third floor she had shared with her parents. Elena said they were servant's quarters and she wanted Eve to have a bigger, nicer room, so she moved. The bedroom was lovely, with a view over the lawns all the way to the sea. It reminded her of the front bedrooms at Robinswood, but on a smaller scale.

She sat bolt upright and checked the clock – it was five thirty. The garden gate creaked, and she heard it open. Bartley had offered to oil it, but the women said the noise made them feel safer. She heard footsteps on the gravel, arrive and then retreat, then the creaking gate again.

Heart thumping, she got up to check, but the lawn below was empty. She was awake by then, so she got up and washed and dressed. She wanted to write to Aisling and ask her to come up to Dublin for a visit. Elena wouldn't mind, and she longed to see her sister again. Maybe Kate could come too and they could have a sister's reunion.

She made a cup of tea and sat at the sunny kitchen table. It was only when she sat down that she noticed the parcel on the doorstep, just outside the garden doors. Anything to be delivered came to the front of the house – nobody went around the back – so she was surprised to see it there.

She opened the door and picked up the parcel wrapped in brown paper and string. She unwrapped it, even though there was no name or anything on it.

Inside was a wooden box, intricately carved. The box itself was highly polished oak, and it was inlaid with a flower in a much lighter-coloured wood. She opened it. It had tiny brass hinges, and inside was a glass jar holding some kind of ointment with a label on it that simply said 'burns'. Beside the jar was a tiny carved leaf, no bigger than a matchbox, on which was perched a carved bee and a butterfly. It was the most extraordinary thing Eve had ever seen. She lifted the little ornament out of the box, terrified she would break it. The wings of the butterfly were so delicate, the wood was almost translucent, and the little fat bee shone like a conker. She held it up and examined it from every angle. The workmanship was incredible.

'My goodness, what on earth is that?' Elena asked as she entered the kitchen, fully dressed rather than in her usual night attire and dressing gown.

'I don't know… I found it on the step outside there.' She pointed at the garden doors.

Elena lifted the box and took out the jar. 'Bartley.' She smiled. 'That's his writing. He gave me a tincture for a cut in one of those exact glass jars last week, and he had it just like that, with "cuts" written on the label. He saw your burn last night, and remember you said you were like a bee and I said you were more like a butterfly? He must have made this for you.'

'But why?' Eve was confused.

'Maybe he likes you.'

'Don't be ridiculous.' Eve was flustered. 'Of course he doesn't, and anyway, I have absolutely no time for anything like that with him or anyone else, so…'

'You're blushing,' Elena sang out, a cheeky grin crossing her face.

Eve busied herself pulling out the dishes and pans that would be needed for the morning's lesson. 'I'm not. I just don't think it's what you said –'

'He likes you,' Elena interrupted, 'and what's more, he's absolutely handsome. And I think you maybe like him a little bit too.'

CHAPTER 19

*K*ate struggled to wake up. The dawn had just broken, its pale, cold light creeping in the gap in the curtains. Jack was sleeping peacefully in the crib beside their bed. She turned over to cuddle up to Sam, but he was gone. Groggily, she sat up. He was not in the room, and the bathroom door was open, so he wasn't in there.

Creeping out of bed, she wrapped herself in an old dressing gown and went downstairs to find him sitting beside the range reading a letter.

'I woke up and you weren't there,' she whispered, sitting on his lap. 'I missed you.' She snuggled into him, kissing his neck. 'Come back to bed. We'll have to get up soon.'

'I will in a minute – I just needed some time to think. I got this yesterday, and I didn't get a chance to show it to you.' He handed Kate the letter. It was from Lillian.

Dear Sam,

I hope you and Kate and little Jack are doing well, and that things are shaping up nicely back at Robinswood. I can only imagine how lovely it must be now; that old house needs the sound of children.

We had such an idyllic childhood there, didn't we? I think about it often. Austina and I are doing well. She is growing by the day, I am convinced.

As you know, I am currently boarding with Mother and Perry, in the absence of any other plans, I must admit, and one of the many terms of her deigning to put us up is to insist I do not suggest to you the move back to Ireland to live at Robinswood. The fact that it is my home as much as yours seems lost on her. But there has been a development, and I have been speaking to Perry about it.

If you tell on me, she will put us out on the side of the road – hard to believe, but she would do it. At least Perry is on my side. She was always a tough nut, but the war has made granite of her.

The thing is this. I got a letter from Beau's cousin. He is in prison. He did nothing wrong, but the terrible regime under which people like Beau are expected to endure just became too much. He was accused of threatening some white man, but that did not happen. A commanding officer of his, a thoroughly nasty piece of work, was from the same place as Beau and knew about him and me during the war, and he held a grudge. Though what it had to do with him, I cannot possibly fathom.

Anyway, Beau's cousin wrote and told me that he had been arrested and was in prison awaiting a hearing. I don't know what the situation is now. I have tried writing back but got no response, and so I have made a decision. I am going to go to America and see if I can do anything.

I'm going to leave Austina with you – well, not with you, but with the Murphys; they won't mind. Mother is too old, and anyway, she and Perry are always gallivanting somewhere, and on top of that, she knows nothing about babies or children. It was Isabella who reared us, as you know.

It is too dangerous to bring a mixed-race child to Georgia, I am reliably informed, and I could not bear it if anything happened to her. This way, I'll know she's at Robinswood being cared for and loved, and it would be one less thing for me to worry about.

Your sister,

Lillian

PS. Thanks to the generosity of Perry (unbeknownst to our mother), I will not need you to give me the fare.

Kate laughed out loud at the last part. Lillian never lost it, that was for sure.

'Did you ever hear anything like that?' Sam asked, his face inscrutable.

Kate sighed and put the letter down. 'Well, Violet is trying to protect us from the worst of her gold-digging, so that's something.'

'Except that there is no gold to dig. Lillian seems to have always laboured under the illusion that I had a big pot of cash hidden away somewhere. Honestly, Kate, I could strangle her, thinking she can just drop her child off like it's a parcel, not a human baby that needs feeding and changing and washing and all the rest of it. She really is the most selfish person I have ever had the misfortune to know.' His voice was tight.

'I know, she would drive you to drink.' Kate soothed her agitated husband. '"The Murphys won't mind." The cheek of her! But she was always the same. But if Beau really is in trouble, then I want to help him. I really like Beau. What he sees in your sister is a complete mystery, but she's nicer around him. To be fair, I know it's hard on Lillian and the baby to face the future without him. If he is in prison for something he didn't do, then someone needs to fight in his corner, and Lillian, for all her selfishness, really does love him. And I really believe he felt the same way about her.'

'You're right that he brings out the best in her, or curbs the worst at least,' Sam added wryly. 'I know it was brave of her to go ahead with the pregnancy. I had her down as someone who would have gone to certain doctors, as you can do if you have the right money, and had it seen to, to use the horrible parlance. But the reality is that she is a single woman with a brown baby. Her kind of people, while they are grateful to the Yanks, I don't think their hospitality stretches to welcoming a black man's child into polite society.'

'It would be hard with Beau at her side, but without him, it will be horrific,' Kate said quietly, making them each a cup of cocoa.

He took the warm drink gratefully, and she sat on her mother's fireside chair, sipping hers.

'I'm not sure she fully understands that. Lillian is deluded if she thinks the world will just accept them,' Sam replied, stoking the embers of the fire.

'Well, we can't control what the world thinks. We can only control our own world. And in this world, Austina is your niece – our niece now that we're married – and she's Jack's cousin. And Lillian's right. Taking a baby – especially a brown one – to America in search of the black father who may or may not be in jail is madness. The way coloured people are treated over there is hard to believe. They're not allowed to use the same facilities, or inter-marry... It's terrible.'

'Who would have thought that the end of the war would mean we would all make it through, only to have Lillian alone with a child?' He shook his head.

'I know. It's incredible, but a nicer man than Beau you couldn't meet. They went through so much – we all did – so it seems so unfair that we get our happy ever after but Lillian doesn't. Should we just do it, despite the entitled way she asked?'

'I really don't want her over here. Speaking down to you and your parents, you know how she is. And another baby. We are so busy trying to get everything done, it would be you and Isabella who would be left taking care of her.'

'And Ais. She'll be here too. I'm trying to convince her to stay and get Mark to come over. He's working with his father, but he'd be better over here. We need the help, and Ais would be so much happier.' She leaned over and smoothed his hair back from his temple. 'We can do it, and if it means Lillian can find Beau, get him out or whatever she needs to do, then selfishly, she and Austina will be Beau's responsibility, not ours.'

'And if she starts being an insufferable cow to you and your parents?'

'We'll stand up to her. I know she kind of overpowered me when she arrived out of the blue back in Brighton, but I'm on home turf now. I'll be stronger.' Kate was adamant.

'The only trouble is, she sees this as her home turf, not yours.' Sam wasn't convinced.

'Look, she won't be here, will she? She wants to drop Austina off and go to America. We won't have to deal with her at all really.'

'Good point. So will I write back and say yes?'

'Do. We have to do this, if not for Lillian, then for Beau and Austina.'

'We'll have to come up with a nickname or something – I cannot call a baby that ridiculous name. She made that up, you know, calling her after my father, as if he were some saint.' Sam rolled his eyes, picking up his sister's letter once more. 'Mother will go mad as well, but I'll have to calm her down, I suppose. I know Lillian thinks Mother is being a dragon, but she is trying to get my sister to stand on her own two feet. A Herculean task, since she is terminally lazy and feels entitled to be pampered without ever lifting a finger. What a decent chap like Beau sees in her, I will never know.'

'She's very pretty, and she loves him,' Kate said.

'No, she's not very pretty. She is very coiffed and made up – that is a totally different thing. But you, Lady Kenefick, on the other hand, are incredibly naturally beautiful and also a tremendously accomplished and hard-working young woman, the polar opposite of my pain-in-the-behind sister.' He pulled Kate to her feet, wrapping his arms around her.

'It will be fine,' she said. 'At least it's just the baby.'

'I wouldn't even consider it if it was otherwise...' Sam took Kate's hand. 'Now let's get one more hour in bed before your father puts me and poor Oskar back on the chain gang. He doesn't give us a moment's rest, you know?'

'I know perfectly. I'm his daughter, remember? Anyway, I can't go back to sleep now, I'm wide awake...' she said with a slow smile.

'I was banking on that,' he whispered. He led her quietly to the bottom of the stairs, only to have the air fill with the full-lunged cry of their son.

'Looks like he doesn't want a brother or sister.' Kate sighed and smiled.

* * *

LATER THAT MORNING, Kate began her offensive on Aisling once more as they scrubbed the chequered tiles of the huge entrance hallway.

'You know that Lillian is dropping Austina off here, like she's a parcel?' Kate asked, plunging her scrubbing brush into the bucket of hot soapy water.

'I heard. Sam said it this morning. She's a piece of work, isn't she?' Aisling scraped with a knife at something stuck to the floor. 'I don't even want to think about what this might be.' She grimaced.

'Well, between us, we'll manage.' Kate deliberately avoided looking at her sister. 'But it would be so much better if we knew if you and Mark were staying on. Daddy and Sam could really use his help, and me and Mam need you more than ever now.' She sat back on her feet and wiped her brow with her sleeve.

'Kate, I told you, I don't know Mark's plans. He's busy and –'

'He's with his father, who managed fine without him all during the war. Surely he doesn't need him as much as we do?' Kate knew she was pushing it, but if she could get them over, she knew everything would be so much better. There was a sadness to her sister, and she wondered if it was being apart from Mark that was the cause. Aisling wrote often but never rang, even though they'd had a phone installed in the farmhouse. She'd been there over a month, and she wasn't showing any signs of going back to Devon, but she refused to be drawn on long-term plans.

'Kate, stop, will you? I'll talk to him when I go back, and we'll see then.' She stood up. 'I'm just getting clean water,' she said, making for the kitchen.

Kate stood as well. 'But if you just ring him, tell him to get the next boat, we'll give you the fare if that's the problem. And I'm sure he'd come if you really pleaded, Ais…'

'Oh, for God's sake, I can't just phone him! He's in prison!' The words were out before she realised. Kate had a way of mithering until you just exploded.

Both girls' eyes went to the door off the entranceway, where Isabella and Dermot were standing, dumbstruck. They'd heard everything. For a moment, all four of them just stood, rooted to the spot.

Dermot was the first to move. He stood beside Aisling and put his arm around her shoulder. 'What did he do, love?' he asked gently.

Aisling started to cry, the first tears since the day she left Portwye. She sat down on the stairs, and the whole story came out.

They let her talk, and when she was finished, Isabella held her hand on one side. Her father sat on the other side and Kate on the lower step.

'My poor girl, what a time you've been through,' Isabella said. 'I wish you'd have told us.'

'I wanted to, I did, but I couldn't. It's not Mark's fault. He just can't cope with everything that happened.'

Dermot asked the question all three of them had been wondering about. 'Did he ever hurt you?'

Aisling's eyes blazed. 'Never! He wouldn't, he couldn't do it. He would never, ever hurt me, Daddy, I swear.' Her eyes raked his face. 'You have to believe that.'

'I do, pet, don't worry. I do.' He soothed his daughter.

'How long will he be there?' Kate asked gently, feeling awful now for badgering her poor sister.

'He got six months. He'll be out mid-March. I've asked him to come here when he's free – I've sent the ticket and everything – and he says he will, but...' Aisling was so torn. She needed her family's support, but she desperately wanted to stay loyal to Mark too. She couldn't bear it if they said anything bad about him.

'Well, then, we'll just have to wait. I saw how he looked at you the day you got married, Aisling. That lad won't leave you. That war hurt so many people, and in ways that nobody can see. It feels like the world will never be the same again.' Isabella squeezed her daughter's hand. 'So now it's just a case of waiting, and hopefully then getting him back here, and you two can start your lives properly.'

Aisling gave her a watery smile. She prayed her mother was right.

CHAPTER 20

*V*iolet was fuming.

'Darling, let her go. She is determined to try to find this chap, and what harm can it do to try?' Perry was sitting up in bed, reading the *Financial Times*, as she brushed her hair furiously at the dressing table.

'It's madness. Lillian haring off to America. Who does she think she is, Jessie James? That girl is incompetent at best, and now that child has been parachuted in on top of Kate and Sam when they are trying so hard to get that crumbling old wreck of a house back into some kind of habitable order. This is Austin coming out in her, Perry, I swear it is. This is typical of him, rushing off half-cocked, with no thought whatsoever. And you know what will happen next, don't you? Oh yes, she will send an urgent telegram needing money or a lawyer, or she'll get herself arrested.' Violet slammed the brush down and got into bed beside him.

Perry sighed and put the newspaper down. 'And so what if she does?'

'What?' Violet did not wish to be interrupted in her rant.

'I mean, if she gets stuck for money or whatever out there, we'll bail her out. It's not a problem, you know that.' Perry smiled.

'But you shouldn't have to, that's the point. She's not even your daughter, and she behaves so irresponsibly...'

He drew her into his arms. 'Darling, you are getting yourself in a tizzy over nothing. Lillian is a brave girl, she knows what's what, and if anyone can get that chap of hers back here, then it's her.' He paused. 'Look, don't get cross, but please, just listen. Sam can do no wrong. You support him and help him in every way you can. But because when you look at Lillian, you see Austin, all the old resentment and bitterness you feel is reflected towards poor old Lillian. She fell in love with a coloured chap, and yes, there are people who would raise an eyebrow at that, but to hell with them. And she got herself in a predicament, but did she do what most girls of her class would do? No, she did not. She had the child, and she loves her, and she is doing her best.'

'But she –'

'Just let me finish, old girl. She is doing her best. She has no resources. Sam got the house, such as it is, I know, and he has had a career. What did Lillian get? Classes in embroidery and deportment and no inheritance. She has no skills because nobody ever gave her any, and most of her peers will marry chinless wonders such as myself, with land and money behind them. So why is she to blame? She made only one error – she had a child out of wedlock – but she is doing her best, and from where I'm standing, she is doing all right.'

Violet sat up and turned to look at her husband directly. 'You gave her the money, didn't you?'

Perry smiled. 'I did.' He held his hands up. 'But before you go mad again, she didn't ask. I offered. And I gave her the name of a legal chap I use in New York. He's going to help her.'

She sighed. Perry was right, of course. Lillian was infuriating, that was true, but she was raised for marriage, and now that the prospect was well and truly off the table, then she had to make do as best she could. Perry saw a different Lillian than the one Violet saw.

'I just want her to step up, take a bit of responsibility,' she said.

'She is raising a child alone, she is going off to try to find her father, she has left her child with kind, caring people who will look after her – that's pretty responsible behaviour in my book.'

'Well, she's hardly raising her alone... If we didn't let her stay here –'

'You would have had her put the child in an orphanage.' Perry wasn't accusing, but she hated to hear the disappointment in his voice.

'I just suggested it as an option...' She was embarrassed.

'Violet, she is your daughter, Austina is your granddaughter – of course she must stay here. I don't believe you'd have gone through with locking her away in some home. This house is huge, and the staff adore the baby...once the initial shock wore off. Let's just accept that they live here with us and stop making her feel like she is imposing every single day, shall we?' Perry was gentle but firm.

'Not all the staff. Mrs King is appalled. She said as much when I went down to discuss the menu for next weekend's after-hunt luncheon.' Violet felt mollified somewhat.

'Mrs Fields is returning this week, and I've had Jenkins explain to Mrs King that her services will no longer be needed. One of the footmen also was overheard making a derogatory remark about the baby, so he too is seeking other employment.'

'You've dismissed staff because of Lillian?' She was outraged all over again.

'No, Violet, I dismissed staff because they could not be kind to a little girl who has done nothing wrong. I will not have people like that in my house.'

'But... You see? Her presence is causing issues here...'

'Do you love your daughter, Violet?'

Perry had a way of being charming but very direct. It served him well in business, but it was a bit disconcerting to those in his personal relationships.

'Of course I do, but...' She was getting flustered under his unwavering stare.

'Are you ashamed of Austina?'

'Perry, I know you must think me harsh but...'

'I love you. But yes, I do think you're harsh on Lillian and, by association, poor little Austina. They are your flesh and blood, like it or not. I never had children, as you know. Though several fecund young ladies from the right class were dangled under my nose, none of them loved me – they loved the money and the house and the titles and all the rest of it – and I vowed to only marry for love. When I announced that to my parents, they were astonished, and my father more or less said I was too short and too ugly for such ridiculous notions. But I persevered and refused every viscount's daughter that was paraded in front of me because they had no interest in me, the person, in Perry. They wanted Lord Goodall. What I loved about you was you were not interested in my money.'

Violet coloured. This was not where she wanted this conversation to go.

Perry smiled. 'I'm not delusional. I know if I were a chimney sweep, you wouldn't look sideways at me, but I have a talent for seeing what people really are. You like the life – of course you do, who wouldn't? But you are more than this.' He waved his hand around the lavish bedroom with the antique furniture, cream damask curtains and thick pile carpet. 'You are intelligent, loyal, kind and funny.

'And that is why, when I met you, for the first time in my entire life, I fell in love. Of course, by then children were out of the question, but you have a family, and how lucky you are to have them. Sam and Kate and her whole family are wonderful people. Not of our class, it's true, but maybe all the better for that. Lillian and a beautiful little girl are available to us, to two old codgers like us. We can have the joy of a child in our lives. I want to do it, I want to be her doting old Grandpa Perry, and I want her to see Framington Hall as her home. And I want you to want that too.'

Violet realised that her feelings about Lillian and the baby were based on what people would think. And she hated the gossips muttering about how not only had the destitute Lady Kenefick taken poor old Perry for all he was worth, but also that she was pouring more shame on the Goodall family name by bringing her raggle-taggle family with her, complete with Irish servants and brown-skinned babies. She blushed, deeply ashamed of her selfish and silly ways.

'You're right, as usual,' she said quietly, enjoying the feeling of his arms around her. 'I... I don't know, Perry. I know Beau and Kate and the Murphys and little Austina are my family, and I am grateful, as they were such a support to me all these years. And I'll admit that maybe, now that I'm back, well, in our set, I was a little bit ashamed of them. It was fine when I was in Hampstead, living life like a normal person, but now that I'm back among my own class, it's more difficult.' She had never been so honest with anyone.

'Those people, they are not our people, the lords and ladies and viscounts and earls. We know them, and I do business with them, and we'll drink their champagne and attend their parties, but they are not our people. Our people are Sam and Kate and Jack, and Dermot and Isabella, and Lillian and Beau and little Austina. They are the ones we must prioritise. They are the ones who stood by you, and who would again, when all the toffee-nosed inbreds are gone.' He burned with intensity.

'One thing I loved about America is how anyone can make it there. You don't need to be connected, from the right bloodstock, like a prize mare. If you work hard enough, and are willing to take chances, then you can rise to the top over there. I loved that about it. I don't voice my opinion often because it doesn't serve me, but I find most of what you call "our class" shallow and boring at best, and downright mean and nasty at worst. We don't need them, Violet, and our family doesn't either.'

She leaned up on one elbow and looked down into her husband's face for a long moment. There was an integrity and an intelligence there that she had perhaps overlooked before. It was as if she were seeing him for the first time. He really was an attractive man, she thought, and she was a very lucky woman.

'I love you, Lord Goodall.' She smiled.

'I know you do. Now, can you love your daughter and granddaughter as they need and deserve to be loved?' His gaze never wavered from hers.

'I can. And I'm not ashamed of Austina, really, you know, not at all. I think she is adorable. I suppose I was afraid you would see us as gold-diggers, and so would everyone else. First, a destitute widow lands one of the wealthiest men in England, then foists her unmarried daughter and her fatherless child on him. What a laughing stock she's made of him. I can hear the gossip mills turning now.'

'And we care about that why, precisely?'

She shrugged. 'I don't know. I don't want people thinking I've made a fool of you.'

Perry laughed out loud. 'Violet, my dear, I inherited this house and a little money, but my father was cautious and nervous, and so when he died, I invested heavily. I gambled on stock, and while it was risky in the extreme, it paid off. I made my money, and continue to do so. I didn't inherit it. If I kept it to what I got from my father, we would be selling paintings and wearing coats in bed. So I may not be handsome, and I'm certainly too short to be taken seriously, but I'm nobody's fool.'

Before she had a chance to contradict him, he went on. 'Austin was a failure in business. I'm sorry to be blunt, but you know that anyway. But he and I were alike in lots of ways. He wasn't afraid of the big stakes, and neither am I. I'm just better at it, and I don't make big decisions under the influence of whiskey. I knew him a little bit, as you know, but I do recall this about him – he was warm. Perhaps it was his Irish upbringing, but he wasn't emotionally retarded as most of my class are. He was able to express the full range of emotions, not just anger and distain, which seem to be the most popular ones. He would have welcomed Austina, after a possible blow-up of course, but he would have loved her as he loved Sam and Lillian, and as he loved you.'

'He had an odd way of showing it, leaving us destitute,' Violet said, the bitterness against her first husband lingering.

'He wasn't equipped, in the same way Lillian isn't equipped. The lawyer in New York I mentioned, I got to know him when I moved over there for a spell in the 1920s before the crash. I wanted to see business and how it worked when you didn't have a title or a big house to hide behind. I met a lot of people there, many young men like myself, born into money, especially from the South. Those chaps put us in the ha'penny place, as Kate would say. They made fortunes on cotton and tobacco. But anyway, that's what I learned there – how to reinvest, how to be smart – and that's why I can do it, I can make money, and I can negotiate effectively. Austin was, like all of his generation, thrown in at the deep end and expected to swim. So few actually can.' He shrugged. 'It's not their fault.'

Violet wondered for the millionth time what lucky star had brought Perry to her. She realised now more than ever that she loved him with all of her heart. She knew that people thought they were an odd couple, but they had no idea. She didn't love him for his money, though she would admit the lifestyle was nice. She loved him for his mind. For his enthusiasm, for his sense of fun and lightheartedness, and now for his sense of fairness. He was a really remarkable man.

'You're right,' she whispered. 'I do see Austin when I look at Lillian, and I am nicer to Samuel. I always was. He looks like my father, whereas Lillian is a pure Kenefick. And I am worried for the future, for Austina. But you're right. There is nothing we can do about that, and the world may not accept her...' She hated the thought of a cruel world rejecting the little girl but knew that it was the reality.

'But this is my point, darling. What the world thinks or feels is irrelevant. We will love her, we will build her up, give her the confidence she will need to face this world. Money does matter. People who say it doesn't either have too much or none, but it does ease a passage through life. And we can't make the world at large kinder, but we can make *her* world a kind, loving, safe place, and if we can do that, then we will have succeeded.'

'So what do we do now?' Violet sat back against the pillows.

'Well, how about a trip to Ireland? Visit our grandchildren, see how things are going in Robinswood?' Perry knew that she had vowed to never set foot there again.

'Oh, I don't think I could bear it...'

'It's just a house, Violet, bricks and mortar, and it's a house that currently is home to our two grandchildren. Come on, it's almost

Christmas – wouldn't you like to see them open their presents on Christmas morning?'

She still looked doubtful.

'And sit down to one of Isabella's legendary Christmas dinners?' He grinned mischievously.

'Well, they may not want us…'

'Sam rang and invited us last week. They really want us to come, and I promised I'd talk you around. They are planning a big celebration.'

'Fine.' She sighed and smiled. He always got his way in the end. 'But we can't stay there, all right?'

'Of course not. We'll stay in Lismore Castle. The Duke of Devonshire and I are good friends. He won't be there, but he insisted we stay. It's fully staffed, and they are expecting us.'

'You had this organised already? How did you know I'd agree?' Violet was too stunned to be annoyed.

'I told you, my dear, I am an excellent negotiator, and I always get what I want.' He winked, and she pelted him with a pillow.

'You really are a sneaky rat, Perry…'

'But I am your sneaky rat, my darling Violet.' He laughed and hugged her.

'You might be right about a lot of things, but you are completely wrong about something,' she said, running her hand over his chest.

'What's that then?' He smiled.

'You said you weren't handsome, and too short and all of that, but I actually find you very attractive…' she said, and meant it.

He looked at her, trying to find the lie in her eyes. To his amazement, it wasn't there. She bent her head and kissed him deeply.

CHAPTER 21

*A*isling pinned her hat on and tried to steady her nerves. She was wearing a dark-green dress she'd made, and she'd borrowed Kate's black patent high heels and a black cardigan. Mark was supposed to be arriving on the bus in one hour.

She wondered how he got on in Dartmoor. He must have kept his head down because they let him out a month early for good behaviour. She had sent the ticket – Sam insisted on paying her a wage, so she had a little money saved up – and a letter begging him to come. His reply was in her handbag, and she took it out once more to make sure she had it right.

Dear Ais,

Thanks for the letter and the ticket. They are keeping the ticket for me; I'll get it when I get out. It feels like a very long time since I saw you, but then in the months before I got sent here, I wasn't really there, was I?

Dad came to see me last week. He and Mum and Delilah take it in turns, and it's the thing that keeps me going, knowing I'll see a friendly face. Delilah sends her love and says to tell you she and the boys miss you. She's doing all right, though I don't know if she'll ever get over Terry. They were together since they were kids, but like everyone, she is just trying to keep going.

I told Dad about your idea that I would go over to Ireland, and of course, he was appalled. He's easily outraged, my dad, but I explained that I had to be where you are, so if you're in Ireland, then that's where I must go.

I'm so sorry for everything I put you through, Ais. You really didn't deserve any of it. I lie awake at night here reliving that time over and over in my head. It makes me cry when I see your beautiful face, all tears and hurt.

There's a chap here, Pendon is his name, and he's in for something similar to me. He was involved the last time too. He turned eighteen in 1918 so was sent to the front, and then again this time. I don't know... I can talk to him – he understands about it. The governor of the prison is a decent man. The place is hell on earth, but he's all right, and so me and Pendon asked if we could be cellmates, and he agreed.

We talk about what we saw, what we did. He knows all about you, and he tells me about his wife, Elsie, who divorced him after he attacked her. He's so sorry, but she doesn't want to know. Can't blame her.

Anyway, he thinks I should go over to Ireland too. I want to see you so badly, but I'm afraid, Ais. What if I hurt you again? Not physically, I would never do that, but what if I'm never able to get back to being the man you married? A bit part of me thinks you'd be better off without me.

In a strange way, coming to prison has been good for me. No booze, up early in the morning, working hard, eating three square meals a day. Dad reckons I'm cured, but I'm not so sure.

I'm glad you are meeting up with old friends and seeing your family again, but I think the Sean you mentioned in the last letter was the chap Kate always called an eejit because he lost you by fooling around. I hope he's not thinking he might get a second chance now?

Anyway, I better go, as it will be lights out in a minute. I love you, my wild Irish rose, and I want so much to be worthy of you.

Yours always,

Mark xx

She folded the letter. Now it was just a case of waiting.

She went downstairs. Before she pushed the kitchen door, she stopped. Her mother and Kate were talking.

'I wish there was some way... I don't want her going down there on her own. What if he doesn't turn up? And I know she thinks Sean

Lacey is a different person now, but I'm not convinced. He'd love nothing better than for Mark to not turn up.'

'Kate, we have to let her do it her way. We're all worried, of course we are. My heart goes out to Mark, but at the same time, Aisling is my daughter, and people who are violent are not people I want my daughters around...'

Isabella's words died on her lips as Aisling opened the door.

'Ais, love, I'm sorry... I only meant...' Isabella began, but Aisling just stood there, dumbstruck.

'You said you understood, that you were on his side...' Tears sprang from her eyes.

'I do! I am!' Isabella tried to reason with her.

'You said he was violent and that you can't trust violent men, so does that mean you don't trust Daddy? He killed people, Mam. You know he did when he was in the IRA. And yet you think he's different or that was different – you're such a hypocrite.'

Aisling barged past her mother. Kate grabbed her arm. 'Ah, Ais, come on, Mammy only meant...'

Aisling spun around to face her sister, hurt and indignation burning her inside. 'I know perfectly well what you both meant. We are not wanted here – you made it perfectly clear, both of you – so we won't burden you any more. If Mark arrives today, we'll turn right back around and go back to Portwye. As far as I'm concerned, I don't have a family. There you all were, pretending to be so concerned for us – poor Mark, it's awful, all the rest of it – but deep down, you just want me to get rid of him. Well, let me tell you something, both of you, with your perfect marriages. I won't ever leave Mark, and he won't ever leave me, so you can forget your plans to break us up.'

She stormed out, crying. As she ran down the rutted lane, all she wanted to do was get away.

Kate tried to run after her, but Isabella stopped her. 'Let her go. She won't want to talk to either of us for a while.'

Aisling rounded the bed of the lane, her tears almost blinding her. How could she have gotten everything so wrong? She should never have come back there. She longed to be in their cottage in Portwye.

Even when things were bad, Mark was always on her side. She just needed to see him. Before she knew what had happened, her head hit the pebbled driveway as she tripped and fell forward. The pain was indescribable, and she realised she had twisted her ankle. She lay on the ground, sobbing, the pain in her ankle and the hurt caused by her sister and mother both fuelling her tears.

'Aisling!' She heard a voice coming from the field on the other side of the lane. It was Oskar. 'Wait, I'm coming,' he shouted.

Within moments, he was beside her, checking her ankle and then trying to help her up.

'I'm all right,' she managed to mumble through the pain, embarrassed that he was seeing her in such a state.

'Let me help you back up to the house, though. That looks nasty.' He pointed to her rapidly swelling ankle.

'No!'

Oskar looked surprised at the strength of her response.

'Sorry, but I don't want to go back there,' she managed to say through gritted teeth.

'All right, how about we get you over to that wall anyway, for a start, and we can take it from there. Isn't your husband due to arrive today?'

'Yes.' She felt the tears well up again.

'Well, I think maybe you will want to change your dress and coat? These are covered in mud and are soaking – you fell in the biggest puddle on the lane.'

He gave her a smile, and she tried to respond. Her ankle was throbbing unbearably. Leaning on Oskar, she hobbled to the wall, relieved to take the weight off her leg.

He bent down again and gently touched her foot. 'I think that might be broken. I don't know, but it is swelling very fast. You'll need a doctor.'

'Can you take me? To Doctor Grahame? His surgery is just in the square.' She thought she might pass out with the pain.

'I can, but would your father not be better?'

'No... Just take me, please...'

He paused for a moment, thinking. 'All right, wait here.' He ran up the lane to the farmyard where the car was parked. Within moments, he was back in the Austin Princess, and she managed, with his help, to heave herself into the front seat.

He drove as slowly as he could, trying not to jolt her. Aisling could feel beads of sweat on her forehead and between her shoulder blades.

'The last time I drove down this lane,' Oskar said, focusing on the road ahead, 'there was another person in the car, in pain. I shot Thomas Hamilton-Brooks in the foot to convince him to tell your father where you girls were.'

She managed to smile a little, though the pain was excruciating. 'I'm glad you did,' she choked out.

'But you managed to get away without help, I believe?'

'Yes,' she managed, unable to formulate any more words, the agony in her foot taking all of her attention.

'Almost there now, not too much longer,' he said as he pulled the car into the square. Everyone stopped and stared as Oskar parked precariously and ran around to help her out.

Once they saw Aisling in pain, several men went to help him, one of whom was Sean.

'Aisling, what happened to you?' he asked, concerned, throwing a suspicious glance at Oskar. Everyone knew he was working above in Robinswood, but he never came into the village or went for a pint or anything, so of course, tongues were wagging.

'I just fell.' She gasped.

'Oh my God, your foot is completely swollen! Here, put your arm around my shoulder, and put the other round him.' Aisling did as she was told, and Oskar and Sean carried her into the surgery.

Dr Grahame confirmed that the bone was broken, and said she would have to go to the hospital in Waterford to have it reset.

'I'll take her,' Sean immediately offered.

Oskar looked at Aisling. He knew Sam needed the car that afternoon to see a farmer, so he really needed to get back.

'Is that all right if he takes you? I could go back and see if Sam can do without the car this afternoon...' Oskar asked.

'No, I need to meet the bus...' She was getting more upset.

'Ais, let me take you to the hospital. You have to get that ankle seen to.' Sean tried to reason with her.

'Her husband is coming from England today,' Oskar explained.

'But Mark...' she began.

'Look, I'll tell you what. I'll bring you over to the hospital, then come back and meet Mark off the bus and bring him to you, all right? The bus won't be in for another hour or so – plenty of time.'

She thought she was going to pass out, as the pain relief hadn't taken effect yet. 'All right,' was all she could manage.

'Very well, but I will tell your parents where you are. I have to, Aisling.' Oskar was insistent.

She nodded. 'Fine, but don't have them following me over to the hospital. No need to make a fuss.' She gasped.

She tried to put at least some of her weight on her good foot, but it proved impossible. Sean ran and brought his car around and then returned, this time scooping Aisling up in his arms.

CHAPTER 22

*L*illian watched as her fellow passengers waved enthusiastically at the people gathered on the quayside below. So this was America. Beside her were a group of girls, the GI brides, finally joining their sweethearts for a life of glamour and excitement far away from the deprivations of post-war England. They were all so full of hope as they reeled off the places they were going – Cleveland, Ohio; Houston Texas; Boston, Massachusetts. They tried to sound knowledgeable based on what Buddy or Danny or Wayne had told them, and there was a time when Lillian would have distanced herself, deemed them beneath her, shop girls and hairdressers. But now, well, now she had no reason to be proud. At least they had a man.

Perry, the saint, had made sure she wasn't penniless and told her just to ask if she needed more. He really was a darling. He had even managed to talk her mother round amazingly. She was actually quite supportive and even hugged her as she left from Southampton.

Lillian took out her photograph. She missed her daughter like a physical ache. She told herself that Austina was being cared for. Kate and Aisling and the Murphys would look after the child, she knew, but she longed to bury her face in her baby's head, to smell the sweet aroma of her, to hear her gurgle and laugh. She really was the sunniest little thing, and so clever too. She was explaining to Kate and Samuel how far advanced Austina was for her age, when she saw them exchange a look. But maybe they were just thinking that Jack had not reached those milestones.

She allowed herself to indulge in her favourite fantasy many times on the voyage over. It took the edge off the fact that there would be nobody to meet her and that she had to navigate her way around the country alone. In her dreams, she pictured the moment when she introduced Beau to his daughter. He would gaze, wide-eyed, in adoration at the beautiful child, then his handsome face would crease into one of his grins that felt so radiant that they could light up the world. Austina would toddle towards her papa – she was not yet walking but no doubt would soon, as she was so advanced – her chubby little arms outstretched. Beau would tower over the little cherub, but he would bend down and pick her up in his big, strong arms – she loved his arms; he was so muscular and manly – and Austina would squeal with delight.

Then, in the elaborate fantasy she created, Beau would turn back to her, with Austina in one arm, and put the other around her and say, 'You did this? You raised this little angel all on your own? I am so proud of you, Lillian.'

The same fantasy, every waking moment, every night, since she found out she was pregnant.

She told anyone on the ship who asked that she was going over to visit friends in Georgia; she didn't go into any details. She had chosen to travel third class, which was a revelation, to say the very least, but she wanted to preserve her funds. Perry had been so generous, but she didn't want to abuse it, or have him think she was swanning about in first class on his money. Besides, she didn't want to see anyone she might recognise. She certainly didn't know anyone who might ever travel in third class – or second, come to think of it – so she could travel more or less incognito.

The crew tied the ship up, and the passengers began to disembark.

First class first; ladies and gentlemen, impeccably dressed, were shepherded off by obsequious crew members, while pursers scurried about to arrange their luggage and liveried footmen busily loaded trunks onto vehicles. Then second class, the nondescript business travellers, the middle-class families, disembarked next; taxis were called, and they soon were gone. And then finally, the remainder. She learned that there were no porters available for anyone coming out of steerage, so she had to carry her own luggage. Luckily, she had packed lightly.

'Taxi.' She raised her hand on the quayside as a disreputable man approached her. He wore a cap over his greasy hair and was in shiny trousers and a frayed shirt.

'Where you goin'?' he asked.

'Excuse me?' Lillian stared haughtily at him.

'Hey, lady, I don't got all day. Where you wanna go?'

'Um…the station, please,' she replied, not entirely sure what it had to do with this rather rough-looking individual.

He placed his fingers in his mouth and emitted a piercing whistle. A yellow car soon appeared beside her. She waited for the driver to get out and put her bag in the boot, but he just sat there. The man approached her again.

'Whattaya waitin' for?' he barked.

'I… I…' She was flustered but finally decided to put her bag in the boot herself. Then she got into the back seat of the car.

The taxi driver looked a little more presentable and turned to face her without saying a word. He was black like Beau, and she instantly liked him. He gestured a question with his face and hands, which she took to mean, 'Where would madam wish to go?'

'The train station, please?'

'Which one?'

'Um…I'm not sure. I want to go to Savannah, Georgia.'

'OK, you want Penn on Seventh Avenue.'

'Thank you. It's my first time to America.'

'You from England?' he asked as he pulled away from the quayside.

'Yes. Yes, I am. Well, I grew up in Ireland, but I live in England now.'

'Nice country. I was stationed in Devon.'

She felt a frisson of excitement – there was a possibility he might know Beau.

'Well, I am here actually to find my…ah…my boyfriend. He's from Savannah, but he served with the 333rd Field Artillery Battalion. Sergeant Beau Lane. I don't suppose you know him?'

His laugh startled her.

'Lady, the 333rd wasn't the only black battalion. If I said to you, I knew a white woman, she was from London, would you know her, what would you say to me?'

He navigated heavy traffic as he spoke, beeping and slamming on brakes, sending her sliding around the back seat.

'I'm sorry.' She felt her face burning; how stupid she must sound.

'Just 'cause I'm black and this guy you knew is black don't mean we know each other, but I'll tell you somethin' for free. You don't wanna go down there to Georgia lookin' for your coloured man, lady. No way, not unless you wanna find him swingin' from a tree.'

He jammed on the brakes again as a down-and-out walked out into the traffic. He shouted something she didn't catch – thankfully – and sped up again.

The combination of the erratic driving and reference to lynching made her feel nauseated. Beau had explained the lyrics of a Billie Holiday song – 'Strange Fruit' – to her once and told her what sort of things went on, and she was horrified. And now she was actively going there, into that very place where such things happened. She swallowed the lump of anxiety in her throat.

'Well, he is in prison for something he didn't do. His cousin wrote to me. I want to try to get him out,' she said.

'And you thought you could jes' roll down there and ask them nice and they'll let him out? You don't got no clue what you is doing, lady! Why you goin' do a damn-fool thing like that?' He caught her eye in the rearview mirror. 'If he's stuck in some jail down South, some white cop put him there, helped out by some white judge. Lady, you're outa your mind if you think you can do anything. Take my advice – get back on that boat, take yourself back to England, and put that one down to experience. It ain't goin' nowhere good.'

Lillian's emotions were in turmoil. On the one hand, she wanted to dismiss this man out of hand. How dare he speak so candidly to her – did he not know who she was? And the other part of her wanted to cry. He was probably right. Even if she did find Beau, what on earth made her think she would be able to get him out of prison?

She took out her purse and found the lawyer's card Perry had given her. Her plan, such as it was, was to first find Beau and determine the situation, then contact him, but now she wasn't so sure. The photograph of Austina was in a little leather frame in her purse.

'We have a daughter. Her name is Austina,' she said quietly. For some reason she couldn't explain, it was important that this man knew that.

They were stuck in traffic. 'Let me see,' he said, and she handed the photograph over.

'She's beautiful. This guy, does he know about her?' Something in his tone had changed a little; it was softer maybe.

'No. No, he doesn't,' Lillian confirmed, suddenly feeling so overwhelmed.

'Look, lady, I know you probably don't want to hear this, but you sure he wants to know? I was there, y'know? And sure it was a war, but it was kinda fun too. And well, people did what they felt, not really thinkin' 'bout no future.'

She could tell he was trying to be diplomatic. 'I know. Believe me, that thought has occurred to me more than once.' She had no pride left, so she might as well be honest.

'So you comin' all this way after getting' a letter saying he's locked up. Maybe he ain't tellin' you the truth, y'know?' He gave her a sympathetic smile.

'I know, and that is a possibility, but I don't think he was that kind of man.' She sighed. 'Either way, I need to know – for me, but also for my daughter. She has a right to a father.'

He nodded. 'You even got a phone number?'

'No. His mother doesn't have a telephone. I just have an address.'

He shrugged. 'Well, if he turns out to be a rat, at least you tried. I admire that.'

'Thanks.' Lillian gave him a small smile.

He helped her with her bag, double-parking the cab on the street, oblivious to the shouting in protest from his fellow motorists. He even walked into the station and showed her where to get a ticket and which platform to go to. Lillian was so glad of his help; the idea of navigating the enormous station, with everyone in such a hurry everywhere, terrified her.

'Best of luck, lady.' He stuck out his hand and she shook it. 'You're gonna need it.'

She carried her suitcase to the platform and eventually managed to board the train. It was a very long journey, and she would have to change trains several times, but no other station could be as big as Penn Station, or as terrifying.

The unfamiliar landscape sped by as she travelled down the eastern coast of the United States. She remembered Beau showing her where Georgia was on a map. She had to travel first from New York to Philadelphia, then on to Baltimore, Maryland, where she would overnight. She had written and booked a room at a moderately priced hotel and was due to continue her journey south the next morning.

She found it hard to believe that she was actually there. After Baltimore, she would travel all day once more, as far as Raleigh, North Carolina, and spend another night. The following day, she would take the last leg to Savannah. That was the easy bit really. Once she was in Savannah, her plan was to check into a hotel, try to find Beau's mother and subsequently Beau and take it from there.

She rested her head against the window, gazing unseeingly at the country outside. She should probably have been in awe, or at least vaguely interested in how different to England it all was – this was the famous America, after all – but all she could think about was Beau. What if the taxi driver was right? What if Beau was fine and just had no desire to see her? What if he was in prison? What if he was dead?

Round and round the thoughts went in her head until she fell into a fitful sleep. A horrible nightmare woke her – images of Beau hanging from a tree, Billie Holiday's song about southern trees bearing strange fruit playing in the afternoon heat.

'Oh, Beau, where are you?' she whispered, fighting back the tears.

CHAPTER 23

Elena caught a glimpse of her reflection in the glass doors of the Royal Marine Hotel in Dun Laoghaire as the porter rushed to open them for her. She looked all right, she hoped. The years since Thomas had disappeared had taken their toll, and she thought she looked older and more careworn, but Eve said she was being mad. She was still slim, and she took care of herself, but she thought there were more wrinkles and a sadness in her eyes that would never leave. She had dressed in black this morning, but Eve was right – she looked too morose. She didn't want to look bright and breezy – she certainly didn't feel like she was – but nor did she want to come across as the grieving widow. She actually didn't know how she felt.

What should she say? Berate him, thank him, sympathise with him?

She scanned the vast lobby with its plush chairs and sofas. Her eyes stopped at a man, and she instantly knew it was Oskar.

He stood up to greet her, and he looked nothing like what she had imagined. She thought he would be tall and thin and austere, but he was the opposite. He was around her height and stocky. His silver hair was swept back off his forehead, his dark-blue eyes were compelling, and his skin had a healthy sun-kissed look, caused by working outside with Dermot presumably. Isabella had written to her, telling her about Oskar's arrival months ago, and she described him as very thin and frail, almost unrecognisable to them. A few months in the country air, plentiful food and outdoor work must have done him good. The most compelling thing about him was his eyes; they seemed to twinkle. He looked no more like a Nazi than she did.

'Mrs Hamilton-Brooks, I am glad to meet you.' He extended his hand, and she took it. Despite the eyes, he looked sombre.

'Mr Metz. Thank you for coming.' She wondered what on earth she was doing there. This was the man who had brought Thomas – her husband, Georgie and Arthur's father – into the lair of Nazis.

'Would you like some coffee?' he asked. A large silver pot and two cups were sitting on the table in front of him.

'Thank you,' she said, sitting down opposite him as he poured.

'Milk? Sugar?' he asked.

Though she knew he had lived most of his life in Ireland, she was still taken aback at his completely Irish accent. She assumed he might sound a *little* German at least.

'Just milk, thank you.'

He prepared her drink and then reached into his jacket pocket and extracted a gold-paper-wrapped chocolate. She must have looked perplexed because he said, 'I've always had one little sweet thing with my daily coffee since I was a boy. Mrs Moriarty in the shop in Kilthomand gets these in specially for me. Everything is still rationed, but I use up my whole allowance just to get a few of these.'

'Thank you.' She smiled and unwrapped the sweet. It was a caramel with a whole nut inside, all covered in chocolate. It was delicious. There was something about him, something she couldn't put her finger on. He was not what she had been anticipating.

As she sipped her coffee, he spoke again. 'I wanted to meet you, to say how sorry I am. I have no words of excuse or mitigation. I was an Abwehr agent, working directly for Hitler, and I kidnapped your husband. I also shot him in the foot. I was on the wrong side, and I realised it too late. I don't expect forgiveness or understanding, so please don't feel you need to be anything but honest with me.' His eyes never left hers.

'In your letter, you explained that you realised that on the U-boat, and yes, it is true you did those things, but I have read and reread Thomas's letters, and all they talk about, apart from his deep desire to get home, was how much he liked and admired you, and how you were the reason he was alive – him and many others too.'

He inhaled, then breathed out slowly. 'May I?' He took out his packet of cigarettes.

'Of course.' She nodded.

He lit one and threw the match in the ashtray. 'What I did, what help I gave to people fleeing, was only a drop in the bucket compared to the damage done by the people I worked for. It didn't come anywhere close to payback, nothing ever could, but I did a little, as best I could. Keeping Thomas alive and getting him home to his family was my goal. I thought that if I could do that, then at least I would have undone one tiny bit of the harm I perpetuated in my life.'

'Do you mean your days with the IRA as well?' she asked. Dermot had told her the whole story after Thomas went missing.

'I will be frank. No. I did terrible things then too. I'm not a good man, Mrs Hamilton-Brooks.' He looked tired. 'But at least that was a fair fight. What the British did here was horrific, wreaking terror on Ireland and her people for centuries – relentless, demoralising terror. They had to be stopped. I know in this war, Britain had right on their side, no doubt about it, but in Ireland, we were right. Your country tried to eradicate mine, outlawing our language, our culture, all of it. So while individually I feel for the boys I killed, and for their families – it keeps me awake at night – it had to be done.'

Life in Ireland for the last twenty years had given Elena a perspective on the Anglo-Irish conflict that was not afforded to her fellow Britons, and she found she had a sympathy for the Irish plight. It was not a popular opinion back on the mainland, as the ex-pats liked to call it, but she knew it to be true.

'This latest thing, National Socialism, is evil personified, nothing less. And I was part of it. My wife, Birgitta, had no time for the Nazis.

She thought they were just thugs and bullies, and I agreed. But some of what Hitler was saying at the start... Well, I was fooled and so were so many others. Not that it is an excuse. We should have stopped them, but instead we joined them.'

'Oh, I didn't realise you were married.' Isabella had never mentioned his wife.

'I was.' He took a long drag from his cigarette. 'My Birgitta was killed by a bomb.'

'I'm sorry,' Elena said, not sure of what else to say.

Oskar merely shrugged. 'She was one of the lucky ones – a direct hit. And she never got to see what became of her country.'

'Did you have any children?' she asked tentatively, almost fearing the response.

'No. No children. She was pregnant when she died...' He nodded sadly.

'I'm sorry.' The words felt inadequate, so trite, but actually that was how she realised she felt. Sorry. Sorry for him, for herself, for her children, for everyone who had been affected by the last horrific six years.

'It was all such a stupid bloody waste, these stupid wars, the death, the destruction, and for what?' she asked.

Oskar gazed at her with an intensity she had never experienced with anyone ever before. It was as if his eyes were boring into her.

'Oh, please, please, don't think such a thing. The last war, yes, that was a waste, but this one, nothing could be further from the truth. It was not a waste. Hitler had to be stopped, he had to be annihilated, and every one of us, every blade of grass in Germany, had to be excoriated of the poison of National Socialism.' His blue eyes never left her face. 'I saw first-hand their plans. Believe me, the alternative to driving every last Nazi to hell is unthinkable.'

'But you were one of them...' She stopped herself from using the word 'Nazi'.

'I was a Nazi, I was a spy for Hitler's regime, I furthered his cause, and that is something I have to live with. I did not want to live with it. I still don't. I think I should hang like all the others, but Dermot has made me promise I will not go back. He wants me to stay, to do some good, and I agreed that I would.'

'I don't understand. You were against the regime, hiding Jews, looking after Thomas. Surely our side would see you as an ally, not an enemy...' She was confused.

'I'm a Nazi spy, Mrs Hamilton-Brooks. That is all they will see, and all they should see...'

'No. I disagree. I think you should go to the authorities and tell them who you are. I will vouch for you, show them my husband's letters. The people you helped would testify in your favour as well, surely...'

He smiled gently. 'I'm tired, that's the truth. I'm fifty-five years old, and I feel a hundred. I have pitched from one conflict to the next most of my adult life. I just wanted to see you, to say I was sorry, to see Dermot and his family once more, and then...' He shrugged.

He said nothing further, but she leaned over and took his hand in hers. She glanced down and saw how several of his fingers were short and deformed.

'Frostbite,' he said by way of explanation. 'The *Schwarzwald* gets very cold in the winter.'

'I want to thank you for what you did for Thomas. He cared very much for you and had nothing but praise for your actions, so no forgiveness is needed on my part. My husband was a British spy, a career that carries certain risks. He knew what he was doing. All over the world, people are having conversations, trying to come to terms, grieving, praying, and we are just two of them. You lost your wife. I lost my husband. So many of my family and friends have lost loved ones. I think the only way forward for any of us is to let it go. I forgive you, Thomas forgave you, Dermot forgives you. So now all that's left is for you to forgive yourself.'

'Mrs Hamilton-Brooks...'

'Call me Elena. May I call you Oskar?'

'Of course, Elena.' His voice cracked. 'Thank you.'

She nodded. 'Let's go for a walk,' she said, suddenly needing fresh air, the finality of it all hitting her suddenly. Thomas was never coming home. She knew before she got Oskar's letter, really, but now, something about meeting him… It felt irrevocable. She was a widow. Georgie would not have her father to walk her down the aisle when she got married, Arthur wouldn't have his father cheering him on at the school's rugby final, she would never feel his warm, reassuring presence ever again.

He helped her get up and held her coat as she put it on. She gathered her gloves and handbag and walked out of the hotel. Oskar kept up with her, and soon they were on the pier, walking into the stiff breeze.

They walked in silence and in step beside each other, not touching, neither saying a word. They walked for over an hour, and she didn't care that she cried. Sometimes she screamed – she wanted to empty herself, to let it all out. All the years of anxiety, the wondering, the not knowing, then the letter and the anger, at Oskar and Thomas and Hitler and the world, and now this. This cold, silent, grief of loss for once and for all. Thomas was dead, and she could grieve.

Eventually, they came to the end of the pier. Oskar put his coat on some big flat rocks, and she sat.

He pulled a hip flask from his pocket, took the cap off and offered it to her. Wordlessly, she took it and put it to her mouth. The alcohol stung and made her want to cough, but she swallowed it, almost enjoying the rough burning sensation in her chest. Anything was better than the gnawing pain of loss. She handed it back and he took a swig.

'Go again,' he instructed, and she put it to her lips once more.

'It doesn't help in the long term, but it takes the edge off the immediate pain, the pain that makes you feel like you could pass out.' He kept his gaze on the grey Irish Sea.

'Did he speak about me?' she asked.

Oskar looked at her now, for the first time since they left the hotel, and she turned her head to face him.

'Every single day. He begged me to be allowed to leave the forest and try to return to you and the children.'

'When? I want you to tell me the whole story, everything. What it was like, from the moment you left here to the day you pulled his body out of that church. Can you do it?' she asked, her eyes locked with his.

'It is not a good story, Elena. It is better you keep your memories –'

'Did you do that when your wife died? Just keep her memories?' she asked quietly.

He sighed. 'No, I clawed at the rubble with my bare hands until they bled, and I, along with others, tried to free our wives, children, all trapped inside. We could hear screaming, so they didn't all die instantly, though I think Birgitta did based on where I found her. So no, I didn't.' He was honest; this was no time for trying to protect feelings.

'So I'll ask you again. Will you tell me about your life with him?' Her voice was even.

'Now?' he asked. There was a mist rolling in off the sea, and as the sun sank, it was getting cold.

'Now.'

* * *

'I SHOT Thomas in the foot because he wouldn't tell us where he had taken Dermot's daughters. Once I did that, he started talking. Dermot, Thomas and I drove to the village of Kilthomand, where Dermot went into the post office to make contact and send a telegram to the thugs your husband had employed to take the girls. The plan was that we would get Thomas to a hospital and get him seen to.

'I waited until Dermot was inside, and I drove off to where I had arranged to be picked up. German intelligence were doing a deal with the IRA. In return for weapons, we would get information from them about British military movements, and also, they would help us get our people into Britain via Ireland.

'I dragged Thomas onto a rowboat, out a couple of hundred yards, to where it was deep enough for a U-boat, and we made the rendezvous.' He turned towards her once more. 'Are you sure you want me to go on?' he asked.

'I want to know. The reality could not be worse than my imaginings.'

'Don't be too sure about that.' He continued reluctantly. 'Well, of course my superiors were informed, but they trusted me to get him to Berlin. The crew of the U-boat had done a reasonable job on his foot and were managing the pain. I had to get him back in something approximating one piece anyway.'

A question occurred to her. 'When did you turn against Hitler and what he was trying to do? In your letter, you mentioned something Dermot said.'

'Yes, I was never a believer of National Socialism in the sense of the perfect Aryan race and all of that rubbish. Hitler himself was a little runt, so that didn't even make any sense, but I suppose I could see where he was coming from. Versailles was so crippling. Germany was virtually starving, humiliated and with no way to get up off its knees, and then he comes along and offers a way out. But to answer your question, it was when I was here actually. I met Dermot, asked him to help me do a deal with the IRA, and he refused. Dermot Murphy is a man of principle. He said he couldn't do anything that might help Hitler, and that was before people over here knew what he was really like. And I realised then that I was on the wrong path.'

'But still you took my husband? Even though you'd had a change of heart?' she asked, but without acrimony; she just wanted to know.

'Yes. I still did that. And for that, I am so sorry.' He lit another cigarette, and she shuddered. It was getting very cold.

'Do you want to carry this on inside somewhere?' he asked.

'Perhaps it would be best. You must be freezing, as we're sitting on your coat.'

They got up and started the walk back.

Oskar laughed. 'Shovelling snow with bare hands, wearing only furs you took off animals you trapped, for months on end, tends to raise the bar on how much cold a person can endure.'

'How did you all survive?' she asked.

'At first, when we took the train to Freiberg, all I wanted to do was get as deep into the forest as I could. I used to go there with my grandfather, so I knew it. Not well, but I knew how dense it was, and I thought it was our only hope. It was. The Romans called it *Silva Nigra* – the trees grow so densely, the light doesn't even penetrate. We made a camp up in the trees. We lived on meat mostly – boar, squirrels, whatever we could catch. There were wild berries and fruits in the spring and summer, but they were at the edges, where risk of being seen was always there. I grew my beard out, battered up my greatcoat, feigned a limp and put my arm inside my shirt, so whenever I went into a town to steal food or to hear what was happening with the war, I looked like an old Great War veteran and people left me alone. I suspect I stank to high heaven as well, which could be another reason.'

She smiled.

'I learned a lot with the IRA. Back then, we lived outside most of the time, but it was nothing like the cold of a German winter. We couldn't have big fires for fear the smoke would be seen, though we did find a cave towards the end of '43, and that was luxury compared to the tree house.' He smiled.

'I can't imagine,' she said.

'So we set traps and caught animals and then cooked them on tiny fires, usually at night. We ate mushrooms, honey, berries when we could get them, leaves sometimes. Then when we started sheltering Jews, some of them had food. One woman showed us how to make flour from pine nuts, to make a kind of bread. It was disgusting, but it filled us. It was good to feel we were doing something.'

'How did that happen, that you were harbouring Jews?'

'On one of my trips to a town, I spotted some people hiding in the less dense part of the woods. They were German, but from the North. They'd managed to get down as part of an escape line, but something had gone wrong. They were not met as was promised, and they were terrified. It was a family, and I brought them back to Thomas, and it started from there. I went to the meeting point every day or two to see if someone would turn up, and someone did eventually. The line had been betrayed, but they reinstated it with new people, and so Thomas and I became a rest point on it.'

'That was very risky,' Elena said as they walked along the street on the waterfront. It was now six o'clock, and people were leaving their work and heading home. They reached the pedestrian crossing and needed to decide their route.

'Shall we go back to the hotel?' he asked.

'You could come to my house – it's not far,' she offered.

'If that's what you want.' Oskar nodded, and they set off once more.

They stopped outside Elena's gate. 'Here we are,' she said, and walked up the gravel driveway. The students were all gone for the day, and Elena saw Bartley cutting some timber for the next day's class. He was keeping one eye on Eve as she hung out a line of tea cloths and aprons.

Eve turned as Elena entered via the garden door. 'Oh, Elena, I was getting worried –' she began. She stopped mid-sentence. Though she had heard Oskar Metz's name her whole life, knew about his history in the IRA with Daddy and Jack's father all those years ago, and she'd heard the story of how he was embroiled in the kidnapping of her sisters in more recent history, she had never met him.

'Eve, this is Oskar Metz. Oskar, meet Eve O'Neill, née Murphy.'

'Hello, Eve.' Oskar met her gaze and smiled. 'The last time I met you, you were a baby. I knew Jack as a baby too. His father, Mick, Dermot and I were in some very narrow scrapes. I was so sorry to hear what happened.'

'Hello, Oskar.' Instinctively, Eve walked towards him, and he wrapped her in a warm embrace.

CHAPTER 24

*A*isling sat in the chair by the range, her plastered ankle raised as she had been instructed. It was so incredibly frustrating to be so immobile, but her ankle was broken, and nothing but time and rest were going to heal it.

She had been in plaster for a month, and while the terrible pain had dulled to an ache that never relented, day or night, the main pain was the one in her heart.

Mark had not turned up as he had promised. Sean went to meet the bus but came back to the hospital to report he waited for both buses that afternoon, but no sign of any Englishmen. Mark never wrote, or even explained, so eventually in desperation, she wrote to Delilah. Her sister-in-law's letter was on her lap now, and Aisling was bewildered and confused.

She read it again.

Dear Aisling,

Thank you for your letter, and I can confirm that Mark is back in Portwye. He is in good health and is not drinking. He is back living at his house, and he asked me to tell you that you should have your solicitor send the divorce papers to that address. He says he'll sign them without any argument, so best get it over with. There is no divorce in Ireland, I understand, so it will have to be here. But he has investigated, and you can have a solicitor act on your behalf, so there is no need for you to come over for the hearing. He will send on your things.

I had hoped, Aisling, that things would improve for you two. Mark did too, I know, but clearly your circumstances have changed. Mark doesn't blame you. He put you through a lot, and for that he is sorry.

He and I wish you all the best in the future.

Delilah

No matter how often Aisling read the letter, she could not understand it. First, Delilah didn't speak like that, all cold and informal. And what did she mean, her circumstances had changed? Mark knew Aisling was at home. She had explained everything, and he assured her in his last letter from Dartmoor that he was coming to her in Ireland.

She had written. Their telephone had been disconnected, maybe Mark never paid the bill, but she was so desperate, one day she even rang the Portwye post office to ask them to request Mark contact her. But still she heard nothing. Finally, when all else failed she decided to send a telegram. She was reluctant, it was a much more public method of communication, but it was her last option. She was humiliated, waiting in the post office in Kilthomand, then having to shout her message to Mossy, the half deaf postmaster. Oskar kindly drove her but waited in the car. Once again, she could almost hear the whispers. Poor Aisling Murphy, jilted in love once more, was the talk of the parish. She remembered thinking the morning of her wedding to Mark in London how she would never again endure anyone's pitying glances. The reason she left to join the WAAF with Kate was because Sean Lacey had humiliated her, but she never in a million years thought Mark would do the same. He loved her; he'd said it over and over. And even since he came back from the war, when he was so broken inside, he would wake from nightmares and cling to her, crying. How could he do this to her?

To add to it, she had to endure her family's pity. They didn't ever mention his name, but she knew every one of them would love to string Mark up. Kate was furious with him, and she sensed Kate had even tried to get Sam to talk to Mark – they were good friends – but she never said. Mammy and Daddy were worried about her, worried for her future. Aisling, even more so than when Sean made a fool of her, desperately wanted to get away. Away from her family, away from Kilthomand, away from Ireland. But she couldn't even get to the bathroom without help.

The only one she could talk to was Oskar. He was nice and he didn't judge Mark. She pointed out how unusual that was on one of their drives; he took her with him when he needed to get things at the hardware or the mart just to get her out of the house.

'How on earth could I ever judge anyone, Aisling? What I was? Who I was?' She heard the pain in his voice. 'Mark sounds like a nice lad. He must be, otherwise he'd never have got someone like you to marry him. But who knows what's going on? I do think he's a fool to let you go, but then us men are foolish sometimes.'

Aisling knew Dermot was hurt that she seemed so close to Oskar these days, but for the first time in her life, she felt she couldn't talk to him. He told Isabella everything, and after overhearing Isabella and Kate talking about Mark, she just couldn't trust them.

She looked up as her mother entered. She, Kate and the men were spending a lot of time up at the main house these days. The farmhouse was perfectly cosy and restored to its former state, and the estate was starting to show a profit. Sam, Oskar and her father worked so hard, day and night, never taking any time off, but it was starting to pay off.

Kate and Isabella were stripping the walls of the small annex, the one Lord Kenefick had used as his private dressing room, bedroom, study and office. It was built later than the rest of the house, which went back to the 1700s, and it wasn't quite as dilapidated. The plan was for Kate and Sam to move in there soon. They would tackle the rest of the crumbling heap in due course.

'Hello, pet, how's the ankle?' Isabella was trying to repair the relationship with her daughter, but Aisling just wanted to get away.

'It's fine,' she replied, knowing she sounded curt.

'Did you get a letter?'

Even though Aisling had stuffed the letter down beside her, the envelope must have fallen to the floor.

'Yes. There are a few for Sam up there, and one for Daddy as well.'

Isabella sat down opposite her, and Aisling could tell her mother was nervous.

'Is it from Mark?'

Under her mother's compassionate look, all the confusion, hurt and pain of the past year made her disintegrate. She wasn't angry at them any more; they were only looking out for her. And anyway, it seemed that they were right to.

Aisling handed her the letter just as Kate appeared in the doorway. Saying nothing, her sister began to read the letter over their mother's shoulder.

'I can't believe it.' Kate was furious. 'Seriously, who the hell does he think he is? He hasn't even the guts to tell you to your face? He's pathetic.'

'Oh, Aisling, love...' Isabella rubbed her daughter's hair.

'You were right. He doesn't love me. He mustn't if he sent this, right?'

'Just forget about him. Honestly, he's not worth it.' Kate was still fuming when Sam walked in.

'What?' he asked, knowing that look on his wife's face.

'Read that.' She gave him the letter. 'He doesn't deserve my sister. Imagine being so cowardly to not even have a conversation with her after all he put her through.'

Kate stormed out, leaving Isabella to comfort Aisling. Sam ran after her. 'Kate, wait.'

She stopped and spun around, her dark eyes flashing and loose black curls in a cascade over her shoulders. 'What?' she snapped. 'Don't try to defend him, Sam – I'm warning you! Aargh... I could choke him!'

Sam had said nothing while he waited for her to finish. 'I don't know, Kate. I... I don't know what's going on with him, and we haven't been close for a while what with everything, but I just don't think he'd do this...' Sam paused to think.

'But he bloody well has done it!' Kate exploded.

'I know, but... I just think there might be something else going on...' He was at a loss.

'She should cut all ties, let the solicitor do whatever, and meet someone nice. And not that eejit Lacey who's been sniffing round like a terrier since she broke her ankle. Once a snake, always a snake.'

It was true – Sean Lacey seemed to find all kinds of reasons to be up at the farmhouse these days. Ais was so upset over Mark, she didn't see what he was up to, but everyone else did.

'I think I should go over, talk to him. What do you think?' Sam suggested.

'What do I think? If I told you what I thought of Mark Belitho at this moment, you wouldn't want to hear it. I'm so angry with him.'

'Look, I know how you feel, but Mark and I were great pals, and something about this just doesn't sit right with me. How about I go over? I need to go back to London to see the solicitors anyway. We won't say anything to Ais. I'll talk to him, and we can take it from there.'

'Fine,' Kate finally agreed. 'But tell him from me that he'd better have a damned good reason for breaking my sister's heart over and over again.'

'Don't worry, I will.' Sam kissed the top of her head.

That evening, after dinner, Dermot suggested to Aisling that they go for a drive. He knew she was going mad stuck in a chair all day. He drove onto the beach. The tide was in, and he stopped the car almost at the water's edge.

The leather seats of the Austin Princess had been covered in rugs to save them from the greasy, mucky overalls of the men. Dermot leaned back and took one from the back seat, wrapping it around Aisling's legs.

For a few minutes, they sat and stared out at the green sea. The tiny white horses danced on the waves as the surface of the water reflected the sunlight, and the black cliffs to the east and west, topped with green fields, jutted out.

Dermot leaned into the back again and this time produced a flask. He unscrewed the cup from the top and poured her some tea.

'Oskar and I ate all the sandwiches, I'm afraid, but despite your mother's best efforts, he's not a huge tea drinker, so at least there's some of that left, and this...' He handed her a Fry's chocolate bar. 'I remembered you used to love those when you were small, so I got Bridie to put one aside for you. I thought it might cheer you up.'

His kindness made everything a hundred times worse.

'Thanks, Daddy. I don't know when I last had one...before the war sometime...' She didn't know where to begin. She was miserable and embarrassed and frightened for the future.

'Drink your tea before it gets cold,' he said.

She knew he would wait for her to bring it up. Silence didn't intimidate her father in the way it did others. He probably knew it all anyway – Mammy would have told him – but they'd never discussed Mark since the day she blurted out he was in prison.

Dermot filled his pipe. He had given up cigarettes on the doctor's orders, as he was coughing constantly, and he'd taken up the pipe instead. Before his wife had a chance to go mad, he explained he had no intention of lighting it, but he would clean it and pack it and roll the tobacco for it, and the process kind of managed the craving. He was true to his word and was constantly seen these days fiddling with the pipe but never actually smoking it.

'I overheard Mammy and Kate a few weeks ago, talking about Mark and about me, and how they thought he was making a fool of me the same way Sean did all those years ago... It hurt me, and I suppose things haven't been great since. And then I broke my stupid ankle, and then Mark never arrived, and I don't know, Daddy... Then today, I got a letter from his sister.'

She reached into her coat pocket and extracted Delilah's letter, which he scanned. He then threw it on the dashboard and leaned over and held her hand. 'What do you want to do?'

'I don't know... I've written and sent a telegram, and I even rang the post office in Portwye – and nothing. And then that from Delilah. It's obvious he doesn't want to speak to me, but I don't know why.'

She looked up at him, her father who could fix everything. 'What should I do, Daddy? I honestly have no idea.'

CHAPTER 25

*K*ate and Isabella sat down for the first time in seven hours and surveyed the scene before them. Jack and Austina were playing happily on the floor. They really did seem to love each other.

The little girl had been confused at the start, and she howled pitifully for an hour after Lillian left, but since then, she had been such an easy baby to care for. In fact, it was as easy to care for two little ones as one, and they seemed to find each other hilarious. Dermot had constructed a kind of playpen for them. There were many sharp and dangerous things lying around while the reconstruction of Robinswood was underway, and it was vital they were kept away from exploring.

Austina took her first steps, much to Jack's fascination, and a few days later, he followed suit. Though she was younger, the little girl seemed to take the lead, with Jack happy to follow his cousin.

Isabella gave them each a piece of currant bread and butter, and they munched happily.

'Is this really happening, Mam?' Kate asked, wiping a smear of dirt from her cheek. 'Are we actually looking after Lillian Kenefick's child while we do up Robinswood to live in it?'

Isabella chuckled. 'I know, it seems so strange sometimes. For so many years, we worked here. How many times did I carry trays up those stairs, or stand at the sink washing dishes, waiting for the bell to ring because one of the Keneficks wanted something? And now' – she handed her daughter a cup of tea and a slice of the currant cake – 'here we all are. Your father and Oskar and Sam making a go of the estate, and us putting manners on this house. It's hard to believe.'

Kate stood and massaged her lower back with her hands; she was stiff because she'd spent the morning scrubbing the floorboards in Austin's old study – there must have been an inch of dust and dirt on them. Even when the Keneficks lived at Robinswood, Lord Kenefick didn't allow anyone to clean in there; it was his own private sanctuary. She felt and looked filthy, but the floor was restored to its lovely oak glory.

'Oskar turning up has been a godsend. Sam was saying he is an incredibly hard worker. You'd wonder what is going on in his head, though, wouldn't you? He's nice and everything, but deep.'

Isabella kicked off her shoe and rubbed her sore foot. She sighed with relief. 'I think that he's seen so much and experienced things… well, things nobody could ever forget, that working hard means he is exhausted by night-time and so he sleeps.' She examined her foot. 'I'll have to get this bunion looked at…'

'You should go to that shoe shop in Dublin, the one that makes special shoes for older people…' Kate winked, and her mother gave her a glare.

'Less of that, you cheeky pup. You're not too old for a clip round the ear, you know!'

Kate giggled. 'Seriously, though, why don't we go to Dublin next week? We need a break from this place. We've been at it flat out for months, and I need a day off.'

'We could see if Eve could meet us?' Isabella said enthusiastically. 'And it would do Ais good as well.'

'Poor Ais, she's so sad. And that Sean Lacey called again yesterday. I'm telling you, Mam, he's got his eye on her again.'

'Yerra, I don't think she's any notions in that direction, so he can

175

be sniffing around all he likes. She chats away to him when he calls, and he seems to cheer her up when the rest of us can't, so we'll let that go, I'd say. At least she's getting this latest plaster off on Tuesday, though maybe walking around Dublin would be a bit too much for her?'

'I don't know if it would be.' Kate sighed. 'But I do know that she's going to crack up if she doesn't get out of that house. Bad enough that she's all up in a heap over Mark, but to be stuck sitting in a chair all day would drive anyone round the bend.'

Kate wished she could do something for her sister. She and Sam discussed it and decided to keep his visit to Mark between them for now. Nothing might come of it, and they didn't want to get Aisling's hopes up.

'Look, we'll drive up – the men can do without the car for one day – and we'll drive straight to Elena's. And we'll forgo the shopping. Let's just stay there and have a chat with Eve and Elena. They are having great success with the school, you know, so I'm dying to hear all about it.'

Kate nodded. 'That's a plan. Though you'll have to convince Daddy to give me the car. With Sam away, he'll be afraid I'd wrap it around a tree or something.' She rolled her eyes. 'Now, are we ready to face the worst bit, the main house?' She grimaced.

The annex that was Austin's private quarters was more or less habitable now. The plumbing was still working, unbelievably, and Oskar had come in and repaired a few leaks. There was gas in the stove, so that was working, and the electricity had been reconnected. The women spent two full weeks clearing out the rubbish and dirt that had gathered in his rooms over the years. The remains of Austin's chaotic life had been untouched since he died. At first, they had worried that Sam might want some of his father's discarded things, but he came in one day, took a look around and said, 'No, all rubbish. Let's get rid of it.'

They built a bonfire in the yard and burned papers, old furniture riddled with woodworm and hundreds of receipts from bookies for bets that never romped home. There was a trailer full of empty whiskey bottles too, but it had been cleared out and scrubbed. From ceiling to floor, everything looked much better. They got some rugs for the wooden floors and unpacked some of the delph that hadn't been good enough to auction when Violet closed the house in 1940. There were plenty of bed frames in the loft, so Sam and Oskar brought one down. Dermot even found an old crib up there, which must have been Sam's, so Jack had a bed as well. Other bits and pieces were all assembled, checked for woodworm and installed. It looked a bit higgledy-piggledy, but it was warm and cosy, and Kate couldn't wait to move in.

Sean Lacey was due to arrive later with a new mattress. Kate didn't mind using all the old things, but she drew the line at a mattress, especially as there were lots of suspiciously large mouse droppings everywhere. Sam assured her it was just mice, but she knew better.

Isabella shuddered. 'We'll have to do it sometime. Let's leave the door into the main hall open so we'll hear these two scallywags, and we'll start there. If we can open those shutters on the front and at least get some light in, we'll be able to see what we're doing.' She stood up and put her foot back into her shoe, wincing as she did so.

'See the rats you mean,' Kate said ominously.

'Stop.' Isabella shuddered. She wasn't squeamish, but she hated rats. 'If I say they're not there, then they're not there.'

As they rose, Kate picked Jack up and gave him a cuddle. Austina stretched her chubby little arms up for one too, and Isabella lifted her.

'Hello, little lady, how are you?' she cooed as the baby nuzzled into her neck.

'Ah, cuddling babies, is that what's going on up here? And we felt sorry for you, thinking you were being overworked,' Dermot teased as he and Oskar entered. Dermot kissed Isabella's cheek, and immediately Austina raised her hands for him to take her.

'She has you wrapped around her little finger.' Kate laughed as Dermot threw the toddler in the air, causing her to squeal with delight.

'Jack jump, Jack jump!' Her son demanded the throwing treatment as well.

'I will in my eye throw you up in the air, and you weighing like a small calf.' Kate went to put Jack back in the playpen, but he cried in protest.

'May I?' Oskar asked.

The family was used to him and his silent, courteous ways. He was quite formal and didn't say much, but he loved them all, and they knew it.

'Be my guest, but mind your back – he must be two stone weight.' Kate smiled as Oskar took Jack up and threw him in the air, and both children laughed and screamed in glee.

Oskar produced two rattles and used them as bribery to get the children back in their playpen. They were fascinated and shook them vigorously to hear the nuts inside make noise.

'What are those?' Kate asked, looking at the ornately crafted toys.

'Rushes. You weave them into a kind of long cone and then pop in something hard, like a nut, before weaving them shut,' Oskar explained. 'I used to make them for babies – my grandfather showed me how back in Germany. We lived for a time when I was young in Federsee, in Swabia. Lots of rushes there. People use them to make furniture, mats for the floor, toys, cookware, everything.'

'They are beautiful, so intricate...' Isabella picked Austina's up, and the little girl stared at her with solemn brown eyes until her toy was returned.

'So to what do we owe the pleasure of your company in the middle of the working day?' Isabella asked.

'Can't a man pop in to see his wife?' Dermot grinned. He was so happy these days; she never realised how much living in a city had taken from him. He was a country man and happiest out on the land. The fact that he had his friend beside him and a personal investment in that land was just the icing on the cake. Though he was fifty-seven, he looked ten years younger than he did when they were in Dublin.

'Hmm...' She pretended to be suspicious. 'You thought we'd make you a cuppa and a slice of that cake I baked last night is more likely.'

'You know me so well.' He grinned and gave her a squeeze.

A van pulled up outside.

'Oh, it's Sean with the mattress,' Kate said unenthusiastically, lifting the net curtain. 'You can earn that tea and cake by helping him lift it in.'

Oskar and Dermot went outside, and Kate and Isabella watched through the window. 'He'll be going mad to discover Aisling isn't here. You may be sure he'd have sent one of his lads with that mattress if it was for anyone else.' Kate laughed.

The mattress was finally in after much pushing and shoving by the three men. Isabella and Kate went into the bedroom and sat on it to check for softness.

'Don't wear that out now with too much bouncing.' Her father gave her a cheeky wink.

Kate blushed to the roots of her hair. She was speechless – her father never made remarks like that. Thankfully, Sean and Oskar were back in the kitchen.

'Don't mind him, Kate.' Isabella smiled and playfully punched her husband, then shooed him out the door.

Kate recovered and sat for a moment. She hoped that moving up to Robinswood would solve their issue. She adored Sam, and he loved her just as much, and though they worked hard, they tried to make time to be together at night. She tried to model her marriage on her parents'; they were the most successful couple she knew, and one of the things they did was have their time alone. They were available to their daughters all day, but at night, their bedroom was their world. Isabella was remarkably open about that side of their lives and told Kate often how important it was.

'Men can't just come out with how they feel, not men like ours anyway. They need to feel connected to you, and that happens when a couple are alone and physically close.'

Kate was embarrassed thinking about what her father had said. Did he know something? Had Sam said something? It wasn't that she didn't love Sam – she did. He was a very attractive man, so she did relish making love with him. But she tried to avoid it because she didn't want another baby – not yet anyway. There was so much to do, and she had such plans for Robinswood, but a baby would slow everything to a stop. She didn't dare voice her thoughts to anyone, as it would sound so selfish and downright immoral, but she just couldn't bring herself to do it in case she fell pregnant.

She knew about French letters. She and Sam had even used them before they were married. But he wanted another child, so he was never going to go back to using them, and anyway, you couldn't get them in Ireland. She would have another baby sometime, but just not now. She wished she had someone to talk to about this. Aisling was so distraught and had enough to deal with, and Eve was all the way up in Dublin.

There were all sorts of things available in England – she'd heard the girls on the base talking about rings and sponges you'd insert to stop you getting pregnant – but she knew that there was no such thing available here. The church banned all forms of contraception. Babies were a gift from God, and to do anything to stop their arrival was a mortal sin.

She didn't really believe that, but if she suggested using anything to anyone except her sisters, they would be appalled. She tried to find information about taking your temperature, as apparently there were times of the month when you were more likely to conceive, but even finding out what or how to do it was close to impossible.

She rose and went out to join the others.

'So how's Aisling?' Sean asked before he bit into a slice of fruit cake. Kate shared a pointed glance with her mother.

'She's getting the cast off Tuesday,' Dermot said.

'I suppose she'll go back to England then?' he asked, his eyes wide and innocent.

'I suppose so.' Kate didn't want to give him any ideas.

"Tis a wonder her husband never came over to see her, and she housebound this last while, isn't it?'

He was definitely fishing now. Isabella and Kate shared a glance.

'He wasn't able to, work commitments and so on. You know how it is, Sean. We're all so busy. Speaking of which, we must get on ourselves. Thanks for dropping the mattress.' Isabella smiled and almost snatched the half-drunk cup of tea from him.

'Right so.' He rose, getting the message. 'Tell Aisling I was asking for her,' he said and left.

Isabella sent Oskar and Dermot to check out the hallway and to try to open the rusted shutters and do a preliminary check for large rodents.

'He's a right eejit,' Isabella muttered to Kate as they washed the dishes and Sean's van pulled out of the driveway.

'That he is, all right, but don't worry. Ais would never look at him. Though to be honest, she hasn't said a word to me about anything, really.' She sighed. 'There was a time when we told each other everything.'

'I know, and you will again.' Isabella gathered her mop and lifted the clean bucket of water out of the sink. 'She's just trying to figure it all out in her own head first. You and Eve wear your hearts on your sleeves, but Aisling was always deep, even as a little one. She'll come back to us. We just need to be patient.'

Dermot put his head around the door. 'Shutters open, and no sign of any mice.' He chuckled.

'Oh, thank God for that,' Isabella said, relieved.

'Plenty of rats though!' Dermot joked, and she threw a tea towel at him.

Isabella was glad to see him cheerful. The letters seemed to have stopped for now. They were just from malicious, nasty people, he told her, but still it rankled.

Dermot didn't want her to say anything to Kate, but Isabella disagreed. The letters were as much about Kate as they were about her and Dermot.

'What?' Kate asked, noting her mother's face.

'Oh, nothing...' Isabella picked up her cleaning things.

'Mam, what is it? The other day, the same – when I came in, you and Daddy were arguing over something. What's going on?'

Isabella sighed and sat back down. 'We've been getting letters, anonymous of course, and I... Well, your father didn't want to tell you and Sam because he said it was nothing, but...'

'You don't think it is? What do the letters say?' Kate sat opposite her mother.

'That your father fought for Irish freedom, and yet here we are living like the gentry who treated us so badly for so long...' Isabella sighed. 'Basically, that we were getting notions of upperosity and that we'd get our comeuppance some day.'

'Are they threatening us?' Kate was incredulous.

'Ah, love, it's only old talk. You know how they are. People don't like to see anyone getting on in life. They feel like we have no right to be up here, living like lords and ladies, when we were just like them – worse off in fact, since we never even had our own house.'

'But that's rubbish. This is Sam's home and I'm his wife – we're entitled to live here. And anyway, we've hardly any money and we pay everyone that works for us. How dare anyone...'

Isabella saw the old familiar temper rise up in her youngest daughter. Kate was the fieriest of the three, and she wouldn't take this lying down.

'They dare because they see it as us selling out to the likes of the Keneficks. In their eyes, they fought hard for independence back in the twenties, but their lives haven't improved. The rich are still here, getting richer, and poor people are still poor. They want to lash out at someone, and they see us going from servant to master, and they resent it.' Isabella was circumspect. 'It wasn't ever going to be easy, coming back. You were a local girl, a servant's child, and now you're Lady Kenefick. That's a bitter pill for some people to swallow.'

'But why would they care? It's not as if I'm like bloody Violet or Lillian being all lah-di-dah around the place.' She stopped. 'Do you know who is behind them?'

Isabella's eyes would not meet her daughter's.

'You do know!' Kate blazed. 'Tell me who is writing them.'

'I don't know for sure, so don't go tearing over there half-cocked, but Charlie Warren has had a set against your father since he refused to carry on the madness of the Civil War. Charlie saw it as a sell-out, and then when Sam said he wanted the land back, well, Warren saw that as yet another slight against him. So we think it's him, but no doubt there are others in Kilthomand who feel the same way.'

'What should we do?'

'Ignore it. That's all we can do. They won't let it go any further.' Isabella tried to calm Kate down.

'Should we go to the guards? It's illegal to threaten people, isn't it?'

'It is.' Isabella sighed. 'But you know how things work in a small community. Calling the guards would only make it worse.'

'But we can't just take it!'

'We are throwing the cowardly letters in the fire, so we aren't taking anything, Kate. Charlie Warren or whoever is behind this isn't brave enough to stand up to your father in broad daylight because they know what they'd get. So we won't give them the soot of it by reacting, all right?'

Kate wasn't convinced.

'It's the only way, Kate. If it turns into something else, we can see about it then, but for now, let's leave them at it. They're pathetic and jealous, so let's make a right go of this place, and that will drive whomever is sending these letters daft. That's our best revenge.'

Kate knew her mother was right, as usual, but it still rankled with her. 'All right, but if anything else happens, we deal with it, agreed?'

'Agreed.' Isabella rose and went back to her cleaning.

CHAPTER 26

*E*lena checked the post and found she was disappointed there was nothing from Oskar. They had talked late into the night on the day he came to Dublin, and he explained about his and Thomas's life in the Black Forest. The reports that were emerging daily on the true horror of the Nazi death camps were unbearable for her to listen to, picturing Thomas as one of the emaciated, corpse-like survivors. To think that but for Oskar, Thomas could have ended up in one of those places gave her nightmares.

It was hard to explain, even to herself, but she felt a connection to the German. There was something about him – it was hard to put into words. He was deeply remorseful for what he had done, and he admitted to her that he still thought he should go back and face the consequences of his actions despite Dermot's pleas. But she pointed out to him how stupid a move that would be.

They talked about Birgitta and their unborn child. He wept bitter tears and confided in her that it was the only time he'd cried for them. When it happened, he was just frozen inside. She knew exactly; she was the same sometimes about Thomas. It was just too much to deal with, so her emotions didn't allow her to feel any more pain or something. It was hard to explain, but Oskar understood. He told her about his days in the IRA, about the feelings of despondent despair he had when the Civil War of 1922 broke out and men he had fought alongside were now the enemy. It was then he went to Germany, sickened by it all.

He had looked into her eyes and said, 'Perhaps I should save the Allies the bother and do the job myself. At least I'd die in my own country. I never saw myself as anything but Irish really. My father was German, and I liked to visit, and I spent some of my childhood in Swabia, but in my heart, I'm Irish, always was. But I got caught up in National Socialism willingly, and I deserve no sympathy. Sometimes, I think that is all I am good for, creating chaos and destruction. I don't bring joy, I don't have love in my life… It feels like I was born to kill and maim and hurt.'

He sat staring at the floor between his knees, and she put her hand on his back. 'Please don't do that. Hasn't there been enough death? Here, in Germany, all over Europe? And for what? What does you leaving this world achieve? Absolutely nothing. You say you don't have love – you loved your wife and she loved you. The Murphys love you. Dermot took you back and gave you a home. Is that not love? He may not say it, but actions speak louder than words. You talk about little Jack and Austina and how you love to play with them and read them stories – is that not love? Please, don't leave all of that. Stay, live, love. There has been too much suffering. Those of us that are left owe it to those who are gone to live our best lives, otherwise what was it all for?'

It got so late that night that he ended up staying overnight in the guest room but was gone early the next morning, before she woke. He never even left a note, so that was the last contact she had from him.

Night after night, she lay awake, thinking about Thomas, what he must have endured. Her thoughts strayed to Oskar and how both he and her husband were victims of that horrible regime. Round and round it all went. She dreamed of Thomas, sometimes seeing him like the photographs that appeared in the newspaper, other times as he was, charming and funny. Sometimes, in her dreams, Thomas's face became Oskar's and vice versa. She was exhausted from it all.

She stopped buying the papers or listening to the wireless. She hoped the children weren't exposed to too much of it in school. They'd had a hard-enough time dealing with it all, though Thomas's letters to each of them were a comfort.

Arthur had been stoic, poor little fellow. She could see he was heartbroken, but then so many of the other chaps at his school had lost their fathers as well, so it was easier for him.

Georgie took it worse. She had stronger memories of Thomas, and she adored him. Elena hated to see the anger and pain in her daughter's eyes as she tried to come to terms with what she already knew – that her father was never coming home.

She wrote to Oskar, thanking him for the visit. That was over three weeks ago, but he had yet to reply. Perhaps he felt it needed no response. He was probably right.

She collected the post and saw Eve sitting in the study at the desk that once was Thomas's but that now the two women shared.

'Eve, can you meet with the head of the Glenvera Nursing Home this afternoon?' she asked as she searched the post. 'She is looking for several domestic staff, and I thought it might be better if you spoke to her, as you might have a better idea who would fit where. They were very pleased with the last bunch, and they've settled in really well. It's sad, but the matron says girls who come out of orphanages are better suited to the schedule of a nursing home. Girls reared in families are either too lonely being away from home or too wild and want to be out and about the town.'

Eve smiled. 'I can, but you'll have to supervise the class here then. We're doing dressmaking, and there are a few lively personalities in this new group, so leaving them alone with sharp scissors may not be a great idea.'

'Of course, no problem.' Elena handed her a telegram. 'One for you.'

Eve scanned it.

Coming to Dublin. Stop. Kate Ais Mam babies. Stop. Saturday 10th. Stop.

A broad smile split Eve's face. 'Mammy and the girls are coming up to Dublin next Saturday! That's going to be great – I can't wait to see them. Will you join us for lunch?' Thomas Hamilton-Brooks's widow had long ago ceased to be their employer; she was now considered part of the family.

Elena hesitated. 'Ah, no, it's a family thing. I'll let you alone. You need a break from me.'

'Don't be daft. We'd love you to join us. Mammy will want to know everything about Arthur and Georgie anyway. And you've never met Aisling, have you? Poor thing is having a bit of a time at the moment. Her marriage is in trouble, and then she broke her ankle, so she could do with cheering up.'

Tears shone in Elena's eyes. The support of the Murphys had made the last years so much easier to bear. She was happy for Dermot and Isabella that they were back in the place they considered home, but she missed them.

'Well, then, thank you, I'd love to join you all.' She paused. She had been thinking about something since the conversation with Oskar. 'I was thinking... Maybe it's a bad idea, but I thought it might be nice for the children, and for me as well, if we had a memorial service for Thomas now that we know for sure he's dead. I know there would be very few people there. Not like an Irish funeral or anything, but just a small gathering, family, a few friends. I know we were not exactly forthcoming about the circumstances of his death, but now that the war is over, I think we can just say he was working for the government, which is true, was captured and died in Germany. What do you think?'

She tried to read Eve's face. The younger woman could never forget the danger Thomas had put the Murphy sisters in, and the fact that for many years, he was on the other side of the political and military divide from their father. Perhaps they would not come to such a memorial? She knew the Murphys were very fond of her and they loved the children, but was this asking too much?

'Of course, we should do that.' Eve rose and stood in front of Elena. 'I know we don't talk about what happened, but I want to say this. Thomas did a terrible thing, and if anything had happened to my sisters or Lady Kenefick, who knows how we would be now, but they got out. We don't think it was ever his plan to harm them. He wanted my father to betray Oskar, and he knew the only thing that would make him consider doing that was to threaten us. And Oskar was a Nazi. Thomas was doing his job, and in a war, the lines of right and wrong get very blurred. My father is a good man, but there are mothers in England who no longer have their sons because of him and others like him. I think leaving the past in the past is the only way to go on. You, Georgie and Arthur should have the chance to say goodbye. I know you more or less knew, but there was always hope. Oskar's letter ended that, and I know it's been a very difficult time. But, Elena, you're here. You're standing up and doing some good. Georgie and Arthur are smashing children, and I know all of my family will stand beside you and them, and we'll all let Thomas go.'

'Thank you, Eve. I don't know what I would do without you.' The two women hugged as they stood together in the morning sunlight.

CHAPTER 27

*L*illian reread the note from Ruth. She had sent a telegram to Ruth's home address, as she had no idea how to contact her in Chicago, once she arrived in Savannah to say she was there and looking for Beau. She hoped she might be at home. When she got back from the police station where she'd been making enquiries, the concierge delivered the note. Ruth was in Georgia thankfully had suggested a meeting.

Now that she was here and witnessing first-hand the hateful Jim Crow laws Beau had told her about, she began to realise exactly what was going on.

The Americans – at least in the South – who had fought so valiantly in Europe to defeat Hitler's evil regime were, on their own soil, openly supporting the idea that one group of people were better than another based on race. It was hard to comprehend.

Ruth was taking a big chance by even suggesting a meeting, and Lillian realised that inviting Beau's cousin to tea in the hotel, which had been her original plan, was a complete nonstarter. She dressed as conservatively as she could, as she wanted to draw as little attention to herself as possible. It was hot and sticky, so she wore a plain navy dress and patent-leather court shoes. Her blonde hair needed to be shampooed and set, but she had no time for such frivolities, so she pinned it up under her hat.

She was given an address – not Ruth's – and a time to be there, which she gave to the taxi driver, a white man who looked askance at her. She assumed it was because he thought it odd that she, a white woman, wanted to go there. He never spoke to her but dropped her off and took her money. She stood outside a ramshackle house on the edge of a town about six miles outside of Savannah. Clearly it had been derelict for some time. Once there, the car gone, she wondered what was going to happen. After a few moments, a young black girl appeared and told her to follow her. Lillian set off on foot with the girl, who was about twelve, down a dirt road, the girl watching warily all the time. At the end of the road was another house, and she was ushered quickly inside.

Lillian felt very vulnerable. Nobody knew where she was; anything could happen.

Standing at the open door was a young woman dressed more like a city girl. She wore a cream dress that hugged her figure, and her black hair was neatly pinned. She looked more glamorous than any of the other black women Lillian had seen, most of whom were wearing the uniform of domestics. Inside the tiny kitchen sat a small, wizened black woman Lillian judged to be in her sixties. She must have suffered from rheumatism, as she was very hunched over and her fingers were deformed.

'Miss Kenefick, thank you for coming,' the younger woman said. 'I'm Ruth Lane, Beau's cousin, and this is my mother, Flora Lane. My father and Beau's daddy were brothers.' The woman had the same accent as Beau, a slow, drawling way of speaking, and even this tenuous connection to him gave Lillian hope.

'Thank you for meeting me. I can see now that it is dangerous for you.' Lillian glanced around the small house. It was immaculately kept and smelled of baking and lemons.

'Can I offer you some coffee, ma'am?' Ruth asked.

Lillian had no taste for coffee, but she didn't want to offend or embarrass by asking for tea; she could swallow it down. 'Thank you, that would be lovely.'

The older woman busied herself with cups and placed a plate of biscuits on the table.

'Those biscuits smell delicious.' Lillian tried to engage the older woman, who had a hunted look in her eyes.

After an encouraging glance from her daughter, the woman spoke. 'Those isn't biscuits, ma'am. If y'all want biscuits, I coulda made them...' She looked disappointed, and Lillian knew she had caused offence but had no idea how.

'I think in England they call cookies biscuits, Mama.' Ruth smiled and her mother relaxed a little.

'Oh, yes, I'm terribly sorry. Beau and I would often laugh at the different words between British English and American English.' Lillian tried to come across as warm, not her strong point generally, she knew, but it was vital that these people trusted her. Otherwise, her chances of finding Beau would go from minuscule to nonexistent.

'So it's true? You is Beau's lady?' His aunt spoke again, her tone incredulous.

Lillian coloured at the description, but inside, she was proud as well – he had told his family about her. He had not forgotten her; he wasn't ignoring her. She knew that in her heart anyway, but it was nice to have it confirmed.

'Yes. All the time Beau was stationed in London, we were together. I...' She didn't know whether the existence of Austina would help or hinder her cause, as they were very religious people, but she decided to tell the truth. 'We loved each other very much, and we would have married if it had been permitted by the U.S. military. He had to return to finish his service and be discharged.' Lillian saw that both women were hanging on her every word.

'I found out I was expecting a child after he was sent home. She is with my family back in Ireland now. Here she is – her name is Austina.' She took out a photograph of her daughter and handed it to Ruth, who gazed in astonishment and then handed it to her mother.

'She's a beautiful child.' Flora handed back the photograph, her eyes giving nothing away.

'And you have come here to find him, is that your plan?' Ruth asked directly. Lillian did not get the impression she was intimidated by white skin the way so many other black people down here seemed to be.

'Well, yes. He wrote to me, saying he was in hospital. Then nothing further. But a few months later, I received a letter from you saying Beau had been arrested. I don't know how or why, and there doesn't seem to be any official charge or hearing or anything. I've been to the courthouse and spoken to the clerk there, and initially he told me that Beau had never been there. But I persisted, and then I said I would have my attorney from New York contact them and request the documentation of Beau's arrest and charge. It was at that point that they told me that they had moved Beau to someplace in Mississippi. That's all I know.'

Ruth and her mother exchanged a look, Flora's obviously warning her daughter against saying too much. It was clear she didn't trust white people.

'It's OK, Mama. Beau told me about Miss Kenefick and what she meant to him. I met him at church when he got out of the service, before I left for Chicago. I've come home to take care of my mother.'

Lillian thought, *she managed to escape the oppressive South. That's where the confidence comes from.*

'Beau was always good to me when I was little, Miss Kenefick.'

'Lillian, please.'

Ruth nodded. 'He was always looking out for me. My daddy died when I was a baby, and Beau and his brothers became my big brothers too. If you want to help him, I want to help you.'

'Well, if you can tell me anything at all about how or why he was arrested, that would help. I mean, was there an incident? Did he start a fight with a police officer?'

'Lillian, first things first. Y'all need to understand how things work down here. Beau didn't do nothin' wrong, and there was no crime. He knew he was in danger from the moment he got back. He told me the

192

whole story after church that first Sunday he was home. There was an officer – Charles Brigg, a white man – over there in Europe with Beau, and he knew that he and you were together. Now, his family owns one of the biggest mills in this state, and this Charles Brigg didn't like the idea of a black man being with a white woman. He's a firm believer in segregation. Beau told me that Brigg asked you to dance or something, and you turned him down? Anyway, he couldn't do anything about it over there in England, but he bided his time until he got back here, and then he sure made certain that Beau was punished.'

Lillian nodded. 'He was drunk, and I refused to dance with him, and he got quite ratty about it. Later that week, Beau and I were walking in Hampstead Heath when he passed and made some remark. I didn't quite catch it, but it was unpleasant. I mentioned to Beau what had happened at the dance, and he said the man was also from Savannah.'

Ruth went on. 'Well, that was Charles Brigg. Beau didn't help the situation by refusing the blue ticket – y'know, the way they try to force black soldiers to take this kind of discharge? It means you can't get the GI Bill, and it makes it really hard to get a job. The clan came one night and pulled Beau out. It was just him there, so he had no chance against ten or twelve of them. He was beat up so badly, but for some reason, they stopped short of killing him.

'He was dropped off outside the coloured hospital, and they patched him up, but Charles Brigg wasn't finished with Beau yet. When he got out of the hospital, Brigg sent the cops to his house – his uncle is the chief of police for this county. Beau was still pretty beat up, so he couldn't fight back, but they got lots of white witnesses to say Beau assaulted a police officer.'

Lillian was trying hard to focus and remember the facts rather than allow her emotions to get the better of her, despite the harrowing images Ruth's story generated in her mind. 'But were there no other witnesses who saw what really happened? Neighbours?' she asked.

Ruth looked at her with what seemed to be pity. 'That's what I mean – y'all need to understand. Sure, lots of people saw it, and that's how come I'm tellin' you, because someone told me. But those are the words of black people, and in a court of white men, the voice of the coloured don't stand for much.'

'But this is outrageous.' Lillian felt so angry. 'I mean, whatever about police brutality, they cannot surely lock someone up without a trial?'

'There most likely was some kind of a trial, but not one that anyone would recognise as any kind of justice.' Ruth shrugged. 'I know it must seem strange, Miss Lillian, but it's how it is, and you and your lawyer ain't about to change that.'

'But we can't just abandon him. I won't.' Passion burned inside of Lillian; she had never felt so strongly about anything in her life before. She loved Beau, and he loved her. She needed him, Austina needed him, and she was determined to get him back.

For the next hour, Ruth and her mother filled Lillian in on what they knew, which wasn't much. They had tried writing to Beau but got no reply, so they didn't know if he even received their letters.

Lillian allowed them to finish, and then decided she would go to Mississippi and try to visit Beau.

Ruth and Flora exchanged a glance.

'Miss Lillian, they ain't gonna let you within fifty miles of him, I can tell you that now. Parchman Farm is notorious. It don't have gates even. It's right there in the Mississippi Delta, and by anyone's reckoning, it's slavery all over again. You don't know what you're dealing with.'

Ruth wasn't trying to be negative, Lillian knew, but Beau's cousin wanted her to be realistic and not to get herself into even more difficulty. She had mentioned to the women how she was being watched by police. Nobody had approached her yet, but she saw them observing her as she made enquiries about Beau or sat having a meal alone in her hotel.

'Well, I appreciate your concern, I really do, but they don't know who they are dealing with either.' Lillian got up to leave. 'Thank you for everything. I understand you have put yourselves in danger even talking to me. I will get Beau released – I don't know how, but I will make it happen.'

The two women looked at her with expressions of pity.

'I sure hope you can, but Miss Lillian, please don't go down there alone.' Ruth stood square before her. 'Bad things happen to anyone who tries to change things, and one white woman fighting for a black man – that's just lookin' for trouble. Back where you come from, I know your family is very high up – Beau told me – but that don't mean nothin' here. Men like Brigg, he's got a lot of people on his side. I'm worried for you, and Beau would be too. I hate to say it, but maybe it would be better if you just go home. You're takin' on something you can't win.'

The oppressive feeling, the atmosphere of fear was very real. Lillian had a moment of doubt. Maybe Ruth was right. How could she expect to overturn generations of prejudice and hatred, and did she really know Beau anyway? Just because he had been arrested and couldn't contact her didn't mean he would have wanted her and Austina anyway. Maybe she was just a wartime romance and was now risking everything. Looking around Beau's aunt's neat tiny house, the subterfuge they needed to employ even to have her visit all of a sudden seemed so overwhelming. She thought of little Austina back in Robinswood; she needed her mother. She thought of Sam and Kate, and the image of her father flashed into her mind.

She had loved her father. What would he do? Despite his drinking and gambling, Lillian knew her father had a strong sense of fair play. He never looked down on people. Irish, English, Indian, women – he was very egalitarian. He would have liked Beau, and he would have had a good laugh at the outrage on the faces of the matriarchs in society when Lillian arrived with the handsome black man on her arm.

He hadn't prosecuted poachers on the estate like so many other landlords did. He just got Dermot to give them a talking to and sometimes a clip round the ear. There was more than enough to go around anyway. He never used snares, deeming them inhumane, and he was very well liked, unlike her mother, who came across as cold and superior.

Her father would encourage her if he were here, she was sure of it. She had Perry's lawyer, and she was going to contact him, see what he had to say about it all now that at least she knew where Beau was.

'Thank you for everything, Ruth, and I do appreciate your concern, but I can't just leave him. I know maybe you think this was just a wartime romance and I'm being like a silly schoolgirl. But I love Beau and he loves me, and he has a daughter who deserves to have her father in her life, so I have to do this. I know the odds are stacked against me, but I do have powerful friends in London who have good contacts in this country, and so I am not entirely alone.'

'I hope you do, Miss Lillian, 'cause you are gonna need every bit of help you can get.' Ruth paused and smiled, her first smile. It revealed a wide, gap-toothed grin. 'And just so you know, I don't think it was just a wartime romance for Beau either. I saw his face light up when he told me about you. He loves you, and I think if he knew he had a baby girl over in Ireland, it would make him the happiest man alive. So good luck. I sure hope you can get him out.'

Hearing those words from Ruth instantly dispelled any lingering doubts she had. Beau loved her, and she wasn't imagining the depth of his feelings for her.

'Thank you, Ruth. I'll do my very best.'

CHAPTER 28

*S*am sat in the bar of the Royal Excelsior Hotel in Exeter, hoping Mark would turn up. The whole space was decorated with holly, and a big Christmas tree stood in the corner.

The crossing had been atrocious; he'd vomited twice on the way over to Fishguard from Rosslare. The trip had to be made, but now he wasn't so sure it was worth the journey. He had written to Mark and said he would be there and had not had a reply.

Mark was a decent chap. He'd been badly affected by all that had happened, but men were not like women, the way they could talk about their emotions and all of that.

And even by women's standards, the Murphys were very emotional. He could never imagine Lillian talking to their mother the way Kate, Eve and Aisling did to their parents. They all discussed everything. Kate even told her mother she was worried about falling pregnant again when there was so much to do at Robinswood, and her mother had explained that there were certain days in a month when a woman was more likely to conceive and how to work that out. Sam had burned with embarrassment when Kate told him about the conversation – the idea that his mother-in-law knew about his sex life! But the Murphys were just like that, open and loving and kind to each other. He loved being a part of it.

He and Kate had had a frank discussion, and she said she wasn't ready for another baby. He understood, and while he'd love to be a father again, he could understand it from her point of view. Of course they could wait until she was ready. They restricted their lovemaking to the safe times according to Isabella, and so far, everything was fine.

He thought about his parents-in-law. They were so worried about Aisling. They had done so much for him, and he wanted to solve this – not just for Mark but for the whole family.

He sipped a pint of bitter, hoping it would settle his stomach after the seasickness, and read the paper. He had said three o'clock, and it was ten past now. He would wait till four. The hotel bar was filled with Christmas shoppers, and there was such good cheer about after years of miserable war. True, the rationing was every bit as bad as it had been, but people were making do as they always did, and at least they had their men back around the table; that was the most important thing.

'Hello, Sam.'

He looked up, and there before him stood Mark.

He got up and shook his old friend's hand. 'Lieutenant Belitho.' He grinned. 'A pint?'

'No thanks, I'll have a lemonade.'

Mark sat down, and Sam gave the waitress the order.

Sam folded his newspaper. He tried not to look shocked at the other man's appearance. Mark had always been a big, burly lad, a typical West Country farmer's son with fair hair, blue eyes and ruddy cheeks, but the man who stood before Sam was lean. In civvies, men often looked, less… He couldn't really describe it, more ordinary or something. But that didn't account for the change in Mark.

'So how've you been?' He began, trying to say the right thing.

'You know, it's been tough. You heard I did a spell in Dartmoor?' Mark accepted the drink from the smiling girl and took a sip.

'I did. Did you manage?'

'Actually, it was probably good for me. Got me off the grog anyway. I was drinking too much.'

Sam felt awkward with his pint, wishing he had ordered a cup of tea or a soft drink.

'How's Kate and the baby?' Mark asked.

'Oh, they are great. We're so busy, you know, trying to renovate Robinswood and get the farm up and running and all of that...' He didn't know how to bring Aisling into the conversation. There was a slight pause, and then Mark spared him having to try.

'And how's Aisling?' Mark's face was inscrutable.

Sam wondered if he should keep going with the jovial chat or just tell the truth. He decided on the latter. 'Heartbroken. She can't understand why you never turned up. She was devastated. She was about to write to you when she got the letter from your sister talking about divorce. She is really upset.'

'I doubt that very much.' Mark smiled bitterly.

'Mark, look, you can tell me to sod off and mind my own business if you like, but she's a great girl and she loves you, warts and all. What's going on?'

Mark sat back and placed the lemonade on the table between them. 'I know about her and that Irish chap from the drapery shop, so I don't know what you want me to say.'

Sam was confused. 'What Irish chap?'

'Oh, come on. You and I go back too far for this nonsense. I met him, and he told me everything.'

Sam could sense the anger and tension. 'You met who?' He had no idea what his friend was on about.

'Sam, why are you here?' Mark's brow furrowed. 'I know about Sean.'

'Sean? Do you mean Sean Lacey? Well, you might think you know something, but you're well wide of the mark,' Sam said with certainty. 'The day you were to arrive, Aisling was running down the lane to meet you off the bus, but she fell and broke her ankle. She was in plaster for ages. Oskar took her to the doctor – Oskar works with us,' he explained, noting Mark's look of confusion.

'I wasn't there, and the doc said she had to go to hospital to have it set. Sean took her to the hospital all right, as he was the only one with a car at that moment. I don't know exactly what you think happened, but I do know you got the wrong end of the stick there, mate. She has had nothing to do with him for years. I know he treated her badly years ago, before you ever met her, so of all the people she was likely to even be friendly with, he'd be at the very bottom of the list.

'I wasn't there, but Kate told me. Years ago, Aisling and Sean were walking out kind of, nothing serious. But anyway, they all went to a dance in the village. Jack – Eve's husband who died – well, anyway, he was there, as well as Kate and Eve. Apparently one of the Conlan sisters – I can't remember which one – was up against the wall outside with Sean when he was supposed to be with Aisling. Well, Kate – and I can well imagine this – had it out with the Conlan girl and Sean Lacey in front of everyone, and it was the most interesting thing to happen at a dance in Kilthomand for decades.

'Aisling was mortified, and that was why she insisted on coming over to London. Kate was coming to be with me, and she had planned to come alone, but Aisling said she couldn't stand the embarrassment of everyone talking about her and pitying her. So she left and joined the WAAF with Kate.'

He took a sip of his pint. 'Aisling has absolutely no interest in Sean Lacey, I can guarantee that. He might have ideas about her, but that's a one-way street.'

The reality of what had happened was dawning on Mark. 'So you're telling me Sean was making it all up?' He was incredulous.

'Definitely. I lived in the same house as Aisling up until recently, and I can assure you, she's not carrying on with Sean or with anyone else. She is just devastated, and she can't understand why you won't even speak to her to explain. When she got that letter from your sister about the divorce, she was so upset. Honestly, you should have just talked to her.' He wanted to wring his friend's neck for his stupidity.

Mark ran his hands through his hair in frustration. 'But that Sean seemed so sure. He just kept saying I'd put her through enough and all of that, that the kindest thing would be to not contact her, let her be, she'd only feel responsible for me and all of that… I've made a right pig's ear of this, haven't I?'

Sam didn't need to reply.

'I was such a mess after coming back. I couldn't sleep, drinking, fighting…' He looked straight at Sam. 'I never hit Aisling, though,' he was quick to clarify. 'I was so ashamed that I couldn't handle what I'd done, and I drank more. And she stuck by me, even with all of that, and I was horrible to her.' He wiped a tear angrily from his eye.

'I've been swimming. Every day in the sea, every day of the year. My father comes with me – he is the one who's got me back on the straight and narrow. He was in the last war, saw so much – worse than us, I suppose, in lots of ways – and he won't let me wallow. It seemed harsh, but it's worked. I'm better, back at work with my father on the farm, swimming, off the booze… I've managed to let it all go.'

Sam remained silent. His friend needed to get it off his chest.

'Should I go and see her?'

Sam tried to imagine what Dermot would do in this situation. 'Look, I won't lie to you. You've hurt her deeply, and I'm not sure how the Murphys will feel about you now. But then, they want her to be happy, and you're the only one who can do that.'

Mark nodded. 'If she'll take me back after being so bloody stupid, I'll give them all my word that I will take proper care of her…if she'll give me a chance to put this right.'

Sam was still frustrated with him. 'But why would you trust the word of a stranger over your own wife? I mean, this is Aisling Murphy we're talking about here. She was so loyal to you from day one, and yet you took a stranger's word rather than give Ais a chance to explain? I don't understand it, Mark, I just don't.' He wanted to do right by everyone, but this was hard to rationalise.

'I don't know. I just was so battered, I suppose. Dartmoor was hard. I was lonely, and fellows in there are always on about their wives going off with other men while they're inside. I used to tell myself that Aisling would never do that to me, but then Sean was there and saying what he said…'

'And has there been anyone else? Because if there was, you'd better tell me now…' Sam warned.

'God, no! Nothing at all. I just work and sleep. I miss her so much it hurts.'

Sam believed him on that score at least. 'All right, look, come back with me now. Can you do that? We can catch the early morning boat if we had a car?' Sam had gotten a lift at the boat from a friend, who took him as far as Bristol, and then he got on a bus to Exeter. His meeting in London would have to wait; this was more important.

'I've a car outside. Let me go home and grab a bag, and we'll be on the way.'

Both men stood, and Mark stuck out his hand once more. 'Thanks, Sam. You're a real pal. Whatever happens, I won't forget you for this. I don't know how I'll ever repay you.'

Sam smiled. 'Just sort things out with Ais first. But I'll warn you, she'll want to stay in Ireland, so you might as well come to terms with that as well. You can repay me in work on my estate.'

'Done.' Mark nodded.

CHAPTER 29

*E*ve was in the garden picking some rhubarb that her father had planted years ago when she sensed someone watching her. She stood up and spun around. Bartley was standing by the kitchen door.

He looked different these days, a little less wild. His hair was still longer than most men wore it, but it was oiled and back from his high brow. He wasn't as brown as he was when he arrived – he spent most of his days working indoors, she supposed. He wore a collarless white shirt and dark, reasonably respectable trousers. She knew the girls giggled when they saw him and were always trying to get his attention, but he was courteous and pleasant with them, nothing more.

His classes with the boys were as successful as hers with the girls. He taught them woodworking, gardening, building, plumbing – all the skills they would need to make them employable. Eve saw how happy he was when each of his young men got a job or an apprenticeship. It was their ticket not just to financial independence but also to lifting the stigma of being an orphan. She could tell, that as with her, to Bartley this was more than just a job; it mattered to him personally that these young people got a fair crack of the whip, something that had been denied them since birth.

'Bartley, good morning,' she said, glancing at the tiny scar on her. She'd used the cream he made, and the angry burn had faded quickly. She didn't know whether to thank him since he had not given it to her directly.

He'd made the little flat in the workshop his own. It was full of books and pieces of carved wood. He was an expert in plants and their various properties, though how he came to be so, nobody knew. He was the school's unofficial doctor, and he solved almost all ailments, from cuts and burns to pulled muscles and even the girls' monthly cramps. Once word got out with the girls that he had this amazing tea for period pains, they couldn't get enough of it. Though he spoke to Eve often, it was always about work and generally short exchanges. He didn't ever talk about himself.

She was thinking of asking him to look at Aisling's ankle when her family came up to Dublin. Her sister had written to say they had taken the plaster off, but it was still very weak and sore.

'Good morning, Eve,' he said, not moving.

She walked towards him, carrying the rhubarb. Her mother and sisters were going to come to the house for lunch later that day. They would take the train to Dublin and get the tram down to Dun Laoghaire from the city centre, as apparently the men needed the car after all.

'I'm glad I met you, Bartley. I wonder if I could ask a favour?'

'Certainly. What can I do for you?'

'My sister broke her ankle a while ago, and it is still very painful even though it's been in plaster. Do you think you would have anything for her? They are visiting me today.'

He thought for a long moment. 'What time will she be here?' he asked.

'Later today. They are on the bus from Waterford now.'

'I have something, but I need to make up another batch, as I may not have enough. I'll see what I can do, though.'

'That would be great, thank you. The students are all raving about your cures. They think you're better than any doctor.'

Bartley smiled. His face was transformed, and the dark eyes that usually looked brooding and deep suddenly sparkled. 'Most medicine comes from plants anyway, so what they get in a chemist's shop is usually more or less what I give them...' He looked pleased that they had acknowledged him.

'How did you learn all about the different plants?'

He paused, and she got the impression he was weighing whether he should respond. He inhaled and then spoke. 'I have always known. I'm the seventh son of a seventh son. My people are travellers, and we know about nature and the land.'

Eve was taken aback. As a child, she had been taught that the travelling people were to be given a wide berth usually, though her father always treated them with respect. They would come in the summertime, with their brightly painted wagons and a seemingly endless stream of children and animals. She remembered Mammy giving clothes that were too small for Kate to one woman who used to call. They were often wild-looking, but her parents insisted they were decent people and should be left alone and not harassed. Not everyone felt that way, though. She remembered old Mrs Lacey refusing to serve them and most people in the village either secretly or overtly supporting her.

'Oh... I thought you came out of...' She stopped herself; she sounded so condescending.

'An orphanage?' He smiled slowly. 'No, I was reared with my family. But when I was a young fella, I got in a wee bit of bother, and they sent me to reform school.' His soft Donegal accent was almost hypnotic.

'Oh...' She was at a loss as to what to say next. 'Was it awful?' she asked.

'Aye, it was.' He was not going to be drawn on that subject. 'Can I help you?' he asked, pointing to the vegetables. She had already picked the tomatoes from the glass house and some scallions as well; they were in a basket by the door. She'd had the butcher deliver a chicken, which she would roast and serve with salads and a rhubarb tart for dessert.

'Thanks.' She smiled. Suddenly, it was important he knew she wasn't judging him. People from poor backgrounds were always being put into institutions, often for no reason.

He carried the vegetables in and placed them on the kitchen table. Once inside, he seemed to take up so much space. Eve was suddenly acutely aware of his maleness. She had not been in close proximity to an attractive man in so long that it was a shock. He was different to Jack in so many ways. Jack had been a joker and full of life and fun. He had been the same height as her and handsome in a conventional way. Bartley was different. He didn't make conversation easily and was a deep thinker. He reminded her of the actor Ronald Colman, whom she had seen with her sisters in the film *Kismet*. She remembered Kate swooning over Colman as he appeared in some kind of Arab outfit, all dark-featured and black eyes. Eve had to suppress a smile. Though Kate was mad about Sam, she was sure her sister would have something to say about the brooding Bartley Doherty.

An awkward silence fell between them once more.

'I'd better get lunch prepared,' Eve said, just to break the quiet.

'Right.' He moved to go, then stopped and looked at her as if he was going to say something, but then he left. She sighed, suddenly disappointed.

A few moments later, he reappeared at the door. 'I can look at your sister's ankle later on if you like?'

'Thank you, Bartley, that would be great. I'll let you know when they get here. Well, you'll see them anyway coming up the avenue...' Eve was flustered; something about him made her nervous. She wasn't afraid of him, nothing like that – he was a very gentle person actually – but he was such an enigma, she never knew what to say to him.

'I will, aye.' He nodded. Again he paused. 'Eve, I was wondering...' His head was down, and his voice seemed quieter even than usual.

'Yes?' she prompted.

'I was wondering if you'd like to come out one night, maybe to the pictures or something, or for tea or a drink or something.' He never looked up; this was clearly very hard for him.

'Oh...' Eve was totally taken aback. Whatever she had expected, it wasn't that. Elena teased her about how she thought Bartley liked her, but she had dismissed it.

'It's fine if you don't want to,' he began, obviously embarrassed.

'No... I mean, I'm not saying I don't want to, I just...well...I don't usually...' Eve had no idea what to say next.

Elena breezed into the kitchen. 'Oh, for goodness' sake, she would love to go out with you, Bartley, thank you. How about tomorrow afternoon?'

Both Bartley and Eve looked appalled at being railroaded.

'What?' Elena looked at them innocently. 'Bartley likes you, Eve, and why wouldn't he? You are a beautiful woman, but you lock yourself up here day and night. Go out and have some fun! If that war taught us anything, it's that we must live our lives and take our chances. So many had their lives cut short – don't waste yours.'

Losing her husband the way she did had changed Elena. She was much more about living in the moment now and not worrying too much about the future. She was probably right. Since Jack died, Eve had felt like she was living underwater, the world above her there but blurred and far away. Bartley was handsome, and while she couldn't say she knew him, he was much loved by his students and Elena had great time for him. She wasn't ever getting Jack back, not in this lifetime anyway, so maybe it was time to move on. She knew in her heart he would want her to, just as she would have wanted it for him if she had been the one to die.

She turned to face Bartley, who looked like he wished the ground would open and swallow him.

'Look, we'll leave it...' he began, desperate to get away.

Her heart wrenched. How hard it must have been for him to come in and ask her out, especially being a traveller, as there was terrible prejudice against them. So if she refused, he would assume it was because she wouldn't go out with someone from his world.

Eve smiled. Kate brought home Lord Kenefick, and she was going to the pictures with a traveller. She could just imagine the gossip mill in Kilthomand. Kate had mentioned some of the poison-pen letters they were getting when she last rang, so her bringing a traveller into the community would no doubt be another reason to dislike the Murphys. A surge of rebellion coursed through her veins. To hell with them, or anyone else. Bartley was a nice man, and she was going to do it.

'Thank you, Bartley. I would love to go out with you. I haven't done this for many years, so I'm a bit rusty. That's why I hesitated, not because I don't want to.' She tried to soothe his discomfort.

'Are you sure?' His dark eyes met hers.

'Yes.' She smiled and he smiled back.

'Is tomorrow all right?'

'Perfect. I'll be ready at two?'

'I'll see you then so.' He exhaled, and it sounded like relief. 'And don't forget to send your sister over to me when she gets here. I'll be in the workshop.'

'Hey, Mr Doherty, you're only getting one sister now, don't be greedy!' Elena called as she searched the cupboard for something.

Bartley rolled his eyes at Eve and she giggled. He really did have a very nice smile.

* * *

THE MURPHY WOMEN arrived amid much hugging and squealing with delight. Jack and Austina were in the middle of everything, yelling their heads off, joining in the excitement. Elena had pulled out Georgie and Arthur's old toys, and Eve had constructed an enclosed play area in the corner of the bright sunny kitchen where they could potter around but couldn't escape. It was too cold to play outside; the crisp frost glinted on the shrubs so lovingly planted by Dermot. It was only ten weeks to Christmas.

'Ais, oh my God, I can't believe how long it's been!'

Eve and Aisling clung to each other. They had not seen each other since Mark and Aisling's wedding over two years ago. They wrote every week, of course, but it wasn't the same.

Isabella was deep in chat with Elena, who was filling her in on Georgie and Arthur's progress in school.

'They miss you and Dermot so much,' Elena said. 'They ask after you all the time. Georgie likes it, I think, but poor little Arthur is very lonely. He writes such sorrowful letters.'

Isabella looked sad. 'We miss them. They are like our grandchildren, every bit as much as Jack and...well, I'm not sure technically what relation that little fairy is.' She smiled and waved at Austina, who was blowing everyone kisses. 'But she's one of ours as well.'

Eve knew that Elena was going to mention the memorial service that day and that she was nervous about it. The story surrounding Thomas's capture and death was difficult, but Eve assured her that her family would be fine about the service. In fact, Eve had forewarned her mother by letter, so she knew for a fact that Isabella would be open to the idea.

'Georgie told me in her last letter that they were getting the boat on the twentieth to be home for Christmas.' Isabella knew the memorial service was planned for early January, at the end of the children's Christmas holidays, so she was giving Elena a way in to say her piece. 'So maybe you could come down? Dermot wanted me to invite you and the children to spend Christmas with us this year. We'll have Oskar and all the girls, and I think Perry and Violet are even planning a visit. Don't ask me where we'll put everyone, but we'll manage. We always do.'

Elena had always hosted Christmas because of the Murphys. The first year after Thomas went missing, she thought she would die with grief. Eve had been still in deep mourning for Jack, and the other two girls were in England, but Dermot and Isabella did everything they could to make it magical for Georgie and Arthur. This was going to be her family's first Christmas without them, and she had been dreading it. An invitation to Robinswood was like a dream come true.

'Are you sure, Isabella? Won't it be a hugely unmanageable crowd?' Elena wanted to be sure the offer wasn't just words.

'Elena, you and your children are family now. We've been through so much together, so of course you must come to us – this year and every year for as long as you want to. It won't be like here, with matching delph and beautiful furniture, but it will be fun and with plenty of food for the first time in years, and we'll have a great time.'

'Thank you.' Elena hugged her friend. 'The day you and Dermot walked in here was the best day of our lives – I mean it. I don't know how we would have survived these last years without you all.'

The lunch was noisy and full of laughs and chatter. The babies were cuddled and passed from one woman to the other, and they loved it.

As they finished dessert, Eve spoke. 'Now, Aisling, do you see that workshop over there?' She pointed to the shed. 'Go down there. There's a man inside who is quite incredible. He's the seventh son of a seventh son and a traveller, but he works here with Elena and me, and he will have something to help with the pain in that ankle.'

Aisling looked sceptical.

'She's right,' Elena said, tickling Austina, who was loving the attention. 'He is a wonder. Better than any doctor, and he's very easy on the eye as well.' She winked and the women all laughed.

'All right, but I'm bringing Kate with me.' Aisling wasn't convinced.

'Dead right you are. If there's a dreamboat in Elena's shed, I want to see him.' Kate jumped up, and her mother made a swipe at her with the tea towel she had picked up to start the cleanup. 'You are a married woman, Kate Kenefick!' she said, pretending to be shocked.

'Ah, Mammy, just because you're on a diet doesn't mean you can't look at the menu!' Kate winked and ran out the door, pulling Aisling behind her.

'Leave those dishes, Mam. I'll do them later,' Eve said as she hugged the sleeping Jack to her chest. The poor little lad was exhausted after all the excitement.

'Not at all. You made a lovely lunch, Eve, really delicious. That crumble is better than mine, and that's saying something,' Isabella joked.

Twenty minutes later, while Eve, Elena and Isabella sat companionably chatting over another cup of tea, Kate and Aisling came back.

'Oh my God,' Kate announced. 'Where did you find him? He's absolutely dreamy! Those eyes and the curls and that accent... I nearly melted in a puddle on the floor. Aisling of course kept him distracted with her stupid old ankle, but Elena, I don't know how you control yourselves with him at the bottom of the garden, I really don't.'

Everyone knew how loyal Kate was to Sam, but she was an incorrigible flirt at the same time. She couldn't help it, and she was still the dark beauty she always was.

Eve allowed Kate to lift her sleeping son and place him in his pram, gently kissing his soft cheek as she did so.

'Well, actually...' Eve said, and then flushed red.

'What?' Aisling encouraged her. 'Tell us.'

'Bartley and I are going out tomorrow. It's the first time, so maybe nothing will come of it, but he asked me and I said yes.' She couldn't help the grin that spread across her face.

'Oh you lucky duck!' Kate whispered, not wanting to disturb her son, who she was settling under his blankets.

Everyone knew how hard the last few years had been for Eve, losing her husband at such a young age, not having any children. She had been heartbroken for so long.

Isabella leaned over and placed her hand on her daughter's. 'I'm delighted, and it's what Jack would want too. He would never want you to lock yourself away, pet.'

'And for once, I agree with Kate. He is absolutely divine, and so nice and gentle as well. I hope it goes great, Eve.' Aisling smiled at her sister.

Nobody mentioned Mark, and she hid her own sadness. Eve had been through so much; she deserved something nice to happen.

Kate glanced at her watch. Sam was on his way with Mark. He'd phoned Robinswood last night with the entire story, that Sean Lacey had told a pack of lies. Kate wasn't sure how yet, but she would get her own back on that snake in the grass if it was the last thing she ever did.

The men had got the boat early that morning, and she told Sam to bring Mark to Elena's. They would be there shortly. She couldn't wait to see Aisling's face.

Twenty minutes later, Elena had brought up the memorial and

the Murphy women were full of plans for the day, when a taxi pulled into the driveway. Elena and Kate looked out the window, and Kate smiled to see her handsome husband and Mark getting out of the car.

'Ais,' Kate said gently to her sister who was playing with Austina, 'Sam went over to England. He was convinced that Mark wouldn't just cut you off like that. Well, he'll explain himself, but Sam brought him back. They're outside.'

The colour drained from Aisling's face. 'Mark is here?' She was shocked.

'Yes, I'll let Mark explain, but it was all a terrible mistake. So if you'll hear him out?' Kate asked, afraid that Aisling might put the run in him after everything.

Isabella, Elena and Eve said nothing, but Aisling ran outside.

Mark stopped and dropped his bag, and Sam paid the taxi driver and went indoors. The couple needed to be alone.

'Hello, Aisling,' Mark said shyly as the taxi pulled out of the driveway.

'What are you doing here?' Aisling asked, unsure of what she should do. He looked different, thinner, and the puffiness that the drink had brought to his face was gone.

'I'm here to see you, to beg you to forgive me for being such an idiot.' His eyes were bright, and he blinked away a tear. 'I… I don't even know where to begin…' He plunged his hands into his trouser pockets.

'Let me get my coat. We'll go for a walk.' She hurried back into the house, retrieving her coat and hat from the hall stand.

Sam was coming out of the downstairs cloakroom. 'Hear him out, Aisling,' he said, before turning to join the others in the kitchen.

She fixed her soft moss-green hat on her head in front of the large mirror over the fireplace in the entrance hall and realised she was so pale. The contrast between her dark, straight hair and her pale skin was stark. Seeing Mark again had been such a shock. She wanted there to be a perfectly rational explanation for his treatment of her, but it was hard to see what that might be. She was torn between delight and relief that he'd returned and trepidation. What if he was going to hurt her again? She couldn't take much more.

She joined Mark on the driveway and wordlessly began walking down the avenue towards the gate. The garden was a glorious riot of autumnal colours, and the lawn was covered in a carpet of fallen leaves in hues of bright yellow, ruby red, rich copper and forest green. Mark fell into step beside her, not touching her. She was acutely aware of him, his bulk at once familiar and strange.

At the bottom of the garden was a wooden seat, obscured from the house by a hedge. Despite the cool afternoon breeze, she turned to him and asked, 'Should we sit here?'

He nodded and sat down. She sat beside him, leaving space.

'I'm so sorry, Aisling, for everything. I've been such a fool.' His hands were resting on his knees, and his head was downcast. He stared at the damp grass between his feet.

'Go on,' she simply said.

The whole story came out: his time in Dartmoor, his excitement at coming to Ireland to show her that the man she married was back, his determination to put everything right, the realisation that once he had Aisling in his life, he could achieve anything. And then Sean Lacey: his conversation at the bus stop that day, how he was able to capitalise on every one of Mark's insecurities – that he was not worthy of her, that he was the wrong man for her, that she would be so much better off with Sean.

Aisling was dumbfounded. Was this true? Was Sean capable of such duplicity? She turned to Mark, forcing him to make eye contact for the first time since he started telling the sad story. 'And you believed him, rather than just asking me?' She was furious, not only at Sean, but at Mark as well.

'I did. I know now how stupid that was. I should have just demanded to see you, but he kept saying I'd done enough damage and to leave you alone. That your family too were so much happier now that you were with someone they knew and trusted, not a volatile British ex-convict,' Mark admitted miserably.

'How did he know you'd been in prison?'

'I don't know, but he said that he knew all along where I was. I assumed you'd told him.'

'I never told anyone except Kate and my parents.'

Suddenly, Aisling knew. Mossy often asked Sean to empty the postbox outside the draper's shop and bring the letters over to the post office in the evenings. Mossy had arthritis, and he found the fiddly key on the postbox difficult. Aisling was in the post office in the village one day when Sean arrived with the bag of post. She had joked with him about his change of career. She had just posted a letter to Mark. Sean knew Mark's surname, so he would have seen the address. Kate was right – once a snake, always a snake.

'So you took his word and then what?' Aisling's voice was hard.

'I went home. I told my family that I'd lost you, that it was my own stupid fault, and they were good to me, my parents and Delilah. I was tempted to go back on the booze, but my father put me to work instead. I worked like a dog from dawn to late into the night so that by the time bedtime came, I fell into an exhausted sleep. Delilah offered to write to you for me when I just couldn't bring myself to. I knew offering a divorce was all I could do now for you, but I couldn't bear to let you go.

'When I got Sam's letter saying he wanted to meet me, I didn't know what to think, but I went. A tiny glimmer of hope inside me, I suppose. He told me that Sean was a liar and that…well, what I should have known – that you would never do that to me.'

He turned and faced her. A little robin was perched on the now bare beech tree behind her. 'Can you give me one more chance? Just one more? I swear I will make it all up to you.'

'I… I want to, Mark, but you hurt me…' she said quietly.

'I know I did. I was a total eejit, as you'd say.'

She gave him a weak smile.

'But I swear, if you take me back, I will spend my life trying to make you happy, to be worthy of you. I love you so much, Aisling. You are the only girl for me, and that's all I can say…'

She looked at him. The boyish lad with the easy wit and the gentle humour was gone forever – the war had killed him. But this man, this new Mark, was in front of her, offering her happiness if only she could trust him again.

'We'd have to stay here…well, here in Ireland,' she said.

'Absolutely. If you want to live in Timbuctoo, I'll go there. Home for me is where you are.' He offered her his hand, palm up, and she placed her hand in his. His fingers closed over hers, and when he leaned in to kiss her, she knew. Mark was home.

CHAPTER 30

*L*illian took a train back to New York once she'd determined that Beau wasn't in Georgia but in Mississippi. She needed to speak to Walter Finkstein. She had an appointment at 9 a.m. at his Manhattan office overlooking Battery Park.

She took the subway all the way from 7th Avenue where she was staying down to the bottom of the island and emerged into the freezing-cold New York morning. Snow and slush were piled high, and commuters went about their business, seemingly oblivious to the bitter winds coming off the water. She hailed a taxi and gave the address, feeling quite pleased with herself at how well she was managing.

Walter was a tall, morose-looking man with protruding ears and incredibly long fingers; he reminded her of a basset hound her father once had. He was a man who spoke very few words, but he listened keenly to her story. When she was finished, he asked a few pertinent questions, which she answered as briefly as she could.

'And Lord Goodall sent you to me?' he asked.

'Yes, he did. He said you were the best.'

He raised his eyes to hers. 'He's not wrong.'

She didn't know if that was a joke or not, so she smiled but didn't laugh.

'And this man, you attest, is now being held, either with a trial that called no witnesses or without any trial at all, in the state of Mississippi?'

'Yes, I believe so.'

'You believe so or you know so?' He didn't look up from his pile of notes. It was most disconcerting, but she carried on.

'I can't say for sure, as nobody would engage with me officially, but Beau...Mr Lane's cousin seemed sure that he was at Parchman Farm in Mississippi.' Lillian swallowed, wishing she didn't sound so nervous. 'I've spent the last few weeks trying to make contact with other people who have relatives there, trying to find out if he is being held at that prison, even if the confirmation is unofficial. Eventually, I learned from Beau's pastor that another member of his congregation had been sent to Parchman. On the pastor's request, that man's mother wrote to her son, asking if Beau was there, and this young man wrote back to say he was. That is the only proof I have.' That whole process had taken several weeks, but Perry had warned her not to arrive to Finkstein with a half-baked story.

The lawyer lifted the receiver on his desk telephone and spoke. 'Can you get me Lord Goodall on the phone, please, Nancy?' He hung up and went back to his notes.

Lillian thought quickly but didn't dare say anything. Did this Walter Finkstein not believe she was who she said she was? Did he need to verify it with Perry?

Within a minute, the phone rang.

'Perry, it's Walter.'

No general chit-chat among old friends.

'Yes, she is.' He paused. 'Well, she's saying he's in Mississippi, and Gerald Grosvenor is governor down there now, so do you want to call him?'

Another pause while Perry spoke. Lillian wished she could hear.

'I would say so.' He listened to Perry once more. 'Very well, I'll leave it with you.'

Walter Finkstein hung up the phone and raised his head. Then he walked to the door and opened it. 'Miss Kenefick, Lord Goodall will be dealing with it from here. There will not be a fee. It turns out your stepfather is ideally placed to help you on this occasion.'

She stood. She had so many questions, but he held the door open and clearly was not going to discuss this or any other issue any further.

The traffic was bumper to bumper, and the snow piled everywhere was impeding its flow. It took over an hour to get back to her hotel. Once she did, she was frozen to the bone. She planned to telephone Perry and then take a long soak in the bath – or the tub, as Americans insisted on calling it.

As she crossed the lobby, the concierge approached her. 'A telephone message for you, Miss Kenefick.' He held out a yellow slip.

She remembered to tip him this time; this tipping business really was most trying.

Call me immediately – Perry

She got to her room, picked up the telephone receiver and gave the receptionist the number.

'Framington Hall.' It was Dawson, Perry's butler.

'Oh, hello, Dawson. It's Lillian. Could I speak to Perry, please?'

'Certainly, miss, please hold.'

A few clicks and then, 'Lillian?'

'Yes, Perry, it's me. I went to see your friend, but… Well, I don't know. He said you would deal with it… What on earth is going on?'

The line was crackly, but she could just about make out what he was saying. 'Go to Mississippi as fast as you can, tonight if possible. Beau will be released. You will need to pick him up from that prison at 2 a.m. sharp, so take a car and a driver, but time is of the essence.'

Blood pounded in Lillian's ears. Could this be true? 'How? I don't understand,' she managed to say.

'I'll explain when you get home, but for now, just get yourself down there. He will be released, but if his enemies get wind of it, you could both be in serious danger. I know the governor, and shall we say, he owes me a favour. I'll tell you about it another time. He said he will arrange to have Beau released at two in the morning so the press don't get wind of it. He is running for re-election next year, and freeing black men is not how you get back in office in Mississippi.

'Once Beau is out, you two are on your own. And it is not safe, Lillian, a white woman and a black man travelling together, so you'll have to hide him or something. Get yourself down there to that prison, and when you arrive, ask to speak to...' – she heard a rustle of paper – 'a man called Mortimer Bell. He will release Beau to you, but you must then get out of the state and up to New York without delay, do you understand? I have booked you both to fly back from LaGuardia Airport with Pan Am. You need to be there on the twenty-first of December at 9 a.m. I'll arrange his paperwork on this end, just pick up his passport at the desk. Don't ask. Being a peer of the British realm has some advantages. Lillian, you and Beau will be home for Christmas.'

She was so shocked and excited, her heart was thumping in her chest and she felt queasy. She couldn't speak.

'Lillian, are you there? Can you hear me?' Perry's voice was faint.

'Yes, Perry, darling Perry, I can hear you. Thank you so much...' she managed through her tears.

'Leave the thanks until you get home. That plane will stop at Shannon on the Irish coast. Get off there. Your mother and I will meet you at Robinswood – we are all congregating there for Christmas.'

'Thank you, Perry, thank you. We'll see you all in Robinswood.'

'Bye. Good luck.' He hung up.

Lillian forgot how cold she was. She replaced the telephone in its cradle, then lifted the receiver again.

'Good morning, Miss Kenefick, how may I help you?' the receptionist said.

'Can you book me on a flight to Memphis, please?'

'Certainly, ma'am. When would you like to go?'

'As soon as possible today.'

'Oh...well, let me see. I'll call the airline. I'll call you back, ma'am.'

'Thank you.' Lillian hung up. How was she going to get Beau out of that state without anyone noticing? Then she had an idea. She picked up the telephone once more.

'Good morning, Miss Kenefick. I'm still trying to connect with the airline…'

'Yes, that's fine. Can you also contact Hertz at Memphis airport, please? I will need a rental car.'

'Very well, ma'am. Shall I see about a driver?'

'No, I'll drive myself,' Lillian replied, grateful for her driving experience with ambulances towards the end of the war.

A brief pause. 'Very well, ma'am. I'll get right on it.'

She went downstairs to the concierge she had tipped so handsomely earlier. He was younger but about Beau's build.

'Excuse me, may I have a word in private?' she asked.

'Certainly, ma'am.' He led her into the concierge area, which was in a little glass booth by the front door.

'How can I help?'

'I would like to buy your uniform,' Lillian said.

'Excuse me, ma'am?' The man blushed. Perhaps he thought she was suggesting something untoward.

'Please, I need a uniform for someone. It's not illegal or anything – it's for a surprise birthday party, and the person is about your build, so I would like to buy your uniform.'

He looked totally baffled. 'But, ma'am, the hotel supplies our uniforms – there's a store of them in the back. It's not even mine to sell…'

She opened her purse and extracted a fifty-dollar bill. The man's eyes widened.

'If you can get a uniform in your size, maybe a little bigger even, to my room – I don't care who owns it – I will give you fifty dollars in cash. Nobody will ever know,' she whispered.

'Room number?' he asked quietly.

'332.'

He nodded, and she returned to her room. As she was packing her things, the phone rang.

'You are booked on the 4 p.m. flight to Memphis from La Guardia with Northwest Airlines. And I have booked a car for you to drive with Hertz at the airport. Will that be all, ma'am?'

'Thank you, yes. I really appreciate your help.'

'My pleasure, ma'am.'

Moments later, there was a gentle tap on the door. The porter was there with a large brown paper bag. She took the bag, and he stood inside the room while she gave him the money.

'Thank you,' she whispered.

The uniform was dove grey and had the name of the hotel on the sleeve, but it would have to do. The trousers might be a little short, but the jacket, shirt and tie, and most importantly the hat, would surely fit him.

The flight was uneventful. She should have been more excited since it was her first time flying, but all she could think about was Beau. What if she went to this place and this man refused to release him to her? Or had no idea who she was? A million thoughts spun round in her head, but she tried to calm herself. She needed to appear confident, even if she was quaking inside.

She received a few raised eyebrows at the car rental desk, but she signed her name as Lady Lillian Kenefick and was as condescending and toffee-nosed as she could possibly be. When the young man on the desk asked her if she was sure she could drive, she replied, 'I should imagine so, considering I spent most of the war driving around bombed-out London while you were presumably at your mother's knee.' She gave him her most withering look as she walked away in the direction of the Buick Super – a car she had never driven before.

It was 9 p.m. and pitch dark. After placing the bag containing the uniform and her few possessions on the back seat, she sat into the car. She inserted the ignition key and prayed it was like the old Bedford van that had been converted into an ambulance she used to drive. She found the choke and pulled it out to prime the engine, then turned the key. Miraculously, it started the first time. The engine roared to life as she put it in gear, gently pressed on the accelerator and released the clutch. It was a bit jerkier than she would have liked, but she could see the two men behind the car rental desk watching her. She drove away, glad she had not made a total fool of herself.

According to the map she had bought, the prison – or farm or whatever it was – was about a hundred miles away. She had no idea what the terrain would be like, but she hoped she could do it in time.

The city soon gave way to swampy marshland, which she assumed was where all the cotton fields were in summer. The landscape was inky black, and she tried to tell herself it was just her imagination, but it felt oppressive. It was still and eerie, and apart from the dark shapes of a few old colonial houses beyond the tree line, the land was empty. Mile after mile she drove, seeing only an occasional farm vehicle. There wasn't a soul walking on the road.

Eventually, she came to a sign, black writing on white. Mississippi State Penitentiary. She checked her watch. It was eleven thirty.

There were no fences or wires, just more of this marshy land as far as she could make out. She drove on, the lights of the Buick illuminating a single-lane road. Finally, she saw the outline of some low buildings on the horizon.

It was close to midnight. She had two hours to wait. She pulled the car into an area on the side of the road and switched off the engine. The stillness was eerie, and she could hear her heart thumping in her chest. Her hands gripped the steering wheel though the engine was turned off. She tried to picture Beau, Austina, her mother, Perry, Sam. Then she did something she'd not done in years.

'Papa,' she whispered, 'I don't know where you are – heaven, I hope – but if you can see me now or hear me, I really need help. I need you to be beside me for the next while because I am so far from home and everything I know and understand, but this is my only chance to get Beau out of here and for Austina to have her papa in her life. So please, help me.'

She looked out into the dark night, and to her amazement, a shooting star shot across the night sky. She wasn't alone.

Minute by protracted minute, the time went by. She'd never known time to go as slowly. The darkness was oppressive. She longed to turn on the headlights, but it would draw attention and she had no idea what or who might be in the darkness. Sitting still, she tried to remember lines of poems she'd learned at school – anything to occupy her mind. She looked at her watch again – ten to midnight. Had she only been there twenty minutes? It felt so much longer.

Suddenly, she heard voices. It was impossible to make out what they were saying, but they were male voices, and more than two. They came from behind the car, about fifty yards back, she guessed. Her mouth was dry, and she tried to breathe to steady her heart rate, but as she exhaled raggedly, she could feel pinpricks of perspiration break out on her back. The doors were locked, but she had nothing she could use as a weapon. She should have brought a knife or something, though given how her hands were trembling, she doubted she could even hold one, let alone use it.

The voices stopped; they must have seen the car. What should she do? Sit? Drive on? *These people do not want to release Beau. What if the prison governor agreed to release him but tipped someone off? Arranged to have us intercepted?* Her thoughts raced round and round in her head. The silence was deafening, but she knew there was someone there, watching her. Was it Charles Brigg? Or someone in his employ? She had to get away.

She turned the key, and mercifully, the engine roared to life. She drove forward, knowing she was too early for the meeting. She assumed the ribbon of road led only to the prison. She had no options – there were no turns either left or right. After a few minutes, she saw a light coming from a sentry box. It was impossible to tell if the box was occupied or not. Surely it would be safer to park near that place? Then she thought, *No, these people do not want to release Beau.* The authorities were not on her side. It was safer to keep moving. Sitting in the car, she was a target. The road widened slightly, so she stopped and did a three-point turn, driving back the way she came. She would just drive up and down that road until the appointed time; it was the only thing she could think of to do. She kept her eyes peeled for signs of life, and she was sure she saw a pinprick of light off the road to the right. A torch? She accelerated slightly, focusing on the road ahead.

Eventually, it was ten to two. She passed by the sentry box with its yellow light, but nobody was there. She came to a gate, dark metal with vicious spikes on the top. It was fifteen feet high on either side for about ten yards, and then the gate ended – there was nothing stretching out into the delta. It was as if the landscape itself was prison enough. The terrain was flat and marshy, and she assumed that it was impossible to walk on it, hence the lack of a fence. Even the land itself seemed threatening and inhospitable.

A little in front of the gate, two armed men sat in a wooden booth, lit by a pale-yellow light. She stopped and felt her mouth go dry. She swallowed and rolled down the window as one of the men approached. She adopted her best bored aristocrat demeanour.

'What is your business here, ma'am?' he asked. He was white and in his forties, she guessed.

'I am to see Mr Mortimer Bell,' she said with as much confidence as she could muster.

'Your name?'

'Lady Lillian Kenefick.' She sighed impatiently.

He stared at her. His cold grey eyes bored into hers defiantly, but he said nothing. After a long moment, he sauntered back and opened the gates for her to drive through.

She continued up a long road until she saw a colonial-style house, two storied, with a porch. It looked incongruous with the setting, but it was almost a replica of the lovely homes she had seen in the white part of Savannah.

As she approached the house, a uniformed man appeared and indicated she should turn in and park, which she did.

The front door of the house opened. Light spilled out onto the porch, and a short, heavyset man wearing glasses and a brown double-breasted suit emerged and approached the car.

'Miss Lillian Kenefick?' he asked, his tone icy.

'*Lady* Lillian Kenefick,' she corrected. 'Are you Mortimer Bell?'

A nasty smile played around his lips. 'Y'all got some airs and graces for a nigger-lover.'

Lillian was shocked and quaking inside, but she managed to maintain her façade of disdain. 'Where is Mr Lane? Bring him to me immediately.' She decided that being in any way grateful or deferential to this man was going to give him the upper hand, so she defaulted to her best British upper-class condescension.

He gave a snort of derision and went back into the house.

Long seconds ticked by. She had no idea what was happening. Should she get out? Follow Bell? As she deliberated, Lillian watched the door of the house and then could hardly believe her eyes. Beau, her darling Beau, was on the porch. He was still tall and powerful-looking, wearing black striped trousers held up by braces and a white cotton shirt. He was shackled at both his hands and feet. Behind him was another uniformed guard, this one armed. Beau towered over both guards.

The first guard bent and unlocked the shackles while the other kept his weapon trained on Beau. The black man kept his head down; he didn't dare even look in her direction. Lillian watched from the car, her mouth dry. She longed to run to him but forced herself to remain seated and still.

Once Beau was free of the restraints, the second guard butted him in the back with the gun, pushing him in the direction of the car. Beau walked ahead of the weapon, not catching anyone's eye, eventually reaching the car. He opened the back door and got in.

Lillian started the engine and reversed. Her passenger didn't say anything. She turned the car as expertly as she could as the two guards stared her down, one with the gun still cocked and ready.

Her hands were shaking as she tried to find first gear. She thought she had it, but the car stalled, spluttered and cut out. The two guards remained still. She turned the key once more and heard a soft voice from the back seat.

'Gently now, sweetheart, don't flood it.'

She slowly released the clutch and increased pressure on the accelerator, and they were off back down the long driveway. The whole thing had taken less than ten minutes.

The gate was open this time, so she just drove straight through. She didn't dare stop. She would get away from Parchman as quickly as she could, and then she would give him the uniform. At night, nobody was around, but as daylight broke and they drove to more built-up areas, they would be noticed.

'Get down, Beau. There are some men lurking about out here. I don't know who they are, but we need to get out of here as fast as we can.'

'Yes, ma'am,' he replied, and in the rearview mirror, she caught his broad white-toothed grin and returned it.

Beau was beaming that smile of his that felt like it could light up the whole world. 'I always said you were one of a kind, Lillian Kenefick, but I sure had no idea just what a woman you are.'

She smiled. 'I can't believe it's actually you. I thought I might never see you again, I –'

Before she could finish her sentence, the car gave an ominous jerk, chugged along for a few feet, then gave a shudder and stopped. Lillian panicked. Beau sat up, and together they peered out at the darkness. She tried the engine again and again, but nothing. The engine ticked over for a moment but died.

'Sounds like we're out of gas,' Beau whispered.

He got out and she followed him. The crescent moon and stars twinkled in the blue-black night sky. She shuddered. Those men were out there, and she was convinced they were there because of her and Beau. Now they were stranded. She felt tears sting her eyes but blinked them back. This was no time to fall apart. Beau took the dipstick and stuck it into the tank. Pulling it out, he just managed to read the calibrated stick in the pale moonlight.

'Well, we got enough gas, so it ain't that.' He sounded relieved.

'What's wrong, do you think?' Lillian whispered, her eyes darting anxiously into the bushes and trees that lined the road before the land became marsh.

Beau shrugged. 'You got a match?'

Lillian nodded. She retrieved her handbag and dug around until she found her lighter. She flicked it and held it as Beau examined the engine. He took her hand and moved it closer to the workings so he could see better, and even in these circumstances, it felt so good to touch him again.

'Check the trunk – there might be a tool kit or somethin',' he whispered.

Lillian went around and opened the boot, and to her relieved amazement, there was a small bag containing a wheel brace and a few other smaller tools, along with a spare tyre. She took the canvas rolled-up bag and returned to Beau.

'This is a Hydramatic transmission. We had this on some military vehicles during the war – it's sensitive to the engine throttle position. Let me see if I can adjust it,' he whispered.

She stood watching as he tinkered, taking off hoses and wiping them on his shirt, and she prayed that he could fix it – and quickly. A rustling noise from off somewhere to the left disturbed the eerie night silence. She swallowed and placed her hand on his arm. He stopped and listened. There were voices coming from the vegetation behind them. Beau eased the bonnet down without a sound and placed his finger to his lips as he crept around to the driver's side of the car, sat in and pulled the door closed almost silently. Lillian carefully opened the door on the other side and slid into the passenger seat.

A torch flashed in through the back window. The voices were closer now. Lillian could feel beads of perspiration run down her back. *Please God, and Papa, and anyone else who can help, let the car start,* she begged silently. Beau pushed the choke in so as not to flood the engine and turned the key. Mercifully, the engine roared to life. He turned and grinned then put the car in gear and drove away from the men and their torch. They didn't dare look back, or even speak for a few moments. Lillian felt her heart rate and breathing gradually return to normal.

'Are you all right?' she asked him, her gaze fixed on his handsome profile.

He reached over and took her hand in his, giving it a slight squeeze. 'I am now, thanks to the good Lord and my incredibly brave lady. I sure am now.' He shook his head in amazement.

CHAPTER 31

Georgie was helping Isabella stir the gravy on the hob of the huge gas oven that took up almost one wall of the kitchen at Robinswood. It would be served with the turkey and ham at the feast the following day. The whole house was a hive of activity, and despite the biting cold and pitching snow outside, the house smelled and felt wonderfully warm and cosy.

Georgie was regaling Isabella with how truly dreadful the food was in her boarding school and how she dreamed every night as she lay in bed of the wonderful dinners and desserts Isabella made. Isabella made all the right noises of horror and disgust as the girl described lard instead of creamy butter and dry bread with no jam. The food supplies in England were still very scant, and people were barely surviving. Georgie and Arthur had been eating like horses since they came home to Ireland. Despite missing everyone, the girl seemed to be thriving at school, playing hockey, learning Latin and making lots of new friends who – she assured Isabella – knew all about her and Dermot. One friend had thrown a pillow at her for describing Isabella's steak and kidney pie, oozing with gravy and chunks of beef in buttery flaky pastry, as they lay in bed after a dinner of boiled potatoes and cold Spam.

All her friends were jealous that she was going home for Christmas, and the invitation to come to Robinswood had been greeted by squeals of delight according to Elena. Isabella and Dermot were delighted to be reunited with their little charges again.

The children insisted on Dermot tucking them in, just like he did when they were in their house in Dublin, especially because they loved to hear stories about how naughty they were when Isabella and Dermot first arrived at their home in England. Dermot embellished their acts of terror for maximum effect. The tales of their exaggerated antics had both children in paroxysms of laughter, which could be heard all over the house.

Wherever Dermot was, there was Arthur; the boy had not let him out of his sight since he arrived. Unlike Georgie, the poor lad hated boarding school and confided in Dermot that the other boys bullied him because of his Irish accent. It broke their hearts to see their happy little lad so downhearted, and Dermot vowed to speak to Elena before the holiday was over about letting him stay and attend school in Ireland.

Georgie hated the cold, so she was happy to remain in the kitchen, helping with taking care of Jack and Austina and acting as chief taster for the endless stream of food Isabella was preparing for the gathering.

The kitchen of Robinswood had fared better over the years than the rest of the house, so after a good scrubbing and a few minor maintenance jobs, it was up and running again. The big black stove only needed a few valves replaced, and the enormous worktop had been scrubbed with carbolic soap and disinfected so often, it was almost white. The copper pots and pans shone as they hung from the ceiling, and the larders were full once more.

Food was still rationed, but Robinswood was close to being almost self-sufficient again. They grew their own vegetables and fruit, all of which were stored and preserved to be available all winter. They had cattle and sheep, goats and hens and a few very grumpy and aggressive pigs who, much to everyone's delight, were now sausages and bacon. Isabella had been studiously saving her herbs and spices, growing what she could and storing and sparing the rest to do the Christmas baking. She and Dermot were determined to make this the best Christmas they ever had.

She was conscious of not usurping Kate as the woman of the house – it was Sam and Kate's house after all – but her daughter was quick to point out that it would still be a rodent-infested, draughty ruin were it not for her parents, so it really did feel like a family project. Isabella lay in bed at night, Dermot beside her, in their old farmhouse, but it felt different. This time, it was not a grace-and-favour house, and they were not there on the whim of the aristocracy. It was their own home, and it felt wonderful.

Having Oskar and Austina living with them was lovely, and the German was besotted with the little girl. He took her for walks in her pram, and at night, she sat on his knee as he read her stories and sang her songs. It was as if she was healing him somehow. He smiled more these days, and all the talk of returning to Germany to face the courts had stopped. He was Irish, and he felt at home there.

One day, just a few weeks previously, as Isabella was cleaning the windows, Oskar came in. 'Isabella, may I ask you something?'

She got down off the chair she was standing on and replied, 'Of course, what is it?'

He was always very courteous and friendly, but he rarely saw her alone. He was up early every morning and worked hard all day, and when he wasn't out in the fields, he was in his little bedroom reading.

'Do you mind me being here?' He stood before her, his cap in his hand, and she felt a wave of affection for her husband's oldest friend. 'You have not said or done anything to make me think it, please understand that, but Dermot invited me without ever speaking to you that day I just turned up out of the blue. And I wanted you and I to talk without him there. Please, be honest.'

She smiled and invited him to sit, then put the kettle on. 'No, I don't mind, but thanks for checking. In fact, I like having you here. I will admit, at the start, I was a bit doubtful – not you as such, but having anyone living with us. But you're family now, Oskar, so asking if I mind you being here is like asking do I mind Aisling being here or

Sam. So to answer your question, I love having you here. You are a great help around the place. Dermot is delighted to have you back, and we would not be anywhere near as close to renovating the place without you. And if that wasn't enough, this little one adores you. Don't you, pet?' She picked Austina up from the floor, and the child immediately put her pudgy arms out to Oskar.

He took her and gave her a cuddle. 'And I love her. Thank you, Isabella. It's been on my mind. I thought it was all right, but I wasn't sure.' He exhaled, relieved. 'I wish you could have met my Birgitta. You would have liked her, I think. She was a lot like you – strong, kind, a good person.'

'You must miss her terribly,' Isabella said. Oskar so rarely opened up about his life before Robinswood, she was careful not to overstep the mark.

'I do. Every day. But I am glad as well that she didn't live to see what her country became. She was a librarian, loved books, and to see the Nazis burn them, to kill free thinking, to end any debate or dissention except their own twisted version of things... She would have hated it.' He took the cup of tea she offered. 'She would probably have ended up in a camp because I know she wouldn't have been able to keep her mouth shut.' He smiled. 'She was a very opinionated person.'

'The best women are.' Isabella winked.

'Aaskah!' Austina yelled, and Isabella and Oskar looked at her, astounded. Her first word!

'Aaskah!' she said again, delighted to have their attention.

'Who is that, Austina?' Isabella asked, pointing at Oskar.

'Aaskah!' she said again.

'Good girl! Yes, that's Oskar. Well done, darling.' Isabella kissed her.

'And who is that?' Oskar pointed at Isabella.

'Ella,' the baby announced, thrilled with herself. 'Ella, Ella, Ella, Ella...'

'We'll have to knock those out of her before her mother gets back,' Isabella said, grinning.

'Any news of that situation?'

'Nothing. She just turned up. She had asked Sam if she could leave Austina here – she gave us a lot of money, to be fair to her – and left to go to America to find Beau. I don't know any more than that. Though she was distraught at leaving the baby, so she seems to have grown some bit of a heart.' Isabella rolled her eyes. Lady Lillian had a lot of making up to do with her.

'I hate the thought of her coming back and taking her away,' Oskar admitted. 'I know she's her mother and everything, but Austina feels like she's part of us now...'

'I know. It's going to be hard, all right.' Isabella caressed the baby's curls and handed her a bottle of milk. The child could hold it herself, so she settled into Oskar's arms to drink it. He adjusted his position to make her more comfortable. Looking down at her contented little face, he said, 'And at least here, she is one of us, the oddball crew that we are, so the colour of her skin doesn't matter. But I can't imagine life for her in the drawing rooms of the aristocratic homes of England. Will they be kind to her?' Oskar nuzzled her head and she snuggled into his chest.

'Well, if Lillian can find Beau and bring him back, she has some hope. He's a lovely man, really nice and decent, you know?' Isabella shrugged. 'Then at least she'll have him to protect her, and Lillian does love her. So I'm not saying it will be easy, but they could manage. And Perry is being a great help to her. He loves Austina too.'

'Enough love and she can survive anything, I suppose.' Oskar stroked her cheek as she closed her eyes and dozed in his arms.

'And how about you?'

'How about me in what way?' He smiled.

Isabella had suspected for a while now that there might be a blossoming of a relationship between Oskar and Elena. He had visited her in Dublin, and Elena wrote afterwards. It took him a while to reply.

Dermot had told her that Oskar was agonising. He really liked Elena but wasn't sure it was appropriate. Dermot encouraged him to get to know her, and eventually he wrote back. He visited her in Dublin a few more times, and now they wrote regularly. He lit up when Dermot announced she and the children were coming to Robinswood for Christmas.

'You know what I mean.' Isabella raised her eyebrows.

Oskar stood up and passed the sleeping Austina into her arms. As he did so, he kissed his friend's wife on the cheek. 'There's a herd of sheep to be rounded up. Thanks for having me, Bella. Dermot's a lucky man.' He winked and was gone.

Georgie's singing of a Christmas carol brought her back to the present.

'Ding, dong, merrily on high...' the girl sang tunelessly.

They had all worked day and night, Christmas being the goal, and now it was here, the family was gathered, and she could not be happier.

She and Georgie had put the finishing touches to the decorations earlier with big red ribbons on the Christmas wreaths Isabella had made with the children the previous day. They hung one huge one on the front door and another in the hallway over the big gold-framed mirror. They loved pinning in the dried fruit and the holly with its bright-red berries. Oskar made some beautiful stars and crosses out of reeds, and they had pinned them on as well, so they looked very festive indeed.

'Mummy is talking to Oskar again. He makes her laugh.' Georgie was a precocious thirteen-year-old now and wanted to be treated like an adult. She was peering out into the yard where Oskar was chopping logs for the fire; Elena had brought him out a cup of tea. They were chatting while he took a break to have his drink. Their breath could be seen on the cold air, and they leaned side by side against the old wall that enclosed the cobbled stable yard.

Isabella looked at the girl she and Dermot had raised. She reminded her in so many ways of Kate when she was that age, full of fun and mischief but deeply sensitive under it all. 'What do you think of him?' Isabella asked as she peeled potatoes.

'I like him, and Daddy said lots of nice things about him in his letters to me.'

'How are you doing with that?' Isabella asked gently.

'I was very sad when I got the letters. I wasn't able to read them for a while, but then I did, and it was like Daddy was speaking to me. I know he's dead, and it's so sad that he almost made it, but he would want us to be happy, I think.' The child suddenly looked so sad.

Isabella turned and gave her a hug, and she felt the girl relax against her. 'Your father would be very proud of you, you know?'

Georgie nodded. 'And are you and Dermot proud of us?' she asked, suddenly looking much younger than her thirteen years.

'We are as proud of you two as we are of our own girls. You and Arthur are like our grandchildren, and we love you both very much.'

Georgie grinned. 'Do you think Mummy likes Oskar?' she asked.

Isabella smiled. She had mentioned it to Dermot in bed the previous night.

'It would be an odd match,' Dermot had said as she lay with her head on his chest, his arms around her. 'But sure, if any two people deserve a bit of comfort and happiness, it's them. What do you think?'

Isabella agreed. There was a time when she would have found it bizarre that Elena would fall in love with the man who had kidnapped her husband, but life wasn't that simple, and she agreed with Dermot – let people find love and happiness wherever they could.

'Would you mind if he did?' she asked Georgie.

'No, I like him. He's nice and he always has time for you, you know? And he was Daddy's best friend. If I'm talking, he always takes me seriously and he really listens.' Georgie seemed happy enough. 'And Mummy has been sad for so long, I'd like someone to make her happy.'

'Well, you never know,' Isabella said as she saw Elena throw her head back and laugh at something Oskar told her. The body language was good.

CHAPTER 32

The dining room, set for sixteen guests, looked wonderful.
Enough crockery had been unearthed from various boxes
and lofts, and Dermot and Oskar had left Mark in the workshop
making chairs all week. He was a great help on the estate being
already a farmer's son, but he was also a talented woodworker.

Everyone was so happy to see him back, and Aisling looked like
there was a light switched on inside her. There had been a long and
painful conversation between her and Dermot and Mark when he
turned up.

Isabella recalled that conversation at the farmhouse table that first
night, when everyone else had made themselves scarce and it was just
Aisling and Mark and her and Dermot. She would never forget the
shock of hearing Mark say, 'I got into fights, but I never would hurt
Aisling. I know it's what you're worried about, and I don't blame you,
but I'm a different man now. Back then, I was drunk and angry, and to
be honest, not right in the head. That's not an excuse, but I'm just
trying to explain. I don't drink any more, nor will I ever, I swear. And
I won't say I'm cured, mentally I mean, but I'm much better. I promise
all three of you – Ais, and you, Isabella and Dermot – that I will never
again raise my hand in anger to anyone.'

Isabella looked at her daughter and saw the pleading in her eyes. She wanted her parents' blessing and for them to forgive Mark as she had. A silence hung over the table.

Dermot was the first to speak. There was a steely edge to his tone that Isabella rarely heard these days but knew of old. 'It's our daughter's choice who she shares her life with, and she wants you. I think you are a decent man, Mark, I always have, but let me be very clear on this.' He paused and locked eyes with his son-in-law. 'If you ever hurt her again, in any way, I will ensure you are cut out of her life forever. In the future, you only listen to each other. Not stupid gossip. You need to straighten up and trust her. Our daughter is loyal and honest and did not deserve what you put her through, but you know that. Do you understand?'

'I do,' Mark replied.

No more was said on the subject, and he started work on the estate the very next day. They needed lots more hands if the hotel that Kate envisaged was to come to fruition. It seemed a long way off, and sometimes Kate got despondent at it ever happening, but Sam was quick to reassure her, reminding her how far they'd come.

Aisling worked alongside her mother and sister, doing all that was necessary, from mending and cleaning to caring for the babies. It was just like the old days, only without the spectre of Lady Violet Kenefick looking down her snooty nose at everyone and everything.

Aisling and Mark had made the decision to leave Portwye and all its sad memories and start their new life in Robinswood. They went back to Devon for a week to box up their things and gave Mark's parents back the house. Though his mother and father were sad their son was leaving to live in Ireland, they saw how miserable he was without 'Ashley', as they now called her, and they were happy he was almost back to his old self. Mark tried correcting their pronunciation of her name over and over, until eventually she begged him to stop. She didn't mind. Delilah apologised for the curt letter, but she had believed Mark when he told her what Sean had told him – she was so embarrassed.

The two women had a cup of tea and a long chat on one of the days when Mark and his father had taken the boys fishing.

'I don't blame you, Delilah. I'm the same with my sisters. If they told me that one of their men was going behind their backs, of course I would take their side. You were sticking up for your brother.'

'Thanks, Aisling. There, I said it right, didn't I?' She smiled.

'You did!' Aisling laughed.

'I got Mark to teach me. I know my parents struggle with it, but it's not on purpose, I promise.' Delilah laughed too. 'I'll have them trained properly for your next visit.'

'I'm just glad they are happy for us. I don't care what they call me.'

'It's all been so hard.' Delilah topped up her teacup with the watery beverage Aisling remembered. 'Mark being in prison, and then him back here moping about like a wet weekend, and that horrible man saying all those things...' She shook her head. 'Why would someone do that?'

'Oh, don't worry. He won't get away with it. Already my family have decided we won't be ordering anything from his shop ever again, and Robinswood is his biggest customer. He tried to see me a few weeks back, but I won't ever speak to him again. Kate told Biddy Casey what he did – she's called "News of the World" in Kilthomand – so the whole place had it within minutes. He's mortified and rightly so. I think, though, the worst punishment is seeing me and Mark so happy. He lost and we won.'

Tears shone in Delilah's eyes. Immediately, Aisling regretted her words. 'Oh Delilah, I'm sorry! I know how hard it is for you, and me being all happy ever after isn't helping, I'm sure...'

'No...no, please. Don't be sorry. I'm so happy that you and Mark sorted it out. He is so in love with you, and he's been torn apart since you left. We are all just relieved, to be honest. I just... I...' She wiped her eyes. 'I miss Terry so much. Every single day. The boys are growing up without him, and now Mark will be in Ireland, and I'll just miss him – and you.'

She leaned over and held Aisling's hand. 'You calling to me for a cuppa in those early months was so nice. Nobody wants to be around the weeping widow, you know, but you always called in, played with the boys, and we all looked forward to your visits.' She pulled a handkerchief out of her sleeve. 'I don't have a sister, and I felt like I was getting one, and now you'll both be over in Ireland. I know it's the right thing for you, but...'

'Delilah, it's only Ireland, not the moon. Come and visit. Seriously, my sister has an enormous house now, and the boys would love it – a big farm with animals, rivers and trees and so much more food than here. Please say you'll come?'

Delilah smiled. 'We'd love that, if you're sure?'

'Absolutely sure. We're sisters now. And you haven't met Eve and Kate because you were pregnant when me and Mark got married, but you will love them, I promise you. And your boys will love my dad. They can go fishing and climb trees, and he'll probably even let them fire the rifle.' Aisling giggled.

'Oh, Lord, can you imagine? Don't tell them that.' Delilah laughed through her tears.

'And you need taking care of.' Aisling squeezed the other woman's hand. 'My mother's apple crumble with creamy custard and a good strong cup of tea is the answer to every problem on earth. Come over when the weather improves, and you won't all be thrown all around the Irish Sea.'

The week had passed quickly, and the night before they left, Mark's parents hosted a dinner. His father made a speech about how proud he was of his family, all of them, especially his Irish daughter-in-law, 'Ash-Ling'.

His correct pronunciation caused a cheer at the dinner table. As they left, Mark hugged his sister and pushed an envelope into her hand. Aisling knew it was the fare for her and the boys to come over to visit.

Once back in Robinswood, they stayed for a while at the farmhouse with her parents, but with Austina and Oskar there as well, it felt a bit crowded. And anyway, they needed their privacy, so they rented a house in the village.

Aisling happily walked home in the evenings hand in hand with Mark for all of Kilthomand to see. His arrival was of course a nine-day wonder, but soon Mark became a member of the community. He joined the local football team and made lots of friends. He even went to the pub after matches sometimes but never indulged in anything stronger than lemonade.

There had been an incident at a match. Mark had scored a winning goal, and everyone was congratulating him after the final whistle. As the village gathered in celebration, Charlie Warren muttered a remark about how the Murphys were really getting too big for their boots, and Mark heard him. He didn't react with his fists as he might once have done. There was silence as the big Englishman turned to face Charlie. Tension bristled in the air.

'You have a problem with my wife's family, don't you, Charlie? Why don't you just say whatever it is you have to say, and we'll deal with it now in the open instead of whispering and muttering and hiding behind anonymity?'

Dermot had received a letter in front of Mark one day, so he told him what had been going on and who he thought was behind it.

Mark's eyes never left Charlie's. Despite a show of bravado by snorting in derision, Charlie coloured, his eyes betraying his guilt.

'Nothing to say?' Mark faced him down, towering over the Irishman. Mark was wearing the green and gold jersey of Kilthomand, and though he still spoke in his West Country accent, he was seen as a local now.

'Yerra go on back to England. We drove your kind out once, and we'll do it again.' Charlie spat, anxiously scouring the gathered crowd for support. Eyes were downcast, and while one or two of the men looked like they might agree with Charlie, nobody backed him publicly.

'My parents-in-law, Sam, the women and all of us are trying our hardest to turn Robinswood into something – not just for us, but for the whole community. A hotel, where there'll be jobs, and we'll need all sorts, supplies, tradesmen, all of it. This development will be good for Kilthomand, and what's more, it will be done by locals. I've only married in, this isn't my place yet, but I think people should be supporting the Murphys and Sam, not hindering them. It will be good for everyone. It's not easy, and I know they'd appreciate your support.'

There was a murmur of conversation.

''Tis true for you, Mark.' Mossy from the post office jumped in. 'And people around here wish you all well, don't we?' Mossy looked around the gathered crowd for confirmation. Several people nodded and smiled. 'God knows we could do with a bit of action in Kilthomand, and if young Kate Murphy gets her way, she'll fill the place with returning Yanks with loads of dollars to spend. And won't the people of the village be happy then?'

Dermot had appeared by now, and the gathering hushed. 'Thanks, Mossy,' he said.

'Well, 'tis true, Dermot. We all owe you men a debt.' Though it was never openly said, everyone knew Mossy was referring to Dermot's IRA past. 'But those days are over, and we are a free independent country thanks to Dermot and men like him. But 'tis time to build up the country now and let go of all the old gripes from the past.'

A cheer went up as the referee called the team onto the pitch to receive the cup. Mark put his arm around Aisling as they walked.

'Well done,' she whispered, so proud of him for standing up for the family.

He winked down at her and gave her a squeeze. Her Mark was back.

The plan eventually was to build a house on the Robinswood estate, but that would be in the future. For now, they were just happy rekindling their romance. Mark was full of remorse for everything he'd put her through and vowed he would spend his life making it up to her.

It wasn't all roses and sunshine. He still woke some nights in terror, recalling his wartime experiences, but now he talked to her. Sometimes they got up in the early hours and went for a long walk, and day by day, he was managing to put the horrible memories behind him.

He spoke to Oskar too. They enjoyed each other's company and both understood the horrors of war. They were quickly becoming firm friends.

He loved long days on the farm, and at night, he and Aisling cuddled up together in their little house. They were happy.

CHAPTER 33

*R*obinswood looked magical. It had snowed for a few days, so the entire house and grounds were shrouded in white. The rich foliage of the evergreen trees and shrubs was only broken by the red berries on the holly bushes and the red Christmas wreath on the enormous front door. The house looked so inviting, candles burning in all of the windows. Dermot had dragged in a huge Christmas tree to the main hall, and they had fires lit in all the rooms all week, regardless of the state of decay, to warm the house up.

Sam had invited Perry and Violet for Christmas as well, and while the Murphys had a newfound regard for Violet and they really liked Perry, they had a lot of bad memories of her time as mistress of Robinswood. There was a little bit of trepidation, as Violet had not set foot in Robinswood since the day she left in 1940, nose in the air, not speaking to anyone. But Lord and Lady Goodall had written, thanking them all for the invitation and saying how they were longing to see their grandchildren, Austina and Jack. Isabella knew their affection for the babies was genuine. Violet was taking to being a grandmother better than she took to mothering.

Thankfully, they were staying at Lismore Castle, the Duke of Devonshire's house no less, but they were coming to Robinswood for Christmas dinner. Isabella wanted the place as inviting as possible for Violet's first return visit. Kate and Aisling kept telling her she was mad worrying about what Violet would think, but old habits ran deep. The former Lady Kenefick had such unhappy memories of the house, and Kate and Sam and everyone had worked so hard that she didn't want Violet to say anything to spoil it. Sam and Lillian's mother was much better these days, undoubtedly – Perry was good for her – but Isabella worried that coming back to Robinswood might bring out the worst in her again. The house was Sam and Kate's pride and joy, and they had poured their hearts and souls into the restoration. It was nowhere near ready, but it was getting there.

The downstairs was looking well, the damp patches covered up with decorations for now; nothing could be done to dry them out and seal them before the spring anyway. So the public areas of the house were passable, but the bedrooms and the bathrooms upstairs were still in need of major work. The windows were rotten, and lots of the floorboards were as well. Mark had big plans to replace and renew what was necessary with their own wood, currently drying and being seasoned in a large shed behind the hay barns. Dermot had been impressed with his skills so far, so it was looking like they had a busy year ahead.

To accommodate the Hamilton-Brooks, they had done a temporary renovation job on the least decrepit of the bedrooms, and Elena and the children were settled upstairs overlooking the lawns, and at least it was dry and warm. Kate, Sam and Jack were in their own quarters at the back of the house, and Austina and Oskar were in the farmhouse with Isabella and Dermot.

Eve had surprised everyone by asking if Bartley could come for Christmas, so a room was made up for him as well, while Eve shared with Austina in the farmhouse. The room beside Elena's was a bit draughty as the window frames were in terrible shape, and Isabella apologised when she showed it to him. But they had hung the heaviest drapes they could find and lit a big fire, and she had beaten all the dust out of an Axminster rug that had been abandoned in the attic.

He assured her, in that quiet, gentle way of his, that it was lovely and that he would be very comfortable there.

There was something almost otherworldly about Bartley. He spoke slowly and deliberately, and he watched everything that went on with those almost-black eyes of his. But he was so loving and gentle towards Eve that Isabella warmed to him immediately. He was the total opposite of Jack, not just physically, but in temperament. Jack had been gregarious and outgoing, full of fun and devilment, but Bartley was more serious, and he found company difficult, she thought. He never tried to get his say in the endless, loud conversation around the dinner table, but he seemed content to enjoy the chat and banter. Isabella often saw him catch Eve's eye and smile, and it did their hearts good to see their daughter reciprocate his obvious affection. It was early days, but Isabella had a feeling it was going to work out. Eve was different now too. She was more solemn; the carefree girl was gone forever. She was a woman who had known a great sadness, and it changed her.

She and Bartley seemed very happy in each other's company, often sitting and just reading or walking outside in the snow. He was fascinated by all the plants growing around the house, and if you asked him, he would explain the medicinal properties of each one – but only if he was asked. He treated Eve like she was a particularly rare and beautiful flower, very gently, almost reverentially, and Eve trusted him completely.

Eve told them his background, that he had been raised until the age of twelve with his family. They travelled all around Ireland, but then his mother died, and he and his brothers and sisters were taken into the care of the state. They had done nothing wrong, but the powers that be – the church and the state – decided that his father would not be able to cope with fourteen children, so they were forcibly taken from him. Bartley and his brothers were sent to a boys' industrial school where allegedly they would learn a trade, and his sisters were sent to a girls' institution. Their father drank himself to death; the loss of his family killed him.

His treatment at the hands of the priests who ran the place was horrific; the boys had been subjected to all sorts of abuse. So one day, Bartley attacked a priest who was assaulting one of his little brothers. Immediately, he was sent to a reform school, which strangely wasn't as bad as the first place, and there he learned wood-carving and other skills. His knowledge of plants he said he always knew; it was passed on from one generation to the next. His father had taught him as his father had done before. Being the seventh son of a seventh son, it was believed in the travelling community that he had special powers.

Bartley was proud of his traveller roots, but he spoke so rarely that most people didn't know he was a traveller. Eve hoped when people did learn who Bartley Doherty was, they would be kind and give him a chance, as there was so much prejudice about people like him. Her family had been wonderful; she wondered about the locals in Kilthomand, though. It was one of the many reasons she told her mother she would never move back.

The incredible thing about him was that despite all he endured, Bartley wasn't eaten up by bitterness and hatred. He had let it go.

Both he and Eve took their role as teachers to young people very seriously, and they were so invested in the lives of those boys and girls, it was heartening to see. They were making a real difference in the lives of children who were not given the best of starts, and they loved it. And now it seemed they loved each other too.

Eve spoke of him and his hard upbringing with such tenderness and compassion, her parents were in no doubt that their poor heart-broken daughter was learning to live again, and it was such a relief.

Isabella, Dermot and Eve were talking as they cleared up after breakfast that morning. Bartley was out in the snow with Georgie and Arthur. The previous night, a bat had become trapped inside the house – it must have fallen down a chimney – and they discovered the poor creature that morning. It was still alive, and Bartley was showing them how to put a bat on a height if they found one, because bats can't take off from the ground – they need the wind beneath their wings to take flight.

They stood for a moment at the kitchen window, watching the

scene in the courtyard. Georgie and Arthur were enthralled, hanging on Bartley's every word.

'He's an unusual man, that one you brought us, Evie,' Dermot said, kissing the top of her head.

'You do like him, though, don't you, Daddy?' she asked, handing him a tea cloth to dry up the dishes her mother was washing.

'I do. He's not like anyone I've ever met before, and I've known all sorts, but I do.' Dermot smiled, glad his daughter still cared what he thought.

'I remember,' Eve said to him, 'you promised me the night Jack died I would smile again, and I didn't believe you. And for a long time, I thought I would never feel anything but pain, but I am smiling a lot these days.'

'And would a certain unusual travelling man have anything to do with that, I wonder?' Isabella teased.

'He might,' she confirmed with a smile. 'He's not like anyone in the world, Mammy. I'll admit, when I heard about his background, I was a little bit worried. Was he going to wander off one day and leave me high and dry, or was he so damaged by all that had happened to him that he wasn't capable of a normal relationship? But the more I get to know him, the more I like him. There will never be another Jack, but I really believe he is giving us his blessing. I think they would have liked each other.' Eve watched Bartley as he showed the children a snow-covered nest.

'I think they would have too. He's a special man, and anyone can tell he is mad about you. You'll be fine, my love.' Dermot put his arm around her.

* * *

LATER THAT DAY, Eve, Aisling, and their mother were wrapping gifts at the table when Austina woke from her nap and could be heard calling, 'Bella! Bella!'

'I'll get her.' Isabella dried her hands.

Austina had become part of the furniture now, and even in the village, nobody stared at her any more. She was Austina Kenefick-Lane, and she lived at Robinswood, and that was all there was to it. Neither Dermot nor Isabella offered any explanation except that she was Lady Lillian's daughter. Nobody had ever had the audacity to say anything outright about the child being black, or ask who her father was, though no doubt it was the cause of endless speculation.

Isabella reappeared with Austina in her arms. Eve took her while Isabella prepared a meal for the baby, throwing her in the air amid squeals of delight.

She was the sunniest little girl and walking now, so she was full of mischief. Just that morning, she had pulled a whole box of precious sugar all over herself and the floor.

'Righto, little miss.' Isabella took the baby back and laid her on the changing table Dermot had made. Swiftly and deftly, she changed the little girl and wiped her face with a damp flannel. She had four pearly white teeth that showed when she grinned.

'Aren't you a pretty little girl?' she cooed as Austina gazed solemnly up at her. Kate and Sam had taken Jack for a walk and to build a snowman. They normally took Austina whenever they took Jack, but she had been asleep when they left.

As Isabella gave Austina a piece of a bun to chew, there was a loud knock on the front door. Isabella got a fright at the sound of the loud bang of the heavy door knocker. None of them ever used the front door; they came in and out through the stable yard off the kitchen. She thought it must be Violet and Perry, and she wasn't ready. It was only Christmas Eve, and they were not due until the next day.

Dermot appeared at the kitchen door.

'Oh, Lord, Der, I hope it's not them...' she said, trying to tidy herself up. Eve and Aisling chuckled at how flustered the normally unflappable Isabella had become.

Dermot stood before her and rested his hands on her shoulders. 'Bella, you look lovely, and anyway, even if it is Violet, she's not the boss any more, is she?'

Isabella smiled and took a deep breath. None of the others seemed to care what Violet thought, and they were better off for it.

'You know something? You're absolutely right. She can take us as she finds us.'

Dermot winked at his daughters and whispered, 'Here we go!'

Isabella marched out into the hallway, which did look lovely with the decorated Christmas tree and the blazing log fire. The smell of baking, pine cones and applewood filled her nostrils as she went to open the huge front door. It had expanded over time and was hard to pull open.

As she pulled, the door was pushed from the other side. As it creaked open, she realised it was indeed Violet and Perry, but behind them were Lillian and a tall, handsome black man.

CHAPTER 34

'Welcome! Come in, come in...' Isabella opened the door, and all four of them came into the large entrance hall.

'Oh, Isabella, it looks magical! I can't believe the transformation, and it's so warm and cosy...' Violet gushed, as Perry handed Dermot boxes and bags of food and drink to supplement the feast.

Lillian barely noticed anything. 'Is she here?' she asked almost timidly.

'She is. She's in the kitchen with the girls.' Isabella felt a pang of sadness but relief too – Austina would have both her parents, and that was wonderful. She turned to the man she feared none of them would ever see again. 'Welcome to Robinswood, Beau.'

'Thank you very much, Isabella. It's sure wonderful to see you all again. And thank you from the bottom of my heart for all you have done. Lillian told me how you are taking care of our baby.'

'It was our pleasure. She's a little dote.' Isabella smiled.

She led Lillian and Beau into the kitchen where Eve stood with Austina in her arms. Isabella had shown the girl a photo of her mother every day and taught her to say 'mama', so being the bright little thing that she was, she called 'mama' immediately when she saw Lillian.

Lillian ran to her daughter and threw her arms around her. 'My darling... Oh, I've missed you!' She covered the little girl's face in kisses and then walked across the kitchen with the toddler in her arms to where Beau stood, mesmerised. Eve, Aisling and Dermot were rooted to the spot, not knowing if they should leave or not, but it didn't matter; for Lillian and Beau, the whole world had stopped.

'Austina, this is your daddy.'

Beau looked in total amazement at his daughter. He was rendered completely speechless as Lillian put Austina into his arms. The baby didn't cry or make strange; she simply stared at her father intently. She had never seen another black person before, and she raised her little hand and placed it on his face. He turned his head and kissed her fingers, eventually finding his voice.

'Hello, my angel. I'm sorry I'm only getting here now, but I'm staying, and I'm going to take care of you and your mama.'

He put his other arm around Lillian and held them both close. He closed his eyes, and a tear leaked out as he whispered, 'Thank you, Jesus. Thank you for my family.'

Violet and Perry moved to stand beside the Murphys, everyone observing the reunion.

'That was a good thing you did, Perry,' Dermot murmured.

Lord Goodall shrugged. 'Beau isn't the only one thanking God for his family. In the end, Dermot, it's all that matters, isn't it?'

There was more to what Perry said than just words, and both men knew it. It was time to let the old animosities go and move forward together. The ex-IRA man, the peer of the British realm, the former Nazi, the RAF pilots, the black American... In the end, they were family, and that meant so much more than ancient grudges.

'I couldn't agree more.' Dermot smiled.

Violet greeted Eve and Aisling warmly and complimented them all once again on how wonderful the house looked.

Beau gazed down at Lillian and Austina, shaking his head incredulously. 'And you did this, all by yourself? You carried our baby and gave birth to her and took such good care of her, all on your own? And then you travelled across the world, busted me out of one of the toughest prisons in the United States and brought me back here. You are a marvel. I'm so proud of you, Lillian.'

She smiled, her heart bursting with joy and relief. 'She's called Austina Kenefick-Lane – at least that's what I told people...' she began.

'Let's make that her official name, then, shall we?' Beau smiled so brightly, it lit up the room. Keeping his daughter firmly in his arms, Beau got down on one knee.

A silence came over the room as everyone realised what was about to happen. Kate, Sam, Mark, Oskar and the Hamilton-Brooks family had by now appeared in the kitchen to see what all the fuss was about. Arthur was excited about Perry's car outside, an Alfa Romeo 6C 2500 Freccia d'Oro. They immediately took in the scene, delighted not to miss the big event.

'Lillian Arabella Daphne Kenefick, would you do me the huge honour of becoming my wife?'

Lillian gave up trying to hold back the tears. She couldn't get the words out, but she nodded and pulled Beau to his feet. Never letting go of his daughter, he kissed Lillian deeply.

The group burst into applause and cheers.

'I think that was a yes, Beau!' Sam called from the kitchen door. 'And I do believe I found something in the cellar suitable for the occasion.' From under the kitchen table Sam produced a case of champagne.

Within minutes, the kitchen of Robinswood was a cacophony of voices, all talking and laughing together. Beau's deep Southern drawl could be heard as he answered questions. His release from prison, driving through the segregated South as Lillian's chauffeur in a uniform she'd bought from a hotel concierge, the flight home to Shannon – and it all held the family enthralled. Every telling covered Lillian in glory as the heroine of the piece, and she looked thrilled but bashful. Something about Beau made Lillian a much nicer person; he always had.

Violet and Isabella distributed glasses, even allowing Georgie a sip.

When everyone had a glass, Lillian clinked hers to get some

silence. 'I'm sorry, everyone. I'm not much for speeches, but I do want to say something.' Everyone turned to face her.

'I just want to say thank you. To all of you. To Sam and Kate for inviting us, and to them and Isabella and Dermot for taking care of Austina so well while I was in America. Leaving her was so hard, but the only way I could have done it is knowing that she was in the best possible care. She clearly loves you all, so if you don't mind, we might stay around here – not in your house, you'll be glad to hear, but in the village. Beau and I have talked a lot about this, and we think our little girl stands the best chance of a happy life here with us, of course, and the people she loves. I promise we'll be useful – or Beau will. I'll try. I'm kind of skill-less, but I'm willing to learn.'

Sam grinned. 'You can start with the washing up!' he called, and everyone laughed.

'You're on.' Lillian grinned. 'The other people I have to thank are my mother and Perry. Mother has been a tower of strength for me all my life, sometimes telling me a few home truths' – she locked eyes with Violet and both women smiled, a smile of genuine affection – 'and I couldn't have done it without her. Thank you, Mother. Now, Perry won't want me telling you this, but he paid for me to go to America, he set me up with a lawyer, bought flights, rented cars. But most importantly, in 1926, he allowed a friend of his, a young business student from Mississippi, to use his name when the friend was caught drinking bathtub gin in an illegal speakeasy on the Upper East Side of New York. Perry took the rap, as they say in the USA, and looked for no reward. Admittedly, he was going back to England, so it had no real consequences for him, but had that young man from a very prominent family had such a criminal conviction, he would have been disgraced and would never have become governor of Mississippi.'

Everyone looked confused but intrigued. Why was Lillian telling them this?

'Governor Gerald J. Grosvenor, luckily for us, has a long memory and was willing to pay back a favour for his old friend. And that is how Beau was released from Parchman Farm, also known as Mississippi State Penitentiary. I was just the chauffeur. But because of Perry, Austina and I have him here with us, and for that, we are forever in his debt.'

The gathering burst into applause once more, and Perry grinned and blushed, especially when Violet kissed him on the cheek in front of everyone.

The reunion went on late into the night, ending with a sing-song. Beau sang the songs of the Delta, low harmonious Bible songs, and Lillian even gave a reasonable effort at 'The White Cliffs of Dover'. Bartley amazed everyone by playing an old fiddle that Dermot had found in one of the sheds, and Mark had a hilarious recitation about a three-legged horse that had everyone in stitches laughing. Everyone was in wonderful spirits, and the food and drinks were flowing.

Sam spotted Kate leaving the party and followed her to the entranceway. She hadn't looked well all day.

'Kate, is everything all right?' he asked, catching up with her.

"Yes, fine. I'm just going to check on Jack,' she said, her hand on the ornate bannister of the cantilever staircase, but then she stopped. She had been putting off telling him because she wasn't sure how she felt about it herself yet, but seeing everyone gathered there together and the house filled with such love and family, any doubts she had melted away.

She led him to the huge Christmas tree, decorated with ribbons and bows and twinkling lights. The merriment from the kitchen was muffled, and they were alone. The heat of the fire kept the big room warm. Dermot had filled it with dry logs that were, by now, smouldering in the grate.

'What is it? You're worrying me now.' Sam's brow was furrowed.

'What would you like for Christmas?' she whispered, putting her arms around him.

He grinned and kissed her neck. 'I don't know, my good Lady Wife. What had you in mind?'

'Well, how does becoming a daddy again sound?' She placed his hand on her abdomen, and the dawning realisation lit his face up.

'Are you...?' He didn't dare to hope.

Kate grinned, and a warm glow of contentment dispelled any worries she had about expanding their family. 'Pregnant? I am indeed.'

'But I thought you didn't want...' Sam began, afraid she was upset, but the big grin on her face told him he had nothing to worry about.

'I thought I didn't, but it turns out I'm delighted. It took a few days to get used to the idea, but looking at that bunch in there, this baby will be so loved. Now we'll need this big house at this rate, so it was an inspired idea, Lord Kenefick, to return to Robinswood.'

THE END

THANK you very much for buying my book, I sincerely hope you enjoyed it. The first book in this series, *What Once Was True*, as well as all my other novels are available here.

author.to/JeanGraingerAuthor

IF YOU ENJOYED IT, I would be grateful if you would consider leaving a review on Amazon, it cheers me up no end as well as helping my books become more visible in the ever growing sea of books!

As a special thank you for your support, I would like to offer you a free book. It's called *Under Heaven's Shining Stars* and it is set in my home town of Cork in the 1960s. All you need to do is go to my website, www.jeangrainger.com and sign up for my newsletter. It is 100% free and there is absolutely no catch I promise. You can unsubscribe anytime, even immediately after you get the free book if you like (though I hope you won't of course.) Each month or so I'll contact you with my comings and goings, news about new books, special offers and so on.

Le grá

Jean Grainger.

Cork, Ireland. February, 2019